Through All Time

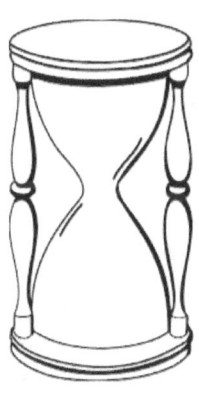

Jen Shaffer

Through All Time
Copyright © 2024 Jen Shaffer
All rights reserved.

ISBN: (ebook) 978-1-958136-88-1
(print) 978-1-964636-29-0

Inkspell Publishing
207 Moonglow Circle #101
Murrells Inlet, SC 29576

Edited By Aubrey Bobak
Cover art By Emily's World By Design

DEDICATION

This book is dedicated to you finally finding your happily ever after.

PROLOGUE

It seemed like he was flying through the streets but even then, he wasn't moving fast enough. He dragged air into his lungs, jumping over a pile of garbage on the sidewalk and wishing he had a horse at least. A horse would get him there faster than his legs, or an automobile. He couldn't shadow walk where she might see. He had to find her before something happened to her. Again.

They were supposed to get married today. He'd been waiting literal centuries for this day to happen.

He followed his instincts and turned into Jackson Square, where he'd first laid eyes on her again.

Where his deadened heart had filled once again.

Something pulled him to the left and sweat ran into his eyes, but he couldn't mistake the shapes of the five men standing there, their black suits stark against the rising sun.

"No!" The word was torn from his very soul and the men looked at him as he ran toward them. If he hadn't known better, he'd think he saw regret on their faces this time. A portal opened behind them, and they stepped in, watching as he slid to his knees and pulled the woman's body to his own before it closed around them.

"No, please, God no." His hand shook as he brushed

the hair off her face, blood streaking across her brow. He looked down, and his stomach rolled at the way they'd brutally killed her this time. Because they wanted it to hurt him. And it did, this time and the five times before this, each one worse than the last. They didn't care about her, they only cared because he loved and killing her tortured him. He pulled her into his chest. His screams broke the air around him, sending the birds in the trees flying. Anyone who heard it had goosebumps rising on their skin.

He kneeled there with her in his arms, rocking back and forth, the tears running unbidden from his eyes. His head went back. "Why do you keep doing this to me!" He screamed it to the heavens.

"Why do you keep doing this to me?" He sobbed it this time as his head came down, holding the woman's body to his own. How was he supposed to let her go again?

A hand landed on his shoulder then. "Come, we have to go."

"How am I supposed to leave her like this?" He brushed her hair back again. He felt her blood seeping into his clothes.

"I'm sorry, friend," the other man said. "I don't know how to make it hurt less, even after all this time."

"Why won't they let me live in peace with her?"

"*Je ne sais pas*, I don't know. What I do know is that we must go."

He laid her gently back on the ground. His very heart and soul. He'd tried to stay away from her this time, but it did no good. They were drawn to each other like moths to a flame. He always knew when she drew within miles of him, from the very first moment he'd seen her. All he could do now was stand and walk back away from her, his eyes on her beautiful face, trying not to see the blood. He didn't know how long it would be before he saw her again.

He had one more chance.

He took another step back before the shadows swallowed him.

CHAPTER ONE

Parker pulled her backpack closer, holding it tightly against her chest. She sighed when the bus made another stop. She should have rented a car, or taken an Uber, instead of being cheap and only spending two dollars on the bus fare. She pushed her glasses back up her nose, checking the map on her phone to make sure she got off at the right stop.

She was heading straight for Café Du Monde.

She wanted to eat a beignet and drink chicory coffee with steamed milk before the two blondes showed up and she had to pretend like she didn't eat food. Those two had intimidated her all through college and she was sure they still would. Parker didn't understand how Theresa and she were friends. They'd met in college and ended up roommates the first two years. The two of them couldn't be more opposite, the only similarity between them was the fact that they both had brown hair.

Theresa was tall, leggy, and thin. She had a big personality and people always knew when she was around. She was in college on a volleyball scholarship and had more friends than Parker could keep up with. Theresa was also smart and graduated with her Bachelor of Science degree in Dietetics. She wouldn't approve of beignets and coffee. Her two friends, the blondes, had also been on the volleyball team and the three of them were very similar in body type.

The two blondes, Samantha and Emily, didn't understand why Theresa liked Parker so much. They tolerated her because she was Theresa's friend.

Parker didn't understand it either.

Parker, on the other hand, was short, she only reached five-foot-two and her body type would be called more curvy than thin. Which was why she hid it under dresses and baggy shirts. No matter how hard she tried, her stomach would never be flat, and her thighs would always touch. Even though she could see her soft, heart-shaped face in the mirror, Parker had never had very good self-esteem, and she preferred to hang out in the background. One of the blondes had once described her as "mousey and pale." When she'd heard that, she'd slunk back into the background. Parker currently held her master's in education with a minor in foreign language. Besides English, she could also speak Spanish and French and was working on learning American Sign Language.

The only part of herself that Parker liked was her dark-gray eyes.

Parker's phone binged at her, and she pulled the cord to let the driver know she wanted to get off the bus. She planned on walking the last mile. It was how she justified eating beignets.

They were here in New Orleans for Theresa's bachelorette weekend. In four weeks, she was marrying the man she'd met in college. He'd just graduated medical school and was about to start his residency. It was almost every girl's fantasy relationship. Parker wished them the best. She hadn't been surprised when Theresa didn't ask her to be part of her wedding party, but she'd been caught off guard when she'd asked her to come for this weekend party. Aside from Theresa and the blondes, three more women Parker didn't know were coming. They were supposed to share a condo somewhere in the Garden District, and Parker was already extremely uncomfortable about sharing a place with these other women.

Parker exited the bus and slung her backpack on. Her purse was the only other luggage she'd brought with her. A lot was shoved in the backpack. She'd bought some compression bags and stuffed enough for two weeks in there without having to drag around her wheeled luggage. She'd taken a different flight than everyone else because she planned on staying after the weekend was over. It was early June, but school was out for the summer, and she didn't have to think about work for a while. Plus, she wanted some time away. She'd never solo traveled. There'd always been someone else around because she was afraid. Her whole life had been lived in some sort of fear. She didn't know where it came from, just like the scar across her jawline. She'd asked her mother once how she'd gotten it, but her mother had squinted at it like she didn't remember or didn't know.

And then there was Max. He'd asked her to marry him, but she couldn't say yes. They'd been dating for two years now and, it wasn't that he was a bad guy, he just… he didn't make her heart flutter. They didn't live together. She was twenty-eight years old now and she'd recently gotten so restless. So, she'd decided to travel more. After this weekend, she had no set plan, she didn't have hotel reservations or a return flight yet. Maybe she'd catch a plane to somewhere else, maybe Galveston, or Charleston, who knew.

Parker turned where her GPS told her to, and before she knew it, she stood in the space between Jackson Square and St. Louis Cathedral. Her head tilted back so she could take in the grand spires of the cathedral. It was one of the places on her list to visit. She was sure none of the other bachelorette partiers wanted to waste their weekend looking at gothic churches, but that sounded good to Parker. She snapped a few photos and looked at them, zooming in on the picture to make sure it wasn't blurry. In the corner of one photo, she happened to catch the image of a man standing there, and it looked like he was staring at her intently. She held the phone closer, squinting at the image of the man, when she felt someone bump her from behind. She took a step forward to keep from falling.

A large, warm hand caught her by the elbow. *"Excusez-moi, mademoiselle."*

"Ce n'est rien," Parker responded without thought, turning to the man who had spoken to find no one there. She did a complete three-hundred-sixty degree turn but there wasn't another body close to hers. That voice had sounded so familiar. Parker tilted her head to the side. Maybe she'd just had her first run in with a New Orleans ghost. A shiver ran down her spine, and she turned so she could walk through Jackson Square to reach the hot, delicious beignets and coffee waiting for her.

Something happened when she stepped into the square though. Her vision went blurry, and suddenly, she wanted to cry. She thought she heard someone screaming in agony and she did another spin, looking for the person in pain. No one seemed unhappy. Tourists like her zipped around the area, most of them posing in front of the statue and taking selfies. Maybe she had jet lag. Her flight had barely been three hours though. "Maybe I just need coffee." Parker smoothed her hands down the purple sundress she had on and checked to make sure the laces on her white Keds were still tight.

Parker stepped out of the square onto Decatur St and saw the line at Café Du Monde. It looked like it would take four years to get through it, but this was literally her whole reason for coming this way. She headed across the street and took her place in line. Her phone buzzed and she saw a message from Max.

Max: *You didn't let me know if your plane landed ok*

Nope, she sure hadn't, the thought hadn't even crossed her mind. Parker supposed that was enough to tell her if she wanted to marry him or not.

Parker: *Sorry, flight went well, currently standing in line for beignets*

Max: *I heard they aren't worth the wait*

"And how about you suck off," Parker was annoyed that she'd answered him at that point. She left him on read this time. Somewhere behind her, she swore she heard a man chuckle. "Look at me, taking charge of my life," she said as she took a step forward as the line moved. While she stood there in line with nothing to do, she pulled the rubber bands out of her hair and ran her hands through it, scratching at her scalp and sighing before pulling it back into a bun again.

The man standing two people behind her almost died at the sight. He wanted his hands in that hair so badly, he had to fist them and shove them in his pockets to keep from reaching for her.

It had been a hundred goddamn years since he'd seen those curls. Her glorious curls. The ones he wanted wrapped around his fingers. Tangled in his fists again. It wasn't fair of her to whip those curls around in front of him and then tuck them away, even if she didn't know that was what she was doing.

It took Parker thirty minutes to get to the front of the line and by then, she was good and hungry. She ordered two beignets and a small coffee to go, and she watched them dump what looked like half a pound of powdered sugar on top of them before folding the bag and handing it to her with the cup of coffee. She didn't want to eat around all these people, so she walked back down the street to Artillery Park and sat on the steps, tucking her dress in under her legs before opening her bag. Parker held up the first beignet and let the wind whip the loose powdered sugar off before taking her first bite and closing her eyes. Yep, most definitely not on the approved dietitian's food list. She sipped the chicory coffee with steamed milk and felt the caffeine jolt through her system.

Across the street, standing behind a horse and carriage, that same man couldn't take his eyes off the look of pure joy on her face. "People are going to notice if you keep staring at her, Gabriel."

Gabriel watched the jolt go through her body. It made

her hips lightly sway back and forth against the step she was leaning on, and he wished it was his lap instead. "It's been a hundred years, Charles."

She pushed her glasses in place with the back of her hand, something he'd seen her do a thousand times, before he saw she was looking across the street in their direction.

Charles turned so his back was to her, leaning in close to Gabriel. "This isn't the nineteen twenties anymore, Gabriel, people notice when you look like a stalker now. I know you've heard of CCTV."

"She's alive and back in this city."

"If you want her to stay that way, you need to leave her alone."

Gabriel turned to Charles. "I already tried that, Charles, three times, and it didn't work. We can stay away from each other like the sun can stop rising." Gabriel's gaze returned to the woman across the street, now sipping her coffee and looking down at her phone.

Charles lifted his phone to his ear and pointed at something across Jackson Square. If anyone looked, they'd think he was pointing out the direction to go. Gabriel had looked back at the man. "You can at least try," Charles snapped at him.

"Excusez-moi, Monsieur, est-ce que vous parlez français?" Parker couldn't believe she'd walked across the street and approached this tall, gorgeous man. Short, little Parker Reed, being forward. The mousey fifth grade teacher from Chicago. She only came up to the top of his chest, and she had to tilt her head back to see his face. His hair was a deep honey-blond, combed back in waves from the angular planes of his face. His nose was straight and his lips full and kissable. Parker didn't think it was fair for a man to have lips that looked like that. When he looked down at her, Parker's breath caught at the dark-blue color of his eyes.

"Oui," he answered.

"No shit," Parker responded.

A little half smile curved on those ridiculous lips. "That's definitely not French."

God, his voice was deep too. "Have we met before?" Parker's eyebrows scrunched together.

"Gabriel," the man next to him whispered frantically.

Parker quickly glanced over at the other man and then watched in detached amazement as the beautiful man in front of her raised her left hand to his lips and kissed the spot where a ring would be if she were married. "May I ask what your name is?" Gabriel asked. It was the only thing about her that had ever changed.

"Parker." She swallowed hard. He hadn't let go of her hand yet. He held it close to his mouth and continued to look into her eyes. Parker shivered as his hot breath ran over her knuckles. Were knuckles an erogenous zone? "My name is Parker."

The man standing next to them said something in a language she didn't understand, and it made the man in front of her lower her hand and sweep his gaze up and down the street behind her. "I have to go, Parker." He looked back down at her. "But I will find you later."

"Ok," Parker said stupidly. He didn't let go of her hand until he stepped back, and he seemed almost reluctant to turn his back on her. Parker watched him walk away from her, back into Jackson Square, the other man beside him, until they were swallowed up by the crush of tourists and the statue sitting in the middle of the square. Parker stood there like a statue in the middle of the sidewalk, not understanding why she couldn't look away from the spot he'd disappeared through, until her phone buzzed again with another message from Max.

Max: *Why didn't you answer me? See, I knew you couldn't do this by yourself. I'm about to fly down there and save you.*

Parker: *I'm perfectly fine.*

He always did that to her, talked to her in a way that belittled. Made her feel like she couldn't do things on her own. That was one reason why she hadn't traveled in so long, because Max didn't like to go anywhere. They'd fought when she told him Theresa had invited her for this weekend getaway and she'd almost declined because of him. Parker had told Max she'd said no but she'd gone behind his back and planned to come anyway. She'd stopped talking to him about it and hadn't told him until this morning that she was leaving. She'd purchased the last seat available on the earliest flight she'd been able to come in on this morning. It hadn't been cheap either, and for some reason, she felt guilty for spending her own money because Max tried to control that about her too. He'd asked for her bank records once, and that was the first time she'd said no thanks and shown him the door. It had taken a few weeks, but he'd sweetly talked his way back into her life. Sometimes, she'd catch him eyeing her phone and she'd been nervous enough about it that she'd fingerprint locked it. Parker had nothing to hide, but that didn't matter. For some reason, him having access to her phone made her extremely nervous.

Max: *I don't approve of what you did by going down there*

Parker's feet actually stopped moving when she read those words. She'd decided to start walking and do some more sightseeing before she made her way to meet the rest of the bachelorette party at the condo.

Who the hell did he think he was? He didn't approve? She might be meek, but she sure wasn't his doormat.

Parker: *Not sure who you think you're talking to, but you can refrain from contacting me for the rest of the time I'm away. As a matter of fact, don't ever contact me again. We're done.*

Parker's heart pounded, and she almost didn't press *send*, but something in her wouldn't let her finger stop as it started for the button. That message went through, and it was like a chain holding her back finally broke. It looked like he was about to reply, and Parker took it one step farther and hit the block number button.

It was after four in the afternoon by the time Parker walked up to the condo she'd shelled out a pretty penny to share with six other women. The reason she'd spent so much was so she could have one of the private rooms in the house. Parker didn't like the idea of sharing that kind of space with any of these women. It had taken her longer to walk here than she'd originally thought it would, and she'd underestimated the heat and humidity of June in New Orleans. Parker was ready to take a cool shower and change her clothes.

The outside of the condo was gorgeous. It shared a deep porch with the condo next door and the owner had decorated the white columned porch with potted ferns, wicker furniture and different fragrant flowers. Parker checked the address on her phone and rang the doorbell. A black- haired woman she didn't recognize came and opened the door. "Can I help you?"

Parker heard laughter coming from the back of the house.

"Hi." She raised her hand in a little wave. "I'm Parker."

"Oh," the other woman said, stepping back, "nice to meet you. I'm Anne, I work with Theresa. You guys met in college, right?"

"Yes." Parker stepped in when Anne stepped back. She closed her eyes at how cool it was in the house. "This air conditioning feels great." Sweat had run down her back, and she was sure the dress under her backpack was soaked.

"Did you walk here?" Anne asked, closing the front door before she headed to the kitchen. Parker followed.

"Yes, I stopped and did some sightseeing after my flight got in. I underestimated the walk," she answered as she stepped into the kitchen. It was like sorority girl central in here. Parker felt her shoulders drop. They were all thin and leggy, aside from the slight differences in height, breast size, and hair color, they all pretty much looked the same. The five other women paused in conversation when Parker stepped into the room, glasses of wine sitting in front of each of them.

"Parker!" Theresa yelled, stepping up to her and putting her arms around her for a hug. "I'm so glad you made it. The other girls and I were talking about ordering pizza tonight before hitting up Bourbon Street. How's that sound to you?"

"Pizza and Bourbon Street? Sounds great," Parker replied, not wanting to go against the group. What she really wanted was some spicy gumbo. Why were they ordering pizza when there was all this food around to be tried? "Do you girls mind if I head upstairs and take a shower? It's extremely humid out and it was a long walk."

"Sure," Theresa said, "I'll show you to your room." Theresa walked out of the kitchen and Parker waved to the other women before following Theresa up the stairs and down the hall. Theresa opened the door to the last room down the hall. "There are three rooms up here and two downstairs. Here's the bathroom up here," Theresa pointed to the door across from her bedroom. Parker opened the door to her room. There was a simple double bed and a dresser with a television on it. Next to the bed was a side table with a lamp and alarm clock. It smelled like bleach cleaner and baby powder and the comforter looked clean.

"This is a nice room," *Not worth what I paid*, Parker thought, *but whatever at this point.*

She slung her backpack off and put it and her purse on the bed.

"Come down when you're done," Theresa said as she turned toward the hallway. She paused for a second, "Parker, I'm really glad you came."

Theresa left before she could see the surprise on Parker's face.

Forty-five minutes later, Parker felt a bit better. She'd taken a long, cool shower and wrapped her hair in a towel to dry. After her shower, she shut her door and sat on the edge of the bed so she could slather her lotion from feet to neck. Parker loved lotion; it was one of the few luxuries she allowed herself. She had at least fifteen different scents at home, and for some reason, it drove Max crazy, and not in a good way. He'd told her once that she should choose the one she liked and stick with it. "I love all of them," had been her response. Since she was here in New Orleans, she'd stayed away from the heavier scents, and she'd brought one that reminded her of how sunshine in a garden smelled. The other one was deep and sensual, like seduction in a bottle. This was the one Parker chose, thinking of a pair of deep-blue eyes as she rubbed the lotion on her body.

She tucked the miniature version of the same lotion in her purse.

Parker dressed in a white sundress. It wasn't a sundress so much as it looked like a long version of a man's dress shirt, with buttons down the entire front of the dress. The sleeves came down to her wrists, but she could fold them up if she got too hot. The one part of the dress she didn't like was that it came with a belt, which formed the dress more across her hips. Parker finished tying her black shoes. She'd brought one white pair and one black pair of Keds, that was it. All that was left was to tackle her hair. Parker sighed as she unwound the towel from her head and let her mass of thick, curly hair go free. It was a mess. She never knew what to do with it, which was why she ended up with it in a bun most of the time. It fell just past her shoulder blades, and it took a good ten minutes to comb it out. She slipped her hair ties around her wrists so she could put it up when it dried.

Parker slung her purse on and grabbed her phone. She'd been charging it while she showered and dressed. Before she headed downstairs, she pulled up her gallery and looked at the picture she'd taken of that beautiful, blonde-haired man from across the street. She'd gotten him in profile, when he'd turned to speak to his companion, who appeared to be talking on his phone and pointing out which direction to go. God, he was freaking hot. She wasn't close to the type that would do so, but she'd definitely have a one-night stand with this man if given the opportunity. Parker bet he knew what to do between the sheets. Her lips were dying to know what his felt like. She'd never been able to orgasm with Max. She faked it every time because she didn't want him to feel bad and then took care of herself after he left. Lately, she'd been avoiding all physical contact with him in general, but she knew she couldn't use the excuse of headache, her menstrual cycle, or end-of-the-school-year stress forever.

The doorbell rang then. Parker heard the other women cheer for whatever pizza they'd ordered. She guessed she'd go downstairs and eat something; all she'd had so far was those two beignets earlier. Parker crept down the stairs and cautiously entered the kitchen. Five large pizza boxes sat on the kitchen island, and thankfully none of the other women currently stood around them. They'd all taken seats around the large kitchen table. She hadn't realized before how loud six women could be. Theresa had set up an account that they'd all deposited money into when they had to pay for things like shared meals and Uber rides together, so Parker didn't feel bad about grabbing a plate and sliding two pieces of whatever pizza she'd ended up picking on it. Parker found a cup and poured herself a glass of water from the sink before standing at the kitchen counter to eat. The last thing she wanted to do was find a seat at the table and eat in front of all those women. She took a bite of the pepperoni pizza and thought about seeing if she'd be able to slip away tomorrow and try one of those muffuletta sandwiches she'd heard about.

"Hey, Parker," she heard from the table. Parker looked over to see it was one of the blondes, she could never remember which was which, who had spoken to her.

"Hey, how are you?" Parker asked, saluting her with the piece of bland, stupid pizza. She lived much too close to Chicago for this to be considered a good pizza.

"So, what have you been doing with yourself since college?" The question was meant as a snub, and Parker almost slunk back into herself at the snarky woman.

"Oh, you know, just teaching elementary school, that's about it." She took another bite of the disgusting pizza and knew she wouldn't be able to finish a second piece. Parker wondered how a crawfish boil tasted.

"Emily," Theresa admonished, "Parker's just being modest. She just finished her master's degree and is working on learning a third language." So, that one with the dark roots was Emily. Emily looked pissed, but the rest of the women, at least the three Parker hadn't gone to college with, looked impressed.

Parker was saved from any more conversation when Theresa looked down at her phone and said the Uber would be there to pick them all up in thirty minutes. The other women cheered and scurried off to get ready. Parker finished her glass of water before dumping the other piece of pizza in the trash and putting her plate in the dishwasher. At that point, she went ahead and cleaned up the rest of the kitchen, putting all the dishes in the dishwasher and condensing the pizza into one box that she slid in the fridge. There were literally only bottles of wine in there. Parker wondered what the hell these women thought they were going to eat all weekend. She started the dishwasher and went into the living room, sat on the couch, crossed her legs, and waited for the other women.

At seven, the Uber van arrived. All six women came stomping down the stairs, each of them wearing heels, and Parker wondered how they thought they were going to walk Bourbon Street in those. Theresa had on some ridiculous plastic crown thing proclaiming her the bride to be and she handed Parker a sash to wear that said Bachelorette Party on it. Parker slipped it on as she followed the group out to the waiting van. The driver dropped them in front of the Old Absinthe House bar, which was where Theresa had decided to start her night. Parker sighed again as the women all cheered when they walked in.

Why had she said yes to this? It just wasn't her thing. She liked libraries and parks and old churches. She wanted to cruise the river, listen to jazz, and go to the botanical gardens. Eat good food and sightsee, not slam shots and carry drinks up and down the street, screaming and yelling and grinding on any man who would let her. And she sure as hell didn't want to hang out with most of these women. Parker finally caved and downed a shot when the next round came because she was so miserable, and she didn't know what else to do. She hardly ever drank because she lost all inhibitions when she did. If one of the blondes decided to get snarky with her after this drink went to her head, she might end up slapping a bitch. Parker drank that shot, and when her head came down her eyes met those of the man she'd seen earlier today. Parker slowly brought the shot glass to the table in disbelief. Gabriel, that was what his friend had called him. Even his name was hot. He was all the way across the bar, but he might as well have been right in front of her. Parker swore she could feel his lips on her finger again.

I will find you later. He'd said those words before he disappeared this afternoon, but she hadn't really believed it. Did he have a tracker on her phone or something? No, that wasn't possible. Someone grabbed her arm and pulled her with the group out the door and onto the street. The group walked to the next location, and Parker looked back at the bar they'd left, hoping to see him step out of it. The sun was going down, and they'd already blocked off Bourbon Street to vehicles. It was Friday, and the street was already getting busy, people standing outside their establishments trying to entice the women inside.

They wandered for a bit before Theresa decided on their next location. This location was bigger than the last, the music louder, and she ordered shots for the table again. This was more like a shot and a half, and the alcohol went straight to her head. Parker then realized she hadn't eaten enough food today to handle this situation. One of the blondes returned to the table from the bathroom, and Parker heard her say something about some hot ass guy at the bar giving someone at this table some sex-me eyes.

Parker started to sweat. Her hands shook. Then she stepped away from the table to head to the bathroom. She sat on the toilet, pulled up the stupid-ass group text Theresa had put her in, and asked whoever would answer what the code to the condo door was. She said she didn't feel well and was going to catch an Uber back but that they should all continue and have a good time without her. No doubt they would. Parker washed her hands and looked at herself in the mirror before she gave herself a disgusted look and headed out the door, trying to tear the sash from her body. She almost had it off when she took a blind step and fell to the side, crashing into whoever was standing there.

"Parker."

CHAPTER TWO

Gabriel could tell she was miserable. It didn't take someone who'd known her through six reincarnations to figure that out. All you had to do was open your eyes and look. What he'd also seen in her eyes was the question of how he'd been able to find her. Maybe Charles was right. This was a different day and age than he was used to dealing with. Especially the women. Nowadays, they were more likely to question whatever move you made than they were before. They were more cautious now than in previous eras. And rightly so. Gabriel didn't like to think of the atrocities he'd seen done against women in his many centuries of life.

Maybe he needed to change the way he handled this situation, because this was her last incarnation, and if he lost her again, he lost her forever. There would be no waiting for the next time she showed up.

Forever was a lot longer than the hundred years he'd had to wait this time. Through each reincarnation, it seemed he'd waited longer and longer for her to return, and he'd nearly lost his mind this time. He never knew when she was going to show up, he only knew when she did. He'd felt that tug in his soul today and followed it until he stood in the shade of the cathedral, staring at her taking pictures with her phone. He hadn't been able to resist bumping her off balance, just so he could touch her to make it right. He'd chosen to speak French to her because he knew it was the language she preferred. Her first language. Gabriel had followed her after that, and when she'd stepped into that park, he'd tried not to remember the last time he was there with her, cradling her body to his own, her blood staining the ground. If he'd been ten seconds faster, he would have killed all those cowards and possibly saved her.

When she'd approached him this afternoon, his heart had swelled again, her voice like the singing of angels to him. It had taken Charles speaking to him in Latin, reminding him of the lead they were currently chasing, to break the spell he'd fallen under with her standing right in front of him.

And here he'd found her again, his soul leading him to her, and her looking so miserable that he wanted to whisk her away, which was what he would have done in a previous incarnation. But not this one. He had to do things differently. Then she'd crashed into him, trying to remove that sash from her body. "Parker." Her name rolled off his tongue. "*Est-ce que tu vas bien?*"

"No." Parker struggled with the sash. "No, I am not alright." She finally got the damn thing off and threw it in the garbage can she happened to be standing next to. Parker squared up to him, her small frame nearly touching his, and he smelled the alcohol on her breath. Then something else, some scent she was wearing, deep and sensual. It made him want to bury his nose in her neck. He wanted to pull her close.

"Are you following me?" She was as close to his face as her tipsy frame would let her get.

"Since I saw you in the last bar? Yes, I am."

His honesty stopped her for a second, but then the two and a half shots with basically no food took over again. "Why?"

"I don't understand. Why wouldn't I?"

"Which one of them put you up to this?" Parker swayed slightly, gesturing behind her. Gabriel was ready to catch her if she fell. "Was it the ugly blonde one with the dark roots? She's hated me since college. She'd do some petty shit like pay some gorgeous hunk to follow me around. As a matter of fact, I'm going to go kick her right now." Parker turned to head back to the table to do that only to find the group had left without her. "Oh, yeah," Parker said, not realizing she said it out loud, "I told them I was going back to the condo." She swayed on her feet.

This time, Gabriel wrapped his hand around her upper arm before she fell. "Parker, let's talk outside. I think some air might be good. There's plenty of cameras out there watching my every move, so don't worry."

Parker squinted at him. "You better not touch me."

"Aside from catching you if you fall, I will endeavor to keep my hands to myself. Deal?"

"I know what that word means," she said, everything slurring slightly. Then she turned so quickly that her purse flew out and almost hit him. Gabriel followed Parker out the door that she used both hands to push open with too much force, hitting the back of whoever was on the other side. She glared at the person, pushing her glasses back up her nose. Gabriel shrugged at the man as he walked by.

"What was in those shots you had? Moonshine?"

"I don't even know." She stumbled slightly to the right and almost fell off the sidewalk. Gabriel fisted his hands to keep from touching her. "Probably called something stupid like the *raging orgasm* or *sex-me-up* or some other dumb name." Parker stopped and held a shaking hand to her forehead. "Why do I do that?"

Gabriel stopped next to her but stepped closer when a large group of people crowded past.

"Why do you do what?"

Parker turned her head and slid her eyes up to his. The group of people had passed, but he remained close to her. She felt the heat from his body. He wore a teal cotton V-neck and black shorts. His skin was an olive tone, like the skin color you imagine everyone from Italy to have. And he

21

smelled good. God, did he smell good. Whatever cologne he had on, Parker wanted to bathe herself in it. She didn't realize she closed her eyes, tipped her head forward, and inhaled the scent.

But Gabriel did, and he couldn't keep himself from stepping even closer to her. He was sure his eyes went dark. He wanted to touch her so badly. He wanted to run his fingers through her hair. He wanted to unbutton every goddamn button on the dress she was wearing and lick her skin. But he'd told her he wouldn't touch her. Parker opened her beautiful slate-gray eyes again and, locked away in his memories, was how they looked when they darkened in desire. Like they were now. "Why do you do what?" Gabriel whispered it this time.

"Agree to things I don't want to." Parker swayed back but was able to right herself.

"Why would you do that?"

"They ordered pizza. Can you believe it? All this food to try and they ordered damn pizza. I've barely eaten anything today."

That would explain why the shots affected her so quickly. "What do you want to eat?"

Parker swayed again. "Why aren't you holding on to me?" Why did she trust this man? It was like she knew he wouldn't harm her.

"You told me not to touch you."

"I want you to touch me." Parker said the words so quietly, but Gabriel heard six incarnations whisper those words through his mind. His fingertips came up and lightly grazed the sensitive skin of her inner arm. She'd pulled her sleeves up at some point, and she was so glad she did because even that light touch made goosebumps raise on her skin. Gabriel ran his fingers from her wrist to her elbow and back again as his eyes held hers. They might as well have been alone on that sidewalk. Neither of them noticed the hordes of people now walking by.

Until someone went by and blew some stupid party horn

in her ear and startled her. This time, Gabriel caught her before she fell to the side. This time, he had an excuse to pull her against him. "You never told me what you wanted to eat." She was so close, and, this time, he was the one who got caught up in the scent of whatever she was wearing. Without thought, his hand burned a path down her spine to rest in the small of her back. He was never letting her go.

"Spicy gumbo," she murmured against his chest. "I wanted spicy gumbo, and they got pizza. It wasn't even good pizza."

Gabriel looked around at whatever street corner they stood close to. He'd had a lot of time to learn about this city, and he knew where the best of everything was. They weren't too far from a little restaurant that served what she wanted, even though it was almost ten at night. "Come with me," he said, taking her hand, "I know just the place."

Gabriel had insisted on accompanying her back to the condo, to ensure she made it inside okay. Earlier, he'd taken her two blocks over from where they'd been and showed her one of those tiny, hole-in-the-wall restaurants and, no lie, she hadn't had high hopes for the food. But she'd been wrong, so wrong. When the waiter had placed that bowl of spicy gumbo in front of her and she tried her first bite, it was worth every penny she'd spent on that plane ticket. "Holy cow," she exclaimed, looking at Gabriel, "that's spicy, but so good." Parker took another bite. "I'm definitely going to be sober after this."

"Next time, food first." Gabriel took a bite from his own bowl.

"Thanks for the advice, Dad, but there probably won't be a next time. That's the first time I've drank in like three years."

"That's too bad." Gabriel sipped his water. "I was looking forward to watching you kick the ugly blonde with the dark roots."

Parker looked down at her food before she looked back

up at him. "It's Gabriel, right?"

He nodded.

"Listen, Gabriel, I really would appreciate you honestly telling me if this is some sort of game. I have a lot going on in my personal life right now, and I don't want to get caught up in someone's sick petty game. So, if one of them paid you to do this, be honest."

"You think someone paid me to do this?"

"I mean, why else would you pick me out of the group of legs and hair and boobs?"

"What? What do you mean?"

"Have you ever seen *Indiana Jones and the Temple of Doom*? Just call me Short Round."

"Short you are but round you are not. Haven't you ever heard of Rubenesque?"

"That's just a pretty way to say fat."

"*Mon Dieu.*" Gabriel leaned back in his chair. This was never a conversation he thought he'd have with her; she'd never had this type of poor body image before. "Peter Paul Rubens loved the way the women he painted looked. Haven't you seen The Three Graces?" Those paintings were some of Gabriel's favorites.

"Oh, you're going way back. I thought we were talking twenty-first century. What are you, an art guru?"

"Yes, I am. But Rubens loved women like that," Gabriel said, "and so do I." He pointed to himself, and Parker's mouth clamped shut. "I don't understand the desire to be skin and bones. Where's the passion in that?" Passion, like the way her hips had swayed when she'd tasted that coffee today.

Parker knew her face went red, and she lowered her eyes to the last few bites of gumbo left in her bowl. She was full now, her tongue was numb from the heat, and she hadn't thought about not eating it in front of him. It seemed like he'd enjoyed how much she'd liked it. For some reason, she felt tears in her eyes. Gabriel stood and paid the bill. It was now almost eleven, and they closed soon. "Come on." He held his hand out to Parker. "Let me make sure you get back to where you're staying safe and sound."

He walked back down the street with her, his hand holding hers, and pulled out his phone with the other. "Here." He gave her his phone with the Uber app open. "Put in the address of where you're staying and get us a ride."

Parker couldn't have been more surprised when he handed her his phone. Nobody had that kind of trust anymore. "Don't you have a car?" she asked, typing in the address and then confirming the ride. The driver was only a couple of minutes away.

"Sure, but I hardly drive it down here to the Quarter," he said as she returned his phone.

"Besides, I wouldn't think you'd be too keen on jumping in a car with me right now."

"Well, that's the funny part, isn't it." She turned to him as the Uber driver stopped in front of them. "We get into cars with strangers all the time now." Parker opened the back door to the car and slid over to the other side so he could get in.

Parker shut her car door and walked up the sidewalk, the Uber pulling away from the condo. The house was dark, so she was the first one back. She turned when she got to the door and saw he hadn't followed her. He stood on the sidewalk in front of the house, waiting for her to step inside. "Parker." Gabriel clasped his hands behind his back. "I'd like to see you tomorrow. Can I stop by, say eleven? We can get some lunch. I'll drive this time."

Parker stepped away from the door and leaned against one of the porch columns. "I'm really supposed to be here for Theresa." He looked so heartbroken when she said that. "But I'm sure they won't mind if I take off for the afternoon."

She saw him smile, even in the dark.

"You don't know how happy that makes me. I'll see you tomorrow then." He moved like he was going to turn around and walk down the street. Parker pushed herself off the column.

"Gabriel."

He stopped and turned back to her. Her heart was in her throat. Something in her didn't want him to walk away. "Isn't this the part where you kiss me good night?"

Gabriel wouldn't have been able to stop his feet from moving toward her if a thousand men held him back. He'd never once been able to resist her. Her heartbeat fluttered in her neck as he crested those steps and pulled her to him, his hand going to the back of her neck as their lips met. Everything in him centered on the feel of his lips on hers again. Gabriel backed her up against that column, and her hands went around his back as her lips opened under his. His other hand slid to her face, moving it slightly so he could deepen the kiss as his tongue swept in, meeting hers that had been searching for him. It was like a hundred years hadn't happened. Gabriel ended the kiss but only shifted his head far enough away so he could see her face.

"Oh, wow," Parker uttered breathlessly. "I've clearly never received a proper good night kiss before." Her hand came up and wound around his neck. "I hope you aren't faking it because you'd deserve an Oscar." Parker pulled his mouth back to hers again. This kiss was deeper and longer, and the hand on her neck fisted in what hair he could while his other hand slid down her neck to her breast, squeezing her through the dress, her nipple tight in his palm.

"That kind of makes me wonder what else you haven't had properly done to you in this life." Gabriel's lips kissed down her neck, tasting her skin again.

"Show me what I've missed," Parker responded.

Gabriel stopped what he was doing. "What do you mean?"

Parker arched against him. "It's okay, I have an IUD. As long as you don't have any sexually transmitted disease."

"I don't but are you sure about this? Because I won't be able to deny you."

"Please don't make me overthink this decision."

Gabriel stepped aside for her so she could unlock the door, but he eased up to her while she was putting in the code and planted his lips on her neck. She got the code wrong the first try and had to wait for it to reset while his hands ran down her back and around her hips. He pulled her hips back against his groin when the door code chimed, and she opened the door. "Second time's a charm." His lips were right at her ear.

"Well, you're distracting me," Parker said, stepping into the door.

"That's how you know I'm doing it right," Gabriel replied. Parker didn't bother turning any lights on when she slipped her hand in his and led him up the stairs to her room, not quite sure where her bold behavior came from. Max had always been the one to initiate sex between them, mostly because he'd never given her a reason to want it. Parker heard Gabriel close and lock her bedroom door as she was kicking off her shoes. She took her purse off, tossing it to the floor, when Gabriel stepped up behind her and wound his arms around her. His hands were on her breasts again, one in each palm, and his lips were back on her neck.

Parker turned in his arms, and Gabriel's hands were back on her face, his lips devouring hers as he slid his hands into her hair. His fingers were almost frantic as he tried to get the hair ties out. He wanted his hands in her hair. "Get these damn things out of your hair," he growled.

Parker reached up to remove the hair ties before he pulled all her hair out and ruined the mood. As soon as her hair fell free, his hands were in it. She also took her glasses off and put them in her dress pocket before they fell to the floor and one of them stepped on them. Gabriel stepped back and tore the shirt over his head before closing the space between them again and kissing her while he unbuckled his belt and shorts and slid everything down to the floor. He felt Parker run her hands down his chest, and every dream he'd had in a hundred years came true again.

His hands shook as they started at the top button on her dress and slid every single one out of its hole, and his lips ran farther down her neck with every button that came free. Parker got impatient and was about to take it off over her head. "No." Gabriel stopped her. "Let me savor it." He inhaled deeply. "All of you smells so good."

Parker had her hands in his hair. He finished unbuttoning the dress to the belt around her waist and ran his tongue over the top curve of each breast. But she didn't want to participate in his slow torture anymore. She unbuckled her belt and let the dress fall the rest of the way off.

"Very well." Gabriel sighed. "If that's how you want it, *mon amour.*"

Gabriel's hands went around her back to unclasp her bra, and it wasn't until this garment came off that he felt her get shy. He backed her up to the bed where she sat on the edge. He leaned over her again and kissed her, an arm around her, sliding her back on the bed so he could join her. He wanted his hands on her body, every last inch of it. Right now. Gabriel lay beside her, his body half over hers before he changed his mind and rose over her, kneeling between her bent legs and sitting back on his haunches to look at her. "I know, it's disgusting." Parker resisted the urge to cover herself.

"I said nothing of the sort."

"You don't have to."

Gabriel reached up, grabbed her wrist, and hauled her upright to him, wrapping her hand around his hard length. "Does this feel like I find you in any way unappealing?" His hand tightened around hers wrapped around him.

He had every intention of lying her back down, but then her hand moved on him, and Gabriel's eyes closed at the sensation. Christ, he'd been waiting a hundred years to feel this again. To enjoy her hands on him. To have her body under his.

Parker was amazed at the feel of him. Max had never liked her to touch him. As she slowly ran her hand up him, she felt his hands slide up her thighs slowly, until he reached her very core. He tried to pull her panties off, but he couldn't accomplish that while kneeling between her legs. "Why did I not fully undress you before laying you down?"

"A silly mistake."

"One I shall never make again." He gently pushed her back down to the bed with the unfortunate side effect of her hand sliding off him. This time, he was able to remove the underwear and he skipped right over his finger touching her. Then straight to using his tongue on her. If there had been a headboard to grab, Parker would have gripped it, but she had to settle for the pillows her head was on at the feel of his mouth on her. Parker felt lust fill her to her very toes, which were currently curled in the blanket. He slowly slid a finger in her, and a groan came out of her mouth.

Parker pushed her hips up to him, purring his name as that long finger continued to move in and out of her body, stimulating every nerve he could. His mouth and tongue slid up over her stomach and then every other inch of her flesh before he reached her breast and drew a tight nipple in his mouth. Parker put her hands in his hair. Her back arched up to him as he switched to the other nipple, her knees raising higher. Her skin tingled, and her moans got louder before his mouth was on hers again as his finger slid out so his body could slide in.

Gabriel buried himself in her as far as he could. "*Mon amour*, you feel just as I remember." Gabriel slid his arms under her shoulders and his knees came up so her legs hung over his, driving him deeper inside. His body was flush with hers, and he thrust in her, staying close to her body, grinding against her. And that was what he wanted, to be close to her, because he'd been away from her for too long. Gabriel wanted no space between them. He wanted to feel all her soft skin. He stimulated her with his body while he drove into her, deep and long. Parker's mouth was right by his ear, and the sound of her moans and pants sent shivers down his back.

Parker's arms wrapped around him, running up and down his back, and he felt her teeth nip his shoulder before her head fell back with a deep moan, like it came from her soul. Her legs tightened over his, and her hips rose with every grinding thrust. He'd brushed her hair back and took her lips in a kiss when they both heard the front door open. Half a dozen drunk women poured into the house.

"Shhh," Gabriel breathed out as they both stilled.

They heard a couple of people stomp up the stairs and some loud, "She must be sleeping," drunken giggle whispers.

"Gabriel," Parker sobbed in his ear, "please don't stop."

"God himself couldn't make me stop right now," Gabriel whispered in her ear. "Not when you're so close."

Then he moved in her again, drinking in her moans with a kiss so the other women wouldn't hear. Nothing would stop him from bringing her to orgasm. Gabriel tried to get closer to her, as deep as he could, his hands framing her face. He wished he could hear her, that those women hadn't returned so soon. Her mouth tore free, and her neck arched as he continued to grind in her deep. Gabriel felt her convulse and shake around him, and she took his hand and held it over her mouth, pressing it down to muffle the sounds of her climax. Gabriel buried his face in her neck at his own release.

"She's sleeping," they heard from the hallway, "what a loser." Whoever said it stomped away as loudly as possible.

"What lovely friends," Gabriel whispered in her ear before he kissed it.

"Only one of them is someone I'd call a friend." Parker ran her hand down his smooth back, her breathing labored.

Gabriel stretched his legs out and lowered his body before rolling off her and lying on his side between her and the door. If anyone happened to open that door, they'd get a good look at his tight behind and not a single view of

Parker. The women downstairs moved around, but it sounded like there were fewer of them now. Probably off to their rooms to pass out. Gabriel, resting his head on his bent arm, ran a finger from her neck down and around each breast, watching her nipples tighten again, before lightly trailing down the rest of her torso. He trailed his hand across her stomach, over her hip, and down the outside of her thigh. Parker turned on her side, so they were chest to chest and hip to hip. Gabriel dipped his head and kissed her, his tongue sliding in her mouth like he'd just slid in her body. Parker's hand rested on his cheek, and Gabriel rolled her body closer to him with the hand on her hip. It was such a tender kiss, and his heart almost burst.

Parker was so confused about what she felt right now. He'd literally rocked her entire world and now he was so tender and loving. How could she find what she'd always been looking for in someone who was practically a stranger? Maybe that wasn't true, because from the very moment she'd laid eyes on him, she'd felt like she knew him. "Can I tell you a secret?" Parker asked after the kiss ended.

"On my soul."

"I was kind of dating this guy for the last two years. He didn't want me coming down here for some reason. He made it sound like I couldn't survive on my own, as if I hadn't made it twenty-six years before I met him. He always said things meant to belittle me. But, when I got here, I didn't let him know I'd landed." Parker traced the lines of the muscle in his arm. "I decided I was done with him this afternoon and blocked him from contacting me. In two years, I was never able to orgasm with him. I faked it."

"That's terrible."

"What I was trying to say was, even before this unbelievably fantastic episode happened, is that I wouldn't forget to let you know I landed safely. So, even if this was a joke, you've at least shown me I'm capable of standing up for myself, even when I think I can't. That there can be something better for me."

"What do I have to do to convince you this isn't, and never was, a prank played on you by some bitch with bad hair?"

"Things like this don't happen to me. I don't invite people into my bed. All my life, I've been too short, too big, too meek, too scared. Too many unknown scars." Parker flopped back; her body half twisted next to his.

Gabriel's hand stayed on her hip, her lower body touching his. "Like scars on your body?" He'd seen the one on her jawline this afternoon and his mind had flashed back to the blood smearing across her face from it. "Or like emotional scars?"

"Both, I guess. I must have blacked out for half my childhood because I don't remember how I got any of the several scars on my body. Good thing it's dark in here."

"Parker, you are perfect. I know you have nothing to go on here but my own words and your intuition but listen to me. What you see in me is true, *mon amour*. Everything you feel and know in your heart about me is true."

Parker turned her upper body back toward him and ran her hand through his hair. "Will you stay here with me tonight?"

"I would love nothing more, but that might be hard to explain in the morning when I try to leave."

"I suppose you're right," Parker sighed.

"Do you have a return flight soon?"

"I have nothing going on. I planned to travel for a couple of weeks after this torturous weekend ended. I currently have no ticket to anywhere."

"So." Gabriel ran his hand over her hip again. "What I'm hearing from you is that you're free for weeks."

Parker yawned and snuggled into his chest, shivering a bit. "At least a couple."

"Here." Gabriel stood up, pulled the blanket out from under her, and threw it over her before he crawled under it and pulled her to him again. "I don't want you to be cold." He couldn't resist kissing her again, his hand in her gloriously curly hair. The house was quiet now, so another round with her was out of the question, and he knew he should probably get dressed to leave.

He wanted to hold her for one more minute though. He'd missed this part the most.

Eventually, he got dressed, with Parker turning on her phone flashlight to help him find his socks and shoes. She'd rummaged around in her backpack and found her pajamas, which she put on before quietly opening her door and peeking out into the hallway. "The coast appears to be clear," she whispered, which made him chuckle. Parker took his hand and led him down the hallway, her bare feet silent. She checked around the staircase to ensure no one was downstairs before they walked down the last of the steps. Parker opened the front door. Gabriel pulled her out onto the dark porch so he could kiss her one more time.

"I'll call a ride when I get down the street," he said, brushing her hair back. "I'll be back for you at eleven on the dot."

Parker watched him step off the porch and down to the sidewalk before she turned and went back in the house, locking the door behind her.

Outside, Gabriel looked back to make sure she wasn't on the porch before he stepped into a shadow and disappeared.

CHAPTER THREE

Parker was getting ready when the doorbell rang at exactly eleven in the morning. She'd gotten up early and ordered two dozen donuts and two large containers of coffee to be delivered to the house. Some eggs and sausage would have suited her better, but she only had so much to work with. Parker ate a donut and sipped her coffee with cream and sugar in the quiet house. Before she was done, Theresa came in and gave her a hug, tears of joy in her eyes at her first sip of coffee.

"I have such a hangover." Theresa winced. "I hope we didn't wake you when we got back last night."

"Oh." Parker waved a hand at her. "No worries. I went right back to sleep. Yesterday wore me out I guess."

"Yeah, last night sure was something." Theresa eyed her over her coffee cup.

"That reminds me." Parker set down her coffee cup. "Did you have anything important planned for this afternoon? I was invited out for lunch today."

"Anyone I know?"

"Extremely doubtful."

"What about Max?" Theresa asked, reading between Parker's lines.

"Max who?"

"I'm so glad you finally dumped that guy. Is that why you bought all these donuts? To butter me up so you can dip out this afternoon?"

"Theresa, you must know you're the only one I care about hanging out with in this whole house. I think everyone else will be happy if I'm not around ruining their good time."

"They all want to go to some wine-tasting thing."

"Ugh." Parker threw her head back. "I almost kicked somebody last night from those two shots. I think I'm done with drinking forever."

"Parker, I wish other people could see you like this, then they'd know why I value our friendship so much."

"It's the other-people part that's usually the problem."

"You could at least try."

"*C'est la vie, mon amie.*"

"I know what those words mean." It was so much like what she'd said to Gabriel last night and a stunned Parker read the truth in Theresa's eyes. "You should make sure to look behind you."

"Oh, my God, Theresa…"

"Parker, please, you think I care? You're an adult. I don't know where you found him, but damn, I'd have left my own bachelorette party for that too."

"I originally intended to come straight back here."

"Were you actually here when we got back last night?" Theresa asked.

"Yes. And I got called a loser because I was 'sleeping.'" Parker did finger quotes around the word sleeping.

"So, you weren't 'sleeping' at that time?" Theresa also did finger quotes around the word. "At least not with your eyes closed?"

Parker fastened her lips shut before more words came out, but she felt her face getting red.

"Parker, tsk, tsk. Do you know how expressive your face is?"

"Yes, and I hate it. Have you ever had to discipline a classroom of fifth graders when all you wanted to do was laugh with them? Because someone said the word *orgasm* instead of *organism?*"

"Can't say I've had the pleasure."

The blondes walked in then. They shared a room, and both groaned in joy when they saw coffee.

"Parker got us all coffee and donuts." Theresa raised her cup. Samantha smiled and thanked her, but Emily with the bad hair looked like her coffee might be poisoned. Parker drew back into herself, downed the rest of her coffee, and threw the cup away. She'd asked the donut place to send cups with the coffee so she wouldn't have to run the dishwasher again.

"Guess I'll go get ready." Parker practically ran out of the kitchen then. She sat in her room for a minute to calm her racing heart, but she underestimated a house full of women with only two bathrooms. It was almost ten before she got a chance to jump in the shower, which was why she wasn't ready when Gabriel rang the doorbell at eleven.

Gabriel rang the doorbell and stepped back, slipping his hands in the pockets of his shorts.

All he'd been able to think about was the sound of Parker purring his name last night. There was no other way to describe the way she had sounded. It gave him chills. With every incarnation she moved through, he'd noticed the sounds she made would change slightly, and he'd thought he'd heard them all, but he clearly had not. During two of her incarnations, they'd never gotten to the point of intimacy, due to the nature of the times and the fact that they'd killed her so soon after he found her. In most of them, she was already a widow.

But those thoughts were not for this day.

A blonde lady, not Parker, answered the door. She didn't have dark roots, so Gabriel figured this wasn't the one Parker hated. Gabriel pushed his sunglasses back off his eyes. "Please tell me you're here to dance for us."

Gabriel's eyebrows drew together. "Excuse me?"

The woman sighed. "I didn't think so. Can I help you?"

"I'm here to pick up Parker."

"Parker?" She said it like she couldn't believe it, her eyes moving up and down his body.

"Yes," he responded. "Parker."

The woman stepped back. "Come in." Gabriel stepped into the entryway when she made space. She turned and yelled up the staircase. "Someone tell Parker she has a visitor!"

Gabriel winced because that brought every other woman in the house to the front room.

They all stood and stared at him, and it made him very uncomfortable.

"Hey," the black-haired woman said. "I know you. You're Gabriel Priveaux. I watched a news piece about you busting some people trying to pass off fake Monet."

"Yes, I'm Gabriel Priveaux."

"He's here for *Parker*?" he heard someone say lightly, and his eyes swept the room to see the blonde with the dark roots in the back.

Parker crept down the stairs and leaned over to look at the same time Emily made her snarky comment. Parker didn't blame her because he looked good enough to eat. Gabriel had on a pair of light gray chino shorts, a blue cotton shirt, and all-white Vans on his feet. The color scheme made his skin seem darker, like he already had a midsummer tan. Parker felt frumpy and wished she'd at least thrown a belt around her waist. She'd decided on a yellow t-shirt dress and her white Keds. Parker had layered it with her jean jacket, but she knew that probably wouldn't last in the Louisiana heat. Her hair was damp from her late shower, so she hadn't put it up yet. Parker sighed lightly.

It had already been a hell of a day. Gabriel looked up at her sigh, like he'd heard it, and his eyes lit up and a smile formed on his lips at the sight of her. Parker gave him her own shy little smile. Every other woman in that house looked up at her then, and Parker's anxiety rose. She literally couldn't get her feet to move. "Save me," she mouthed to him.

"You have to come down here sooner or later," he told her in French.

"They're all looking at me," Parker responded.

"If you want them to stop, then we have to leave."

"Don't make me kick you."

"Come down here and I'll let you."

They held the whole conversation in French, and Parker hoped no one else spoke it. Parker peeked into the room again before she straightened her spine, plastered a smile on her face, and forced her feet down the steps. She stopped in front of him with the fakest smile he'd ever seen. Gabriel lifted her left hand and kissed her ring finger like he'd done yesterday. "You did it, *mon amour.*" Gabriel switched back to English.

"Can we go now?" Parker ground out through clenched teeth.

Gabriel stepped to the side and swept his hand out, *"Après vous, s'il vous plait."* Parker stepped out the door before him like he'd asked her to, and Gabriel turned to the room, nodding. "Have a lovely afternoon, ladies," he then followed Parker.

"What just happened?" he heard someone ask before the woman who had answered the door shut it again.

"Parker." Gabriel reached for her arm before she continued to walk off down the sidewalk.

"Slow down. What's wrong?" She was shaking.

"I want to vomit," she said, facing away from him.

"Why?" Gabriel slowly pulled her back to him. Before she knew it, he was right behind her. She felt the heat from his body, and it comforted her.

"I don't know, it's something about all those people staring at me."

"Maybe they're jealous of you. Because of how beautiful you are." Parker felt him lightly run his fingers through her curls.

"Doubtful. Probably wondering how a two like me got

a ten like you." Parker shook her head.

"You are more beautiful than any of those other women, Parker. Inside and out."

"Did you bump your head this morning?"

"All I could think about this morning was you."

"Really?" Parker had a hard time believing him.

"On my soul." Gabriel ran his fingers through another curl again. "As much as I would love to stand here all day, playing with your glorious hair, we should probably go before the bachelorette parade comes out."

Gabriel turned her to his car, which she had unknowingly stopped next to. He drove a sleek black Mustang Shelby. It was exactly the type of car she'd expect him to drive. Gabriel pressed the button on the key fob to unlock the doors and opened the passenger door for her. He winked at her as she slid into the car. Gabriel walked around to the driver's side, glancing up at the house as he did so, and he caught a couple of faces in the window.

Gabriel waved at them as he slid into his car.

Parker was looking out her window when he shut his door. "Gabriel." She turned to look him in the eyes. "I don't want to come back here."

"Sounds good to me." Gabriel started the car. "I can ask my assistant to come pick up your stuff later."

"I'll need to find a place to stay."

"I know just the place. It comes with an extremely comfortable bed."

Gabriel drove them back down to the French Quarter and parked in a paid parking lot. It was starting to fill with tourists, and Gabriel got one of the last spots available. Parker stepped out of the car and stripped off the jean jacket. It was hot and humid already. This was a different humidity than she was used to in Illinois, and, by August, she bet it would be oppressive. Parker peeked over at Gabriel. He was looking around, watching the people walking by, as cool as a cucumber. She liked those sunglasses on him. "How long have you lived here?" Parker asked as they met at the back of the car. Gabriel took her hand and they stepped onto the sidewalk to head down Decatur Street.

"I was born here." He then told her the story he'd come up with to explain his life here. "I spent about ten years away studying in France and Italy. The building I own has been in my family for almost a hundred and fifty years. What about you?" He looked at her. They slowly made their way past Jackson Square, and Gabriel felt the ghosts of the past in there.

"I grew up in Indiana. Went to college in Indiana. Very Midwestern upbringing. Visit the lake in the summer, watch the leaves change color in the fall, sledding down the biggest hill in the winter. No studying whatever you studied in France or Italy."

"That sounds like a fantastic way to grow up." Gabriel kissed the hand he held. He always liked to hear about her childhood.

"Both my parents are still alive. They're both teachers, so I guess that's what inspired me to also become a teacher. I live near Chicago and teach fifth grade at a little suburban public school. I finished my master's last year at twenty-seven."

"That's impressive."

They stopped in front of a little store painted red. Parker read the sign over the door.

"Central Grocery and Deli. What are we doing here?"

"*Mon amour*, you want to taste New Orleans, then here is one place you get a muffuletta sandwich." Parker bounced on the balls of her feet. Gabriel smiled at her excitement. "Had I known you'd be this excited, I'd have brought you here sooner." They went in and ordered a sandwich to share and a couple bottles of water before they walked across the street and found a bench near the riverfront to eat. A nice breeze came from the river.

"*Ç'est magnifique.*" Parker wiped her mouth with a napkin

when she was done, smiling shyly at Gabriel. He'd seemed to enjoy her enthusiasm for the sandwich more than eating it himself, just as he'd done last night. She lowered her eyes when he ran his thumb down her cheek. "What did you study?" she asked, raising her eyes to his again. "In France and Italy?"

"My family has dealt in art and antiques for generations." It wasn't a complete lie; he *had* dealt in art and antiques for generations. "I spent a lot of time studying with the master classical painters. Black market art fraud costs hundreds of millions of dollars a year." Gabriel had amassed a fortune over the last few centuries dealing in art and antiques. It was easy when you had that much time to do it. Now, he also had people asking him to authenticate different items. Many of his clients were from museums around the world. Considering he'd been studying these artists since they started painting, there was no more experienced. But he also donated anonymously to different organizations around the area. Every eighty years or so, he'd "die" and will everything back to himself. Charles was very good at forging the documents they needed for new social security numbers and identification.

"Is that where you learned French?"

"Where I perfected it, yes."

"I assume that means you also speak Italian."

"I can teach you, if you'd like." She'd left her hair down, and Gabriel caught a curl around his finger.

"What about your parents?"

"I have no family left." Also, not really a lie. He'd lost track of his bloodline many centuries ago.

"How old are you actually?"

"Thirty-three." It was the age he'd turned on his last birthday. When he was mortal.

"But sometimes, it feels like centuries."

"Ewww, you're old." She smiled at him as she said it.

"What? I'll show you old." Gabriel reached out and started to tickle her sides and

Parker's laughter rang out over the river.

They headed up Dumaine Street, walking hand in hand, and Gabriel got to enjoy the streets of New Orleans for the first time again. He'd walked these streets for over two centuries. There was nothing he didn't know about this area. He'd watched it change so much, the cycle of life, the ebb and flow, even more recently when Hurricane Katrina hit. But he'd remained the same, caught in the middle of something he'd never wanted to be a part of. They made a pit stop so Parker could use the bathroom in a restaurant and Gabriel, standing out on the sidewalk, used the opportunity to call Charles. "Charles," he said when the man answered, speaking in Italian. "I need you to do me a favor."

"I'm afraid to know," the man answered. Charles hadn't been happy when Gabriel walked out of a shadow and into Charles's living room last night. The older-looking man had glared at him over his spectacles, the glasses were a hundred and fifty years old, but he still used them. "You couldn't even stay away from her for twelve hours?"

"No, Charles, I can't. I can't," he said it again, flinging himself into a leather chair. "I don't want to stay away from her for twelve seconds." Gabriel leaned back and closed his eyes. He felt her on his fingertips. "You should see the scar on her jawline." Gabriel clenched his jaw. "From the last time those cowards found her." It attested to the brutality of her last murder, that she would carry the scars into this life.

"She has no time left after this life."

Gabriel shot to his feet. "You think I don't know that already, Charles? You think I haven't obsessed over this for the last hundred years?" Gabriel ran his hands through his hair and paced the room.

"And then you lose your soul."

Gabriel sat back in the chair and closed his eyes again. "Losing her hurts more."

"You say that now."

"I've said it six times."

"You've found nothing in any of those books you've purchased?" Charles checked something on his paperwork.

"If it was a curse, I'd know how to break it by now, but it's not."

"You can always try marrying her again," Charles offered. "Even *he* might not be able to tear apart the sanctity of marriage."

"Must you remind me of my every failure?"

"It is not your failure, Gabriel." Charles also leaned back in his chair. "We don't know if it would make a difference."

"But she would at least be my wife for however long I got." The very idea nearly brought him to tears.

"What favor do you need?" Charles asked, bringing Gabriel back to the present.

"I'm going to send you an address. I need you, as my assistant, quote unquote, to head over there and get Parker's stuff out of the room she was staying in."

"You want me to go to this vacation condo, gather up all her belongings, and take them where?"

"To. My. House." Gabriel enunciated each word.

"This is different."

"I'm getting desperate."

"I think this is a good choice," Charles said.

"You do?" Gabriel saw Parker out of the corner of his eye, and he turned so he was facing her, reaching out for her hand. "Okay, I'll send you the address. Thanks, Charles." He finished the conversation in English. Gabriel hung up and slipped his phone in his pocket. "Charles is my assistant."

"You don't have to explain anything to me."

"He's going to get your stuff for you," Gabriel continued. He resumed walking with her again, and they turned onto Bourbon Street.

"And where, exactly, is he taking it?"

"Are you going to kick me if I tell you that I asked him

to take it to my place?" Gabriel stopped and turned her to face him.

Parker looked at him, but all she could see was her reflection in his sunglasses. She reached up and removed them so she could look into his eyes. "There, now I can see your eyes when you ask me if I want to stay with you."

Gabriel brought her hand to his lips again, kissing her ring finger, never breaking eye contact. He lowered her hand down. "Will you come and stay with me?"

"That wasn't so hard, was it?"

"Not yet, it isn't."

Parker raised an eyebrow in a very teacher-like fashion. "Was that a sexual innuendo?"

"One hundred percent."

Parker shook her head and smiled, putting his sunglasses back over his eyes. She started walking back down the street with him.

"So." Gabriel drew the word out as he stepped next to her. "Is that a yes?"

"Your bed better be super comfortable."

Gabriel stopped walking, pulled her back into a hug, and kissed her, not caring about the people walking on the sidewalk. "I promise, *mon amour*, you will never be disappointed in my bed."

Parker felt a thrill of desire run through her at the memory in his words. "You've already proven that. Quite thoroughly, I might add."

Gabriel slid his sunglasses up again, his little half smile curving on his lips. He wanted her to see it in his eyes. "I do like to be thorough."

"Excuse me," they heard a voice next to them say, and they both turned to look. "Could you two move along or step to the side? You're blocking the sidewalk."

"Oh my God." Parker's face flamed red in embarrassment. "I'm so sorry." She turned and stepped off the sidewalk, hauling Gabriel to the other side of the street. Her face was still red as they continued walking.

"You're adorable when you're embarrassed." Gabriel took out his phone and texted Charles the address. These devices had made life a lot easier.

It took Charles twenty minutes to drive to the condo. Sometimes, he wished he could move through the shadows like Gabriel did. But stealth was Gabriel's innate ability. It was what he had been born into. Charles did a mind-sweep of the house before he rang the buzzer, and he didn't like what he found. A blonde woman answered the door. "Can I help you?"

"I am Charles Guarder, assistant to Gabriel Priveaux. I was asked to come by and gather the belongings of one Miss Parker Reed."

"Theresa," the woman said, turning and walking away from the door.

Charles remained standing on the porch. She opened the door and held a conversation with someone inside before she looked at him again and held up a finger. After a minute, the woman returned to where Charles was standing. "I'll get it for you."

"Mr. Priveaux was quite adamant that I assist you." The woman looked Charles up and down, and he knew this body did not present an outward threat. Charles pushed the thought into her mind.

"Okay, follow me, but be quick. We're leaving soon."

Parker hung up with Theresa and looked at Gabriel. "You didn't waste any time, did you?"

"I assumed they would be busy doing whatever." Gabriel shrugged. "They might not be back until late again, and then who knows when you'd get your stuff."

His explanation made sense, but Parker did squint at him some. He just smiled. Parker had stopped at a souvenir shop, saying she wanted to get her parents a magnet or something, and had just checked out when Theresa called her. They crossed another intersection, and Parker paused in front of a little voodoo store. "Marie Laveau's House of Voodoo." Parker read a sign out front that said the psychic was in. "Let's go in here." Parker started toward the shop door, but Gabriel didn't move a muscle. "What's wrong?"

"You want to go in here?" He remembered the real Marie Laveau. Gabriel had no doubt her spirit still wandered. But that wasn't what stopped him, it was the idea of being in the same space with a psychic. A voodoo psychic at that.

"You can wait out here if you want."

What he wanted was for her to not go in there. "No, I'll come with you." Gabriel held his breath as they walked through the door.

Parker thought his reaction was somewhat strange, but not alarmingly. Like, it didn't make her want to run in the other direction. Alarm bells didn't go off like the ones she'd ignored with Max for two years. Parker wandered around the small shop. It was full of kitschy tourist stuff, but she could tell there was real power in this place. It was something she'd always been able to feel, the power in places and objects. It was why she liked to touch things, to feel them. Her students loved going on nature field trips because she got as excited about holding a frog as they did.

It didn't take very long to circle the shop, and she'd practically run her hand over everything in there. Parker saw some jewelry she liked, but nothing that spoke to her. She was about to grab Gabriel's hand and leave when a small, dark woman came out of the back room. The woman was shorter than Parker. She walked right up to Parker and stopped. Parker saw something swirling in her eyes. Gabriel's hands were on her shoulders then, and he pulled her back slightly. "Seven times you've walked this earth and yet your life remains unfulfilled." The woman's eyes went to Gabriel. "Immortal, you cannot save her soul."

"Yes, I will," Gabriel answered.

"It does not need it. Her soul is pure. Hers is not the soul to save. Six times tragedy and yet still the same." The woman stopped and listened to something in her head, her eyes swirling faster. "Perhaps," she said, "this time, you will discover Bondye lives in more places than you thought. Perhaps, this time, you will get what you desire most. But you must give up the ageless. Give your soul freely."

"There is no more time. What is my life worth after this? I would give everything I have."

"Hold nothing back," the psychic whispered this last part before her eyes landed on Parker again. The woman took Parker's hand and held hers over it. Parker felt the energy move between them. "Your soul remembers what your heart desires. Do you agree? Do you desire it to be?"

"Yes." The word came from deep inside her and it sounded like she had more than one voice.

"And you, Immortal?"

"With everything I have."

"So it shall be." The old woman's eyes cleared then, and they no longer swirled. "I'm sorry, dear," she said, her voice now so different from what it had been. "I didn't hear you. What can I help you find?"

Parker stared at the woman because she didn't know what had happened. Was the woman crazy? Gabriel took his hands off her shoulders. She didn't know what he was doing until he held a few hundred dollar bills out to the old woman. "A donation."

"Many blessings on you and your new marriage." The woman made some sort of movements with her hands. It looked like she was sprinkling pixie dust or something. She then took the money from him, folded it into her pocket, and returned to the room she'd come out of. Parker stood there, speechless, and gave no reaction when Gabriel led her back onto the sidewalk. Before she knew it, they were back at his car. He insisted on opening the door for her. Parker stood looking at him, then the door between them.

"What just happened?"

"Something I never thought would," Gabriel responded.

Gabriel drove them back to the building he owned in the Treme District. It was a beautiful old antebellum building that had been new when he'd purchased it. He drove around back and pulled into the carport he'd had installed after cars had been invented.

Parker got out of the car before he could open the door and looked up at the three-story building. "This is your house?"

Gabriel pointed to each floor. "Shop, storage space, my apartment."

"Of course, you would live on the top floor."

"There's an outside entrance on the side." Gabriel pointed to the set of stairs. About ten years ago, he'd had the staircase rebuilt and a larger deck area added to the side entrance to the living quarters. He could get in there by this door or through an internal door in the building. "I can give you a tour later." He ran his hand down her hair. She'd never been in his home, and he wanted her there, right now, in his bed.

He wanted to seal what the voodoo priestess had done.

Parker turned and saw these thoughts in his eyes because he'd never lowered his sunglasses back down. His eyes went dark as he looked at her, and something in her melted. Parker reached up and pulled his head down to her at the same time she rose on her tiptoes to meet him. It was nothing more than raw passion when their lips met. Gabriel moved her back against the garage wall, his hands fisted in her hair, tilting her head so he could kiss her from all angles. His sunglasses slid down his face, and he tore them off and threw them. He really didn't care where they landed.

Parker moved her hands from his neck, over his shoulders, and around his back, holding him tighter as their lips devoured each other. Then his lips slid down her neck, his teeth nipping her and his tongue running over the spot. She arched her back, wanting more, her breathing already labored. "Gabriel," she ground out, searching for the button on his shorts. "I want you right now." She felt like she was drunk. This was how she responded, without inhibitions, after drinking. But she wasn't, and she'd never in her life had the guts to act like this.

He stopped her hands, grabbing her wrists and raising them above her head as he held them in his own. "I like how you think, but not here, not this time." Gabriel kept one wrist in his hand and led her around the building to the staircase. He fumbled around, getting his keys out of his pocket, and almost dropped them as they walked up the stairs. Gabriel managed to get the key in the lock, opened the door, and then turned. He picked Parker up in his arms and carried her over the threshold of the door.

He'd employ whatever tradition he had to at this point.

Parker was startled and threw her arms around his neck; afraid he would drop her. No one had ever picked her up before. "Oh, my God, please don't drop me."

Gabriel kicked the front door shut with his foot. "Parker, that's the complete opposite of what I want to do to you."

"I know you're going to drop me. I weigh like a hundred and forty pounds."

"You weigh nothing."

"Gabriel."

"Look, *mon amour*, you weren't paying attention, and now we are in my bedroom."

"I'm not looking around," she said, "that might make you go off-balance. I think my life flashed before my eyes."

"Parker," Gabriel whispered with such emotion that she felt it in her bones. Parker met his eyes then. "Your life was never in danger from me. You can always trust me."

There was something there in his words that she felt, something buried in her subconscious. She heard his words echo. The fingers attached to the hand she had around his neck rubbed lightly, and she watched his eyes go dark again. "Gabriel, are you going to put me down?"

"No. I'm never letting you go." Gabriel kicked the door to his bedroom closed before he carried her to his bed. He turned and sat on the bed, lowering her to his lap. Parker tightened her arms around his neck.

"I think you need to kiss me more. I didn't get enough downstairs."

Gabriel didn't respond. Instead, he tightened his arms around her and brought her lips to his. Parker ran her hands through his hair, trying to tell him without words how much he meant to her. It was like she'd known him forever. His hands were in her hair, running down her back. She felt the warmth from them, and she knew what those hands could do. Parker kicked off her shoes before she slid off his lap and stood in front of him. Her heart pounded, but the look in his eyes made her hot, hotter than she'd ever been. She'd only been with one other person besides Max, and Gabriel was light years away from both. Parker drew a deep breath and pulled her dress over her head.

Parker took her dress off, and Gabriel's hands were instantly on her hips, pulling her to him, his arms going around her as he centered her between his legs and laid his head on her. She ran her hands through his hair and along his arms, then up his sleeves as far as she could. Gabriel let go of her only to take off his shirt before he tugged her right back to him again. This time, her hands traveled down his back. "Parker." Gabriel had his nose against her skin. "You smell so good."

"It's lotion. I apply it liberally from neck to toes."

Gabriel's arms tightened more, and he slid his hands up her back to unclasp her bra. He looked up at her as the garment fell away and brought his hands up to cup each breast, teasing her nipples into tight peaks. Gabriel kissed her skin then, his hands running over her and pulling her to him. Parker swore she felt his emotions as she stood in front of him. Before she knew it, he had her underwear down, squeezing her, his hands dipping between her legs from behind.

"Parker, I need you on this bed right now." He said it in a way that made her understand the choice was hers. Instead of words that she wasn't sure would make it around the lump in her throat, Parker eased closer to him. That hand moved around the front of her, running through the folds of her body, and her knees dipped. At the first moan that escaped her, Gabriel picked her up and turned to lay her out on his bed, tearing off his shorts.

There was no waiting this time.

Gabriel kneeled between her legs and hauled her back to him, grabbing her hips as he entered her. Parker's back arched at the feel of him sliding in. She didn't know what was different about it this time, but it seemed like she was reaching for something so much bigger than a climax. Parker reached up and grabbed the headboard, glad that he had one, as he continued to thrust into her. Then he leaned over her, lifting her hips higher. He grabbed the headboard as well and his thrusts became harder. Parker moved her hands to his chest, pushing back against him.

"You can be as loud as you want, *mon amour*. I'm the only one who will hear it."

Parker let go. His words allowed something in her to break free, and she pulled his mouth down to hers. didn't stay there because he wanted to hear her. He lifted her leg higher on his hip and was just able to get his mouth around a nipple. Every sound out of her mouth was like music. Her head fell back, and her sounds got louder, until she reached for the headboard again and let out one long moan. Her body shook. Gabriel followed right after her.

The one thing Gabriel never thought he'd feel happened for him. Her soul locked with his. The words the priestess had spoken may have been few, but the ceremony was true to that religion and God had heard.

She was finally his wife. Gabriel's heart soared.

Gabriel let go of her leg but stayed on her, feeling her heart beating against his chest.

"Parker, I'm sorry."

Parker was rubbing his back, but her hand stopped at those words. "What are you sorry about?"

"This wasn't my best performance. I just couldn't wait any longer." "So, are you saying your bad is someone else's great?"

"I can only speak for myself." His hand ran up her side from where it had been sitting on her knee.

"Gabriel, I love having you where you are, but I'm having a hard time breathing."

Gabriel lifted his body and lay on her side, pulling himself up so she could rest her head on his chest. "Can I ask what the hell was that lady talking about in that voodoo store?"

"I don't know. She probably had dementia or something." He couldn't tell her the truth right now.

"You seemed to know what she was talking about."

"I read an article once about not trying to bring dementia patients back to reality, that you should agree and talk about whatever they're talking about. It said it's pointless to tell them any differently than what they believe."

"Her eyes freaked me out. I didn't know what to say."

"Maybe she's going blind." Gabriel hoped the voodoo spirits didn't hear him and took back what she'd done. He sent up a little prayer to them, so they'd understand his position right now.

"She said something about blessings on our marriage."

"What did you want me to tell her? Sorry, I've only actually been around her for twenty-four hours? Besides, maybe she knows something we don't."

"You handed her a bunch of money."

"I donate a lot of money to this area. It was only a few hundred dollars." Gabriel pulled her closer to him, rolling her body a bit so they were side by side. Parker lay on his arm, one of hers over his body, her ear by his heart. This felt so right, like something in her life was complete now, some goal she didn't know she'd been reaching for had been accomplished. She hadn't cared that the room was bright with the sun coming in the window.

Parker didn't care that he'd seen the scars on her body.

The mysterious scars that she didn't remember how she received them.

Gabriel had seen them, and it had taken everything in him to not explode at the sight and kill every angel in heaven. He remembered holding her bleeding body to his own, looking down and not believing what they'd done to her. She had one across her left breast, a circular pattern, about three inches, where one of them had plunged their blade in her heart and twisted. That was most likely the one that killed her a hundred years ago.

The hand Parker had around him rubbed his back again, and Gabriel sighed, holding her tighter. "A few hundred dollars could be everything to someone," she finally said.

Gabriel tilted her head up and kissed her, his mouth on hers so soft. Then he ran his hand across her face. His hand slid down then, over her neck, his fingers light when they traveled across the side of her breast. Her nipples tightened against his chest. Gabriel's hand kept slipping down, over her hip, as far as his arm could reach while their kiss deepened. Parker pulled herself up, so she was closer to his face, and her hand went around his neck. Every kiss he gave her was exquisite, like his lips just knew what to do. She could kiss him all day.

That hand down her leg lightly made its way back up but stopped at her waist and went to the space between them. He brushed his hand over her, waiting to see what she'd say. Her answer was to bring her leg up over his hip, giving him room. Gabriel's lips were on her neck when his fingers found her nerve bundle. His mouth was on her breast he'd so lightly brushed, drawing her hard nipple in as his hand slid across her folds and his finger entered her.

All Parker could do was hang on as he teased her again. Her head fell back as his finger slid out, circled her swelling bundle, and then slipped back into her body. His tongue, God, he licked around her breast now and he'd moved her slightly so he could do the same to the other one. But his hand continued, in and out and around, until she was so close. The way she moaned told him it was time to stop.

"Gabriel, please," she sobbed, like she thought he wouldn't finish what he'd started.

Gabriel held her by the leg she had over him and turned onto his back, pulling her with him so she straddled him. Parker pushed herself upright and rose on her knees to slide down him, her head thrown back at the feel of him. Parker rode him, her eyes closed, but Gabriel watched as her hands went to her breasts, holding them, caressing them, squeezing each nipple.

Gabriel set his hands on her hips, pushing her down, grinding her to him as she continued to move on him, his hips rising to meet her. He angled one hand between them to stimulate her more, and she purred his name again. Her moaning got louder, and she reached down and grabbed his wrists, grinding against him. Parker climaxed so hard it felt like she stopped breathing for a moment. She rode him while her body shook, and then he brought her face down to his as his knees came up. Gabriel kissed her before his head fell back. His final moan made goosebumps raise on her skin.

Outside, Charles parked his car next to Gabriel's and he got Parker's bag out of the back seat before locking it and setting the alarm. He was glad he insisted on helping pack her stuff up because that blonde woman would have happily forgotten half of it. Charles headed for the stairs to Gabriel's apartment before he stopped, thought about it, and did a mind sweep of the third floor. Everything came back to him fine, but he turned to the other door instead of heading up to Gabriel's apartment. Gabriel had blacked out his bedroom to him. Charles's mind couldn't penetrate that black wall around his room, and he certainly didn't want to.

CHAPTER FOUR

"I'm starving," Gabriel exclaimed a couple of hours later. They'd laid there together after the last time and had drifted off to sleep for a while.

"What does a crawfish boil taste like?" Parker asked. Her head rested on his arm as she ran her fingers through the light smattering of hair on his chest.

"It's quite delicious, but you have to eat like four hundred and seventy-two of those little things to be full."

Parker sighed. "I don't think I have the energy for that today."

"There might be something in my fridge." Gabriel ran his free hand down her hair. "Charles usually takes pity on me and makes enough for two when he cooks."

Parker stopped rubbing his chest and lifted her head. "Your assistant lives in this apartment?"

"No, his apartment is downstairs on the second floor."

"That's weird."

"What's weird about it?"

"He works for you, lives in the same building as you, cooks food for you. Someone from the outside looking in would wonder about that relationship." Parker laid her chin on his chest.

"He doesn't cook for me; he takes pity on me occasionally when he cooks for himself and you're the only

57

one who's been in my bed. Charles would pick a partner that looked like someone in the bachelorette parade."

"If you say so." Parker shrugged, her hand trailing down his chest again. They'd crawled under his blanket at some point before falling asleep, but Gabriel had pulled it to the side and had one leg sticking out, his knee bent. Parker slipped her fingers down his side and up his leg to the knee before she used her nails to lightly scrape on the way back. "I love touching. I want to touch everything all the time. The way things feel, it speaks to me. Maybe it's why I love to cover myself in lotion. I get to touch all of me." She did the same motion, and his skin tightened under her cheek. "It was something denied me the last time."

"If you're talking about this guy you told me about," Gabriel said, his voice husky, "he sounds like a royal douchebag."

"Yeah, I ignored the warning signs for a long time." Parker's hand flattened and went under the blanket this time. "I've just gotten so, I don't know, restless lately." Her fingers combed through his hairs and Gabriel sucked in a breath when her hand came back up.

"Parker, you can touch me whenever you want. All of me."

"I saw you, standing across the street, and I thought you were the most beautiful person I'd ever seen. I'm jealous of your lips." Her hand went back down again, but this time she didn't stop. She wrapped her hand around him. "You'll never know how much courage it took for me to walk across that street and say something to you." She slowly moved her hand up and down. "I chose French because then I wouldn't look stupid if you didn't understand me, you'd just think I was some dumb foreign tourist."

Gabriel's hips rose a little as she squeezed and ran her thumb over the tip. "Imagine my surprise when you could understand me." She gripped him hard as her hand lowered and Gabriel fisted her hair. "Everything sounds better in French."

Gabriel did what she wanted and switched languages. "Mon amour, you are killing me."

"I'll make it better," she responded, lifting her eyes to his as she slid down his body. Maybe it was the French that made her so bold, maybe it was him. Who knew, but everything felt right. Parker's lips wrapped around him, and he sucked his breath, reaching for the headboard. She pleasured him while he told her everything he wanted to do to her, in French, until he couldn't speak anymore. Parker was more than willing to keep going until he finished, but Gabriel would have none of that. He sat up and flipped her onto her back, where he put his mouth on her until she rode the edge too. It didn't take long for her to get there.

Then he was in her, close to her again, grinding into her like he loved to do. He pushed her to the very limits before he let her go. Her climax made her knees raise, and she tumbled over that waterfall.

The sun was almost down before Gabriel checked his phone and saw a message from Charles. He'd left her bag in the hallway outside his inner door. Parker had fallen asleep again. Gabriel got out of bed, pulled on his boxer briefs, and opened the door to his room, which dropped the black shield he had around it. His phone buzzed in his hand almost as soon as that happened, and he headed to the door. It was another message from Charles.

Charles: *I put in a takeout order for you. I know you have nothing up there. I took a guess on the time and it was just dropped off.*

There was something to be said about the kind of mind powers Charles had. He didn't

guess at much, he only liked to use that word. *Thank you*, Gabriel messaged back.

Charles: *I hate to bring in negativity, but did you know about who was around her in that condo?*

Gabriel: *Yes, I did. That's why I'm glad she wanted to leave.*

Gabriel opened the door to the inner staircase of the building and picked up her bag before shutting and locking it again. He dropped the bag by his bedroom as he made his way to the front door for whatever food Charles had called in. He picked it up and smelled it as he shut and locked the front door. Gabriel set the bag on the kitchen counter and opened it. He hoped she liked chicken lo mein.

He hoped it wasn't as bad as the pizza incident.

Gabriel grabbed her bag again and headed back into his bedroom to place her bag on the foot of the bed before crawling to her. She had the blanket pulled up to her neck and he leaned over her, kissing her cheek. "Let me sleep." She snuggled into the blanket more.

"Already bossing me around after twenty-four hours." Parker peeked an eye open. "Is that all it's been?" "Do you want to eat or shower first?"

"What do you have?" Parker asked, looking over her shoulder at him.

"I ordered some takeout Chinese chicken lo mein." She didn't need to know that Charles had done it.

"I love lo mein. That's way better than pizza. But I should probably eat first. I have a feeling showering might lead to other things and I'm hungry."

"I like other things." He rubbed against her.

"I like other things too. Is my bag here? I need to put some clothes on."

Gabriel handed her the bag. She put her pajamas on before they headed out to the kitchen to eat. Gabriel's apartment was sparse, with not a lot of furniture, only a leather couch and loveseat, a coffee table, and television. They ate the chicken lo mein with chopsticks out of the containers they came in, and Gabriel asked her a lot of questions about her childhood. Parker found her phone in her purse and showed him pictures of her parents and her together.

Gabriel looked at the pictures on her phone in confusion. "Parker, I can't help but notice the difference in skin tone between you and your parents." Her mother was a short Asian woman. He could tell she was short because in the picture Parker showed him, her mother was a bit shorter than she was. Her father was a tall, dark man, he had to be at least as tall as Gabriel's six feet, if not taller.

"I'm clearly adopted."

"What about your birth parents?"

"I don't know who they are. No one can seem to find or recall that information."

Gabriel kept looking at the picture. Something was off. She'd always known her birth parents before. His eyes lifted to hers when she turned the phone and he saw the question in hers. "Is something wrong?" he asked.

"I was going to ask you the same thing."

He felt her pull back from him.

"Do you have some issue with my parents? Because that's the one thing guaranteed to make me walk away from this right now."

"What do you mean?"

"It seems to be bothering you that my parents aren't white."

"I don't know where you're reading that information from, but it certainly isn't true."

"That's good because my parents mean everything to me. They clearly saved me from some abusive situation. Look at the scars on my body." Tears filled her eyes.

"*Mon amour*, no tears, I'm sorry if I gave you that impression. Your parents must be great people. Look how good you turned out." Gabriel moved closer to her. They had stood at his kitchen island to eat, Gabriel just in his underwear. He took the empty lo mein container from her hand as he gazed into her eyes. "Are you done eating yet?" he asked, his voice low.

It had taken Parker forever to eat because she hadn't been able to stop staring at Gabriel's chest. At his muscled arms. At the way his stomach muscles bunched and moved. His body could have been carved from marble. Like a knight of old. Parker watched his eyes darken as he drew near, like a storm rolling across the sky.

"Did you know that your eyes darken?"

His body was right next to hers. Then he slid his arm around her waist.

"Only when I think about you." He drew her body tight against his.

Parker put her hand on his chest and tilted her head back slightly so she could look in his eyes. "Are you sure you're real?" She whispered the question as his mouth inched toward hers.

Gabriel moved his free hand to her wrist, and he slid the hand she had on his chest down his body. He stopped when her hand was over his hard length, and he rubbed her hand over it through his underwear. "Does this feel real to you?" He kept her hand on him as his mouth finally descended to hers. Parker gripped his neck as her lips opened to him, his tongue meeting hers. The arm he'd had around her waist slid up her back and he crushed her into him.

Gabriel ended the kiss and pulled his head back to look at her face. Parker's eyes were closed, and a flush had crept up her cheeks. She opened those amazing gray eyes and he saw how dark hers had gotten. "This feels very real, yes."

He stepped back from her then but kept her hand in his as he led her back to his bedroom. When he shut the door, that black shield went back up. Gabriel showed her his bathroom, and he waited as she showered, breathing in the scent of her soap and shampoo. He jumped in after her and quickly washed as well, thinking he might need a bathroom remodel so they could shower together. When he walked out of the bathroom, with only a towel around his waist, she stood there, completely nude, smoothing that lotion over her body. It was the same one she'd used yesterday, and that deep scent drove him crazy. He was literally frozen, watching her. Parker ran her hands over her chest and up to her neck when she turned to him.

"So very real," he said before he drew her to him again.

In the darkest part of the night, Gabriel rose again, knowing there was only a slim chance Parker would awaken before the morning. He'd made sure to wear her out completely. And he'd enjoyed every single moment of it. He didn't want her out of his bed for days. Gabriel stepped into the shadows, drawing them around him, covering him in darkness from head to toe. When they receded, he was dressed all in black. This was the suit he wore when he hunted.

He stepped back into the deepest shadow of his room and disappeared.

The room he entered through the shadow was still and quiet. Stealth was his ability; he had been born into it. He didn't remember what it was like to be a mortal human anymore. His feet were silent as he moved to the bed, and he saw the sleeping form there. He stepped up and heard movement a breath of time before he struck. The woman in the bed had shifted too late. She was hauled up, a hand at her throat, the black wall Gabriel had put up muffling any sounds from the room. He lifted her and slammed her against the wall, his body shifted to the side, the hand at her throat squeezing. A dagger appeared in his other hand, and he held it to her ear. This woman was the one Parker had called Theresa. "What are you doing here, Angel?"

It wasn't meant as an endearment.

"Assassin," she choked out, her eyes watering. No one, in the history of time, mortal or immortal, had been able to release themselves from his grip. "You should be thanking me."

"For what? Putting her in danger with a member of The Fold directly in your inner circle?" Theresa's eyes grew big as she ingested this information.

"What is it? That tidbit new to you? It explains everything I need to know." The dagger in his hand grew another inch.

"Release me, Assassin. You're lucky I got her here when I did."

Gabriel squeezed harder. "How's that? Clearly, you're new to this. Unseasoned. Untrained. It was too easy to get to you. But now you want me to believe, after all this time and everything that's happened, that someone finally cares? That now they see that she was meant to be mine through all time?" The dagger in her ear drew blood. "I'm to believe this time will be different? That I'll get to keep her, instead of watching her be brutally murdered. Again."

"She is mortal."

"And I've loved every incarnation." Gabriel's voice was rough as he spoke the words. "And it didn't matter. They still let her die." Gabriel lifted her so she was barely on her tiptoes, her hands hanging onto the hand at her throat. "Her mortality should have no bearing."

"Please, release me," Theresa choked out, tears now running down her eyes. Any pretense she'd had of not being afraid was now gone.

"Why should I listen to your begging? Did any of you ever listen to mine? Every time I held her brutalized body, her blood soaking the earth, and begged God for mercy, did it make a difference? I begged on my knees for her life. She isn't evil." Gabriel's voice was like ice. It was the voice that had made men quake with fear.

"It did to some of us. It did to me."

"Make me believe it," Gabriel whispered the words and that was more terrifying to Theresa than the other tone he'd used. "Make me believe in God's great forgiveness. I want to believe in it again." He had the upper hand, and he'd had it from the beginning. There was a reason he was the most feared assassin. A killer of both mortal and immortal. The one being who could kill an archangel by himself.

"The Archangel Michael doesn't know what I've been doing for nearly ten years." Theresa was barely able to get it out with the grip he had on her throat.

"How have you managed to shield yourself from him for so long?" Ten years may seem like an inconsequential amount of time to an immortal being, but the Archangels knew where every single one of the angels under them were. At all times.

"Gabriel." Theresa spoke his name for the first time. "Please, release me."

Gabriel wasn't sure what it was this time, what part made him step back. Maybe it was her use of his name, but, for only the second time in history, Gabriel released his grip on the throat of his prey.

Theresa collapsed to the floor, gasping for air. She looked up and watched the dagger disappear back into Gabriel. She knew she was lucky to be alive, but that didn't mean he wouldn't change his mind and finish the job.

"Don't make me regret my decision." Gabriel stepped back, giving her space to rise.

Theresa crawled on her hands and knees back to the bed because she couldn't rise to her feet right now. Gabriel watched her as he leaned against the wall, arms crossed, deceptively calm. She hauled herself up and sat on the bed, rubbing her neck. Good thing her wounds would heal by the morning. She was sure the bruise was massive. Theresa looked at the man, this assassin she'd heard so much about, his name was whispered in fear. "We all know about your existence."

"You mean about this existence I have no control over? The existence where others feel they can use me as a pawn against each other? The existence where my services can be sold to the highest bidder?" Gabriel threw his arms out, and Theresa winced. "That existence?"

"I didn't choose to become an angel."

"There's worse things you could be."

"I'm not disagreeing, I'm just stating facts."

"Get to the point before I change my mind about sparing your life."

Theresa knew it wasn't an idle threat. She glanced away from him for a moment. When she looked back, he saw the tears in her eyes. "Parker is my charge."

"As in *you* are her guardian angel?"

"Yes."

"Well, you're doing a piss poor job."

"You know I'm not allowed to interfere. There are rules!" Theresa practically yelled the words to him. "But that last time…" Tears fell down her cheeks. "You aren't the only one her death affects. It was your screams of agony that brought me to her. When I saw what they did to her that time, I just, I lost it." Theresa threw her hands in the air.

"Two immortal beings watching over her and yet we keep letting her die. You angels are too passive. At least I've brought her some justice."

"It makes me feel like a failure. After that time, well, I let my displeasure be known. The normally quiet halls were not silent." Theresa had screamed and yelled that night. "Parker was taken from me as a charge after my outburst. As of right now, she has no guardian."

"Are you kidding me?"

"No, and I was pissed. When Parker went to college, I inserted myself into her life. I made myself her college roommate. She was so different than she was before, like she's beaten down."

"Like her soul had given up," Gabriel whispered.

"Yes, like that. I can't believe the scars she carries on her body. Those are soul scars. So, if I couldn't be her angel, I'd be her friend. She was so timid, so scared, so different. It's only when you're alone with her that you see glimpses of who she used to be."

"Or when she's intoxicated." A ghost of a smile ran across his lips.

"I've been trying to get her down here to you for years, but I never could. I carried the glamour of me having a fiancé for so long that even *I* started to believe it. But then she started dating that guy and, it was subtle at first, but I could tell he was starting to wear on her. Petty things. Don't do this, don't do that, why do you want that. Don't touch me." Theresa looked up at him again. "He nearly drove her to suicide."

"What?" Gabriel's heart plummeted to his stomach at that news. That there had been a chance she was alive and never made it to him, the idea was torture. He'd have spent the rest of eternity waiting for her, and her lives had been spent after this one.

"He made her doubt herself so much. She's already soul damaged and so tired and he rode her. It's like he wanted to drive her to it. I had to come up with something because she was fading away. So, bachelorette weekend it is. It was the only thing I could think of that she wouldn't refuse to participate in."

"She told me he didn't want her coming down here."

"If I can be honest, I made the amount she had to pay for her room so high that I knew she wouldn't back out because she spent so much money on it."

"That was probably smart."

"I didn't expect you to end up in her bed the very same day you met her again."

"That was entirely by Parker's invitation." Gabriel shrugged. "You should know by now that I'll deny her nothing."

"You were correct, I am new still. I was only with Parker through three of her incarnations. I've always advocated for you though. I can see how you've changed. They know that I don't think what they've allowed to happen is right."

"Who are her birth parents in this life?" It didn't make sense to him.

"I don't know, nobody knows, or the people who know aren't talking. It was like she appeared in the system when she was about four years old."

"And her parents now?"

"They are good to her. They love her as if she was their own."

"I hope you understand," Gabriel said, "that I will be killing the member of The Fold in this house. She had planned to kill you and Parker this weekend."

"Who is it?" Theresa looked confused.

"I don't know her name, and I don't care, but Parker called her the bitch with the bad hair. I saw it, her hair was blonde, and her roots were dark."

"There are three blonde women in this house and none of them have dark roots."

Gabriel tilted his head slightly as he looked at her. It had been centuries, but he knew how The Fold operated. "Are you saying this woman has a glamour that you can't see through, but Parker could?"

"I bet it's Emily. She's always been rude to Parker, but I never gave it any thought."

Gabriel held his hand up and his eyes zeroed in on the door. "Lie back down," he ordered as he seemed to melt against the wall, "pretend you're asleep."

Theresa did what he said, and a few moments later, she heard the door to her room quietly open. Had she been asleep, she wouldn't have heard it. It seemed like the person leapt from the door to the bed because she was on Theresa so quickly, another hand to her throat. Theresa saw the flash of her dagger.

"It's time to die, Angel." The dagger plunged toward her heart.

Gabriel appeared behind her then, wrapping his hand around her throat and hauling the woman away from Theresa. He slammed her up against the wall, and her eyes went wide as Gabriel's dagger went through her neck. "That was a poor choice," he whispered in her ear. "Speaking allows the enemy to know you are there. And I *am* your enemy." Gabriel pulled his dagger from her throat at the same time he disappeared into the shadows with her.

Theresa sat up in bed, her eyes wide and her heart pounding. This whole situation was beyond her capabilities. She wasn't a soldier; she'd never been trained for combat or even self- defense. She spun when she heard a noise behind her, and Gabriel walked back into her room. "You let her have the room Parker paid for?"

"Like I could stop her? She just took it."

"Angelic passivity grinds my nerves."

"Maybe she wanted to smell you on the sheets," Theresa

shot back before she slapped a hand over her mouth and her eyes went wide.

"There is a little fire in you after all."

"That was Emily." Theresa told him.

"I don't care what she called herself, she's alligator food now." Gabriel watched Theresa almost retch at the thought. "I got rid of her stuff for you. Report her missing to the police so none of the other mortal women suffer consequences. We aren't done talking. I can find you anywhere." Gabriel was about to step into the shadows.

"Wait."

He stopped, only half his body visible to her.

"Thank you, for saving me."

Gabriel nodded.

"Where are you going?"

"Back to Parker," he said as he slipped away.

Parker stumbled her way back to bed. She'd gotten up to use the bathroom, her eyes still half closed with sleep. She hadn't even turned the lights on. The light through the window blinds was weak and pale, like the early morning light. Her entire body was sore, but it was such a delicious soreness that she didn't mind. Parker was sure she and Gabriel had sex more times since she landed in New Orleans than she and Max did the entire last year of their relationship. Max had told her once that the way her body looked, especially the scars, made it difficult for him to get aroused, but he loved her despite it.

That one had hurt. It had brought her so low that she was barely able to get out of bed and go to work for weeks. The kids in her class had noticed. She'd never told anyone, but she'd started feeling so depressed, looking back on her life and seeing what she thought were failures, that she'd thought about just ending it. Parker had sat down and started drafting a letter to her parents.

But, when she pulled the blanket back over her and snuggled down into Gabriel's bed, which *was* super comfortable, his arm went around her, and he pulled her body into his. He didn't seem to have a single issue with the way her body looked. When his arm wrapped around her, she wrapped her arms around his, hugging it to her. His palm ended up laying on the scar over her heart. "*Mon amour*, it is very early. I'm surprised you're awake."

Parker snuggled in closer to him. "My body is still on school time. It doesn't know I don't have to be up this early right now."

"I bet you are every child's favorite teacher." Gabriel kissed her ear before he laid his head on the pillow next to hers.

"I'd like to think I've made a difference to at least one or two of them."

"How are you feeling?" he asked as he lightly rubbed over her scar.

"Like I've been hit with a six-foot, whatever pounds, beautifully sculpted, train of male flesh many times."

"That's very descriptive." Gabriel rolled his hips closer to hers. He'd worn her out so much that she hadn't bothered putting her pajamas back on and had gone to sleep nude. She hadn't had the energy. She never slept nude.

"And not a single second of disappointment to be found."

"That's even better." Gabriel had brushed her hair back with his other hand and whispered the words into her ear before he ran his tongue along the edge of it. Parker's whole body shivered. He rubbed the scar on her chest, like if he massaged long enough, he'd erase it from her body.

"How do you feel?" Parker asked before she couldn't form words.

Gabriel laid his head back down and slid his arm under her pillow, so both were around her. He brought his leg over hers and inserted it between her legs, opening her body as the hand that had been over her heart made its way down to her core. "Like all my dreams have come true," he said before he cupped her. He ran his fingers around every inch of her before he slid through the flesh that was slick for him already. The arm under her tightened across her chest, and he cupped a breast. Gabriel squeezed her nipple at the same time his finger went in her, hooking around to find her g-spot before withdrawing to rub her swollen bud.

One of Parker's arms went up and around the back of his neck. She grasped the arm over her chest. He continued what he was doing, squeezing her nipple as he drew his finger in and out, his leg keeping hers apart. Parker didn't know what he wanted, but he continued. She squirmed as much as she could, the sounds from her mouth becoming louder. This was usually the moment where he stopped and entered her, but this time, he didn't. He only pleasured her, squeezing and dipping in and out. Her hips ground back against him, and she couldn't control the volume of her moans anymore. Until he stopped with the in-and-out and pressed on her spot inside, keeping a slight pressure on it.

Gabriel's hand moved with her hips, never letting up on the pressure, his thumb on her bud. Parker's moans drifted beyond the normal ones, the pleasure he gave her was so great, until it was like she couldn't breathe.

"Oh, God, Gabriel."

He pressed until she couldn't hold it anymore. She exploded in his hands, her climax so intense she could only get out tiny puffs of air. Her hand around his neck held on tight and her nails dug in his skin as Parker arched back against him.

"That's the one I've been waiting to hear." Gabriel removed his leg from between hers and rolled her onto her back. Parker thought he was going to kiss her, but instead, he pulled the blanket back and moved down her, placing his head over her already swollen core. "I want to hear another." He lifted her hips to him.

An hour later, or maybe it was two, he didn't know, and he didn't care, Gabriel closed the front door after gathering the bag of food from outside. He'd pulled on a pair of jogging pants but that was it. At some point, Parker had turned to him and squished his face in her hands. "I am so flipping hungry right now. Are you trying to starve me skinny?"

"Parker."

"I'm kidding," she said quickly before he could feel bad about what she said. "But I'm not kidding about being hungry."

"I can order some food." Gabriel reached over to get his phone off the bedside table. "What do you want?"

"I want biscuits and gravy, bacon, and scrambled eggs. I'm tired of eating donuts for breakfast. Chocolate milk." Parker had been raising a finger on her hand for every item she listed.

"Anything else?" Gabriel asked. "Perhaps the blood of innocents as well?"

"Only on the full moon."

Her retort was so unexpected that Gabriel laughed out loud. It was so much like something she'd have said so many lifetimes ago. It reminded him of what Theresa had said, that sometimes, when you were alone with her, you'd catch a glimpse of who she used to be.

"Was that an actual laugh and not a tiny chuckle?" Parker teased.

"It may have been." Gabriel showed her his phone so she could see the breakfast order he'd placed. They were in his bed, Parker on her side next to him as he reclined on his back. Her hand was on his chest again.

"Fantastic. Breakfast is my favorite food group."

"It says forty-five minutes." Gabriel set his phone down and turned to his side to face her. "That's plenty of time for a few more orgasms." He brushed her hair back and caught a curl around his finger.

"Aren't you tired of me yet? I've barely been out of this bed in like, eighteen hours."

"I will never get tired of you."

"Has it been very long since your last relationship?"

Parker asked.

"Like a hundred years."

"Funny how it can seem that long." Parker ran her fingers through his hair. She ended up under his body one more time, her legs and arms wrapped around him.

Parker was rummaging around in her bag for something to wear when Gabriel got the notification that the food had been dropped off. He watched her clasp her bra around her and pull on some underwear before he sighed, grabbed some jogging pants out of his dresser drawer, and went to get the food.

He was scooping portions onto plates when she came out of the bedroom wearing a blue dress with a belt around her waist, barefoot, and her hair up in a cuter-than-hell messy bun situation. Parker looked up at him and squinted a little. "Do you know where my glasses are?"

"I have no idea," Gabriel replied, walking around the kitchen island with her plate before hooking a foot in a stool and pulling it out for her. Parker sat on the stool and smiled at him as he handed her the plate.

"Thank you." She smiled even bigger when he handed her the glass of chocolate milk. Gabriel brought his plate around and sat next to her, enjoying this moment of sitting with her. He'd never had her in his home before and now he didn't know why he hadn't, it was safest for her here.

He'd never told her about the nature of their relationship during any of her lives because he'd always been too afraid of what her reaction would be. It wasn't every day you find out your soulmate was an immortal assassin, especially when you are a mortal woman. It was a combination that just wasn't done, for obvious reasons. Their situation was different though. How they'd met was a complete manipulation of everything good and holy.

He'd been sent to kill her.

CHAPTER FIVE

Parker stood aside in the staircase while Gabriel shut and locked the inner door to his apartment. The landing outside the door wasn't very big, and when Gabriel turned, Parker stepped back to give him room. She realized then that he was purposefully crowding her against the wall. When he had her pressed against the wall, Gabriel placed his arms on the wall on either side of her head, leaning on his elbows. Parker looked up at him through her lashes, the glasses Gabriel had found while getting dressed sliding down her nose. He pushed them up for her before he placed it against the wall again. "Have I told you how beautiful you are?"

Parker felt a flush creep up her cheeks at his words. Even though she'd spent nearly the last twenty-four hours in his bed and in his arms, this was somehow different. She saw the utter sincerity in his eyes. And something else, something that could almost be mistaken for love if she looked at it for too long. Parker's heart fluttered. "Not since yesterday."

"How remiss of me." He caught an errant curl in his fingers. "I like this messy bun you have today so much more than the other one. Your hair is glorious." Gabriel had said all this without looking away from her.

"It's a mess."

"It's glorious," he repeated.

"Watch out, Gabriel, you might make a girl feel some things."

"Parker, by now, you should know that I want you to feel all the things, as you put it."

"Are you sure about that? All of them is a lot of emotions."

Gabriel moved back only far enough to take her wrist in his hand and place it over his heart. "On my soul."

"Why does it feel like I've known you forever?" Parker whispered the question. It was like she knew everything about him, like they'd shared lifetimes together. She fisted her hand in his shirt, and she drew in a breath as he moved closer. His eyes had gone dark and serious. "I feel like I can trust you with my life this time."

"This time…"

"I don't know why I said that part." Parker's words cut him off.

"This time, you can," Gabriel said to the deep part of her soul that knew.

"You're talking like this is forever," Parker said. "And not a few weeks."

Gabriel took a step back, a look of concern on his face. "What's this about a few weeks? Who said anything about only a few weeks? Why can't it be forever?"

"That's not what you made it sound like you wanted." Maybe she was the one who didn't know what she wanted. Was it possible to feel that kind of love after a few days? Did that make her a psychopath? What if she said it out loud and he laughed at her? That had happened before.

Gabriel watched all these questions run across her eyes. He understood because, while he may remember her, at every new incarnation, she had to meet him over. The urge to tell her everything was so strong in him this time, but Gabriel knew this wasn't the time or place for that conversation. He stepped back to her, so his body touched hers again. "I have not been calling you my love as a light endearment." The hand on the wall then cupped the side of her face, and he ran his thumb over her cheek. A tear slid down her cheek. "Why are you crying?"

"How is this possible? You're gorgeous and I'm just plain Parker Reed."

Gabriel pressed her hand flat against his chest again. "You are the most beautiful woman in this world. I want you to consider the possibility that some things are meant to be. That some people are meant to be. That maybe"—his thumb ran over her cheek again—"our meeting was meant to be. That you are meant to be mine, and I am meant to be yours."

"You want me to consider the possibility that you are my soulmate? Is that what you are suggesting? Dare I use the word *destined*?"

"Do you know a better word to describe it? Because I'm willing to consider your explanation."

Parker had no alternate explanation, but she was so unsure of herself that her brain wanted to reject the idea. She closed her eyes and tried to settle her mind like all the self-help videos said to do. Her heartbeat slowed and sounded loud in her ear. Parker saw flashes of light behind her eyes. Suddenly, with each heartbeat, she saw she was surrounded by figures in black. They taunted her. Why were they taunting her? Parker's body felt fear as she spun around in the vision, trying to run but unable to find an escape route. Where was he? Parker's body arched when the first blade pierced her back.

Gabriel watched her back arch and heard the expulsion of pain from her lips. He didn't know what the hell was going on. "Parker." He shook her lightly. "Parker, open your eyes."

She tried to open her eyes because this was not calming her mind. Something slashed across her chin as she spun again in her mind. "Gabriel," she sobbed, "where are you?"

"I'm right here."

Another blade slashed, this one across her stomach. More of them came, one after another then. When Parker turned this time, she saw the blade aimed directly for her heart. Parker opened her eyes as the vision in her head continued to play. "Why did you let me die?" she asked before the knife plunged in her heart.

"Oh, God. Parker." Gabriel hauled her into his embrace. "I'm so sorry I didn't make it to you on time. I will never forgive myself." Gabriel tilted her head back and kissed her. "I promise," he said between each kiss, "on my soul." Parker's hand went around his neck. "I will never let anything happen to you again." His kiss was deep and searching, begging her for forgiveness. "Let me prove it to you."

"Gabriel." Parker returned each passionate kiss. "I don't know what you're talking about. But I'm definitely interested."

By this time, Gabriel had her pinned against the wall again, both his hands on her face, but his kisses gentled. "Parker, there aren't enough words to describe how happy you make me."

Parker wasn't sure what had happened. All she'd wanted to do was calm her mind to consider what Gabriel had said. As soon as she'd closed her eyes, that vision had started. It felt like it was her, but not her at the same time. Now, with the idea in her head that maybe Gabriel could be hers, that maybe she wasn't an unlovable piece of garbage, her heart felt lighter.

Gabriel stepped back from her. "You are not an unlovable piece of garbage and whoever made you feel that way needs to die."

"I didn't think that came out of my mouth." "It did."

"Okay, then if I'm such a great, beautiful woman, as you claim, why has every relationship I've had sucked so bad?"

"Because it wasn't me." Gabriel smiled at her as he held her hand. He turned and started down the stairs. "Charles should have the shop open by now. He likes to play at being an art dealer some days and unlocks the doors on his treasures for a while."

Parked stopped on the second-floor landing. "You want me to go meet this person I've never met who knows that I've been in your apartment for the past day? Are you trying to embarrass me? He'll know what's been going on."

"I am not trying to embarrass you, I only thought you'd be interested in meeting Charles. It's a little too late to introduce you before anything happened between us. Plus, I thought you might like to see this side of what I do. As for the rest of it." Gabriel shrugged. "Are you just going to hide away for the rest of our lives? Should we pretend like we don't enjoy making love to each other? Is that something you are embarrassed about?"

"No." She glanced away. "Well, maybe. I don't know. Maybe it's that you guys are close, and he went and got my bag for me. I'm not used to all this." Parker thought about all the things they'd done in bed, especially about how loud he'd driven her to be. "Plus, he lives in this building." Parker stopped for a second. "Gabriel, what if he heard me?"

"*Mon amour*, I can guarantee that he did not hear you."

"Unless you soundproofed this building, you cannot guarantee that."

"Parker, I store centuries-old artwork in this building. The thickness of the insulation in every floor and wall is astounding. You could stand on the other side of this wall and scream, and trust me, no one would hear you."

"Now you sound like a creepy old man," Parker teased as she smiled at him.

"It's only a five-year difference in our ages, not five centuries." Gabriel rolled his eyes but was also smiling as he started down the stairs again. Five centuries stood between them, but he wasn't ready to share that information yet. "I wasn't the one who had to take naps, if I remember correctly." Gabriel stopped at the door to the bottom floor. A door that led into the front showroom and another that led outside.

"Shots fired, *mon coeur*."

Gabriel stopped short, it was the first time she'd ever

called him something like that, in any of her incarnations. He hadn't realized how much it would affect him when she did. Gabriel brought her left hand to his lips and kissed her ring finger. God knew his heart was there, wrapped so tightly around it. "Be careful or I'll march you back up these stairs and put you right back in my bed."

"Your bed is super comfortable."

"You see these fingers?" he asked, showing her the ones he was holding. "I'm not ashamed to tell you how tightly I'm wrapped around them."

"It's only been three days."

"Imagine what it will be like after three years then."

"I think I would like you to take me back to bed right now." Parker ran a hand down his arm.

Gabriel's eyes went dark as he stood there staring at her, the sounds of her climax ringing in his mind. He stepped toward her, ready to draw her back up the stairs, ready to do whatever she wanted, when the door to the showroom opened and Charles stood there.

"Oh good, you're here, I have a question for you," he said in English. "And you also don't need to lose another day in bed," he said in Italian.

"It would not be a loss," Gabriel replied, also in Italian. He watched Parker's eyes get big and a flush creep up her face at Charles's voice.

"How many languages do you actually know?" she asked.

"At last count, seven or eight, but I've probably forgotten the ones I don't use as often." Gabriel stepped aside and swept his arm out between the two of them. "Charles Guarder, may I finally introduce Parker Reed to you."

Parker took the hand Charles held out to her. He was an older man, probably in his mid- fifties, his hair turning salt and pepper. Charles wasn't quite as tall as Gabriel, and his body was thinner. The hand he held out to her was soft and finely manicured. Unlike Gabriel's more casual attire,

Charles was dressed in a suit and tie. It was his eyes though, they looked at her over his wire-rimmed glasses, also blue like Gabriel's, like they could see into her very soul. As a matter of fact, she felt something move through her with their brief handshake.

He gave Gabriel a strange look after he dropped her hand. "It is my pleasure, of course, to finally meet you. I hope all your belongings are accounted for."

"Yes, thank you, I appreciate you getting them for me. And it's nice to meet you too."

Charles turned to Gabriel. "A certain buyer from Italy is calling and wants to speak to you directly. Also, I'd like to discuss the new acquisition that came in, the painting called *Wife of the Assassin* just arrived. I'd love to know how you acquired it."

"I will come in and take the call now." Gabriel placed his hand on the small of her back and led her into the gallery behind Charles. "As for the other, we can talk about that later." Gabriel took Parker's hand after she stepped into the gallery.

"Wife of the Assassin, huh? Sounds ominous," she said, getting her first look around at the gallery. A broad assortment of paintings and tapestries hung on the walls. Displays of pottery and porcelain were scattered around the room. Parker heard soft music playing in the background. The lights were dimmer than a normal store, and Parker realized they were the same kind of lights used in museums. This was a gallery she probably wouldn't enter because she'd be afraid of breaking something.

"On the contrary," Gabriel told her as he led her to the front of the gallery, "it is a beautiful work of art. I never thought it would be, but now it's mine."

"How long do you plan on keeping it?" Charles asked, stepping behind a counter and retrieving a cordless phone before handing it to Gabriel.

"I don't plan on ever letting it go." Gabriel's eyes bored holes into Charles's. Gabriel took the phone from Charles and placed it to his ear, greeting whoever was on the other end in Italian. He turned and walked a short distance away as he spoke on the phone.

Parker looked back and forth between the two men, wondering at the unspoken communication that had seemed to go on between the two of them. "So." Charles met her gaze. "How are you enjoying our fine city so far?"

"So far I like almost everything about it," Parker told him honestly.

"Where are you from?"

"Originally Indiana, but now I live just outside Chicago. I teach fifth grade."

"What a noble profession."

"How about you?" Parker asked. "Where are you from?"

"Originally, I'm from Italy. It's where Gabriel and I met." Charles's eyes swept the room and landed briefly on Gabriel, who was still on the phone, gesturing with one hand. "But this is my home now."

"I would love to visit there one day."

"I do hope you get the chance," Charles said, "it is a beautiful country."

Parker watched Gabriel turn and check on her as she stood at the counter with Charles. He appeared to be listening to whoever was on the phone this time, and he gave a strange look between her and the other man. Feeling uncomfortable, she looked around at the items for sale. They looked like museum-quality antiques. The fact that Gabriel knew the difference in each piece, where it came from, who the artist was, and if it was real, was astounding. Sure, she taught school, but even this small piece of his life seemed like an overwhelming amount of information to remember.

Her gaze landed on him again and the forward part of her brain that ruled her life wondered when the joke would be over. There was no possible way he could want her like he said he did. Even in his shorts and t-shirts he looked gorgeous. He had an obscene number of Vans shoes. He'd shown her this morning after he got dressed because he couldn't decide which ones would look better with his shirt. Parker had asked what the difference was, and he'd responded that he wanted to look good for her. She'd looked him up and down. "You already look good enough to eat, what more do you want?" she'd asked.

And what about that vision thing she'd had in the hallway? That scared her, and she didn't know what to think about it. It was something she'd never had happen before. Parker didn't want to think about anything too far in the future, anything beyond the few weeks she'd given herself for travel. What was she supposed to do with this new turn of events in her life? Was this a forever thing? What if he asked her to move here? What if she asked him to move with her? Were they a couple? Would this just be a long-distance thing? Would she come down on school breaks? Maybe see each other a few times a year, have fantastic, explosive sex, and then see you next time? Could she manage a relationship like that? Is that what this was? Or was this lust from what now seemed like a depressing display from former relationships?

"Parker."

She jumped at the sound of her name and focused her eyes on Gabriel, who now stood in front of her, off the phone. "Sorry," she muttered. "I must have spaced out there for a second."

Gabriel brushed his thumb down her cheek, and Parker felt a flush creep up her face. "Don't worry, *mon amour*, he's not standing at the counter anymore."

"It's kind of scary that you knew what I was thinking."

"Your beautiful face pretty much tells me everything I need to know."

"So I've heard."

Gabriel moved in closer to her, his hand cupping the side of her face. "Your face was also telling me about your doubts just now."

"That's not really fair," Parker squeaked out. "That you

can read all that from expressions I have no control over."

Just then, Charles yelled something at Gabriel from a room behind her, and Gabriel responded in the same language. "Is that Greek?" she asked.

"He likes to test my abilities. He hasn't used Greek in a few years." More like fifty, but he wouldn't tell her that. "He said he has a client coming in a few minutes who likes to browse alone." Gabriel took her hand and led her back the way they'd come in. "What would you like to do today?" he asked as he opened the back door for her.

Parker stepped through the door and then opened the other door that led outside. It was already hot and humid. "Well, I am still a tourist." She headed toward Gabriel's car. He started it up with his key fob. "Is the botanical garden open today?"

"Yes, *mon amour*, it is." Parker reached his car before he did and tried to open the passenger door.

Gabriel stepped up behind her. "Parker."

She turned to look at him, and Gabriel caught her face in his hands and kissed her. His kiss was long and deep, and he had her pushed up against his car, pressing his body to hers. She grabbed his wrists.

"Parker, I wish you could see into my heart." Gabriel kissed her forehead. "And then you would no longer need to question."

Parker opened her eyes, looked into his, and decided she would stop listening to the negative voice in her head, at least for the rest of the day. "Ok, *mon coeur*, for the next twenty- four hours, I won't question anything between us."

Gabriel smiled. "It's a start. Before you know it, it will be twenty-four years and you'll wonder why you ever doubted me." Gabriel pressed the unlock button on his keys and opened the door for her.

Parker slightly tilted her head at him. "Are you sure that wasn't your way to make sure you could open the door for me?"

"I'll use any excuse to take you in my arms and press

your body to mine."

"All you really had to do was ask," Parker muttered as she turned and slid into the car. Gabriel smiled as he shut her door and walked around the car. That was more like the Parker he remembered.

CHAPTER SIX

The botanical garden was only a ten-minute drive from his house. Gabriel enjoyed the gardens. It was one of the many places he donated to. All his donations were made anonymously, mostly because he'd been living around this area for nearly two hundred years and that might seem a bit weird. No family kept a first name going for that many generations. Luckily, he'd had an extra pair of sunglasses in his car to replace the ones he threw yesterday. He slipped them on so Parker wouldn't see how often his eyes landed on her. She'd held his hand and smiled out the window the whole ride.

Gabriel held her hand when they got there and only let go of it when he took out his wallet to pay the entrance fee. They passed the dancing fountain, Parker smiling at the way the water jumped from place to place, and Gabriel pulled her into the sculpture exhibit immediately following that. "These are on loan from the Helis Foundation," he told her. "They are all done by an artist named Enrique Alferez. I'll show you my favorite one in this area." Gabriel led her around the sculpture garden and stopped in front of a bronze statue. It was a statue of a man and a woman. He was embracing her from behind and the woman's hand was in his outstretched one. She was leaning back against him.

"*Pas de deux,*" Parker read.

"Yes," Gabriel replied, bringing her hand to his lips. "Not two. Two dancing as one."

"I don't understand."

"No longer two. Two people who become one. A dance meant for two to become one."

Parker understood and turned to Gabriel. "Are you saying this is how you feel about us?"

"Yes." Gabriel nodded. "And before you say anything," he interrupted what she was clearly about to say, "you did say you wouldn't question anything for twenty-four hours and it's only been like thirty minutes."

Parker closed her mouth on the words she'd been about to say. It would've sounded like *it's only been three days*, but he used her words against her. At least he didn't give off creeper vibes. "You're right, I did say that." Parker pushed her glasses back up her nose. She was already sweating, but the heat and humidity didn't appear to affect him. "How are you not sweating? I feel like I'm melting."

"I guess I'm used to it. The humidity isn't this bad in Illinois?"

"No, and I'll never complain about it again."

They kept walking. Gabriel led her around the gardens and past the lily pad pond, pointing out some of his favorite spots. "I've actually never been to Chicago," he told her.

"That surprises me considering you deal in art."

"Most people come to me at this point. But"—he turned to her—"now that I have the prettiest tour guide in Illinois, it may be time to go."

It was that little half-smile that melted her heart every time. "You realize I don't actually live in the city, right? But I feel like Chicago would suit you, so many artsy-fartsy people with too much money to spend. Maybe you could, I don't know." Parker shrugged. "Maybe you could branch out. Charles could stay down here, and you could open another gallery in Chicago." Parker felt a flush creep up her cheeks again, and she hoped her comment wasn't as transparent as it sounded.

"Maybe I will. I'll buy some property up there. We can look online tonight."

Parker stopped walking at his words. "Wait, you would actually do something like that?"

"I'm not chained to this city, *mon amour*. Your idea is an exceptionally good one.

Besides"—he pulled her along a path around the side of a hall on the property—"I couldn't possibly ask you to leave the school and the students you love so much when I can work from anywhere." Gabriel stopped with her in front of the sculpture at the back of the building.

Parker placed her hand on Gabriel's chest and looked up into his eyes hidden behind his sunglasses. "After two years, Max would barely drive across town for me. But, after three days, you're willing to consider moving across the country?"

"Parker, why did you stay in a relationship like that? It sounds abusive and one-sided." Gabriel rested his hand over the one she had on his chest.

"Gabriel, standing here, right now, with you, I couldn't tell you why." Parker wound her arms around him and laid her head over his heart. When his arms went around her, Parker sighed and closed her eyes, breathing in the scent of his cologne. She felt his fingers catch an escapee curl then. "Do you really think my hair is glorious?"

"If you tell me that asshole said something about your hair, I'll fly up to Chicago right now and kick his ass."

"No, but he was fond of telling me that the way my body looked made it hard for him to feel aroused. But he loved me despite it."

Gabriel's arms tightened. "That's not love. There's nothing wrong with your body. Enough is enough."

"I know that now. I knew it then, but..." Parker shrugged. "I've felt so vulnerable my whole life, like I always had to look over my shoulder. I guess I thought something was better than nothing."

Gabriel held her close to him. Guilt ran through him because he knew why she'd felt vulnerable and scared her whole life, and it was because she loved him. Because she was his soulmate.

"What about you?" Parker asked. "What happened with your last relationship?"

Gabriel thought back to that day a hundred years ago when he'd held her bleeding body to his own. When he'd felt her blood saturate his clothing. It had been the most gruesome and messiest of her murders. He'd been hunting every member of The Fold since the first time they'd murdered her, but no matter how many he killed, more kept coming. There weren't as many of them, but they lingered. "She was murdered."

Parker tried to take a step back, her jaw dropping, but Gabriel kept his arms around her. "My God, Gabriel, I'm so sorry to hear that. How long has it been since she died?"

"It was a hundred years ago, *mon amour*. Another lifetime ago."

"Now I understand why you'd feel like it was that long ago."

"I really brought you back here to show you this sculpture." Gabriel let go of her and turned her to the statue. "It's called The Flute Player."

Under one of those giant live oak trees that Parker loved about this area, with Spanish moss hanging off it, was a circular fountain. In the middle of the fountain was the bronze sculpture of a woman, tall and thin, with a flute to her lips. At some point, a piece of moss had fallen from the tree and was hanging off her flute. The look on her face was so serene. Parker wished she could feel like that. The whole area was quiet, and she closed her eyes, listening to the sounds of the fountain and the birds singing in the trees. Gabriel moved up behind her, wound his arms around her, and pulled her back to him. Parker had been taking pictures of flowers she'd liked, and still had her phone in her hand. "Take your sunglasses off," she said.

Gabriel removed them before she flipped the camera around to take a picture of them.

"Take another," Gabriel said, kissing her cheek as she pressed the button. Parker kept pressing it as her laughter rang out because he tickled her sides. Another couple came around the corner then.

"Excuse me," Gabriel said, "would you mind taking a picture of us?"

Parker flipped the camera back around and handed it to the other couple when they said they would, making sure to get the statue in the picture. Gabriel pulled her to his side, and they both smiled for the picture. Parker thanked the couple when they returned the phone, and she made her way to one of the benches so she could look at the pictures. She scrolled through the half a dozen pictures they'd taken until she got to the one the other couple took. She enlarged the photo so she could see the look in Gabriel's eyes. He looked over her shoulder at the picture.

"You have the most beautiful smile in the world, *mon amour*." Gabriel kissed her cheek again.

Parker stared at the picture of the two of them. "Okay, Gabriel." She turned to face him. "I believe you. You can't fake the look in your eyes."

It was late and dark before Gabriel unwound himself from Parker's arms and rose out of bed again. Gabriel dressed in the dark, pulling on a shirt and another pair of jogging pants. He had no need for a suit of shadows tonight. His bare feet were silent as he grabbed his phone, in case Parker woke up and she texted him, and he exited his apartment by the inner back door. Gabriel went downstairs and knocked on Charles's door.

When she'd turned to him that afternoon and told him she believed him, all he'd been able to do was place his hand behind her neck and pull her to him for a kiss. Her hand had also gone around his neck, her fingers lightly running through his hair. Gabriel's tongue had just met hers when they heard a family with children coming, and they both broke off the kiss, but Gabriel didn't remove his hand from her neck. "Let's get out of here," Gabriel said to her, placing his forehead against hers.

"Okay," Parker responded. "What do you want to do?"

"I can think of about fifteen things I want to do to you right off the top of my head," he said as he rose and drew her to her feet.

"Gabriel, I want to cook your dinner."

"You want to cook me dinner?" Gabriel didn't think anyone had made dinner for him before.

"Yes. And we'll talk about all those things you want to do to me while I cook."

They stopped at a grocery store, and Gabriel told her that whatever she'd decided to make, she would have to buy everything she needed to make it, aside from salt and pepper. Parker filled up the grocery cart with everything for fried chicken, potato salad, and strawberry shortcake for dessert. Parker chose a can of whipped cream because Gabriel couldn't tell her if he had a hand mixer or not, and his eyes got a wicked gleam when she placed it in the cart. "It's to be used for dessert," Parker said after she caught the look in his eyes.

"You are a deliciously sweet morsel." Gabriel winked at her when her cheeks went red, and she looked around to see if anyone had heard.

"Maybe say it in French next time."

"*Désolé, mon amour.* I'm sorry, I'll remember for next time."

Parker gave him her best unruly classroom look, and she tossed a set of knives and spatulas in the cart for good measure. At checkout, Parker nearly got sick at the total, but Gabriel happily put his bank card in the machine before she could use hers.

When they pulled back into his carport, Parker's heart fell. "Oh yeah, you live on the third floor. We should have bought reusable grocery bags."

"You make one trip and start doing whatever you have to do, and I'll get all the bags in the house." Gabriel said this as he popped the trunk and got out of the car. So that was what Parker did. She took up as many bags as she could and emptied each bag that was brought in. She searched the kitchen for a large bowl to marinate the chicken in buttermilk and spices and placed it in the fridge along with all the other cold items.

Gabriel kicked the door shut with the last of the bags in his hands, and nearly fell over at the sight of Parker in his kitchen, moving around and putting things away like she'd done it a hundred times before. This, right here, was all he'd ever wanted in his life.

"Parker, are you doing anything right now?" Gabriel kicked off his shoes and pulled his shirt off.

"No, I've got it mostly under control..." She turned and watched him remove his shirt. The look in his eyes told her exactly what he was thinking as he advanced on her. When he reached her, Gabriel backed her up against the counter, kissing her at the same time his hands went under her dress, squeezing her behind. Gabriel lifted her, knowing she'd throw her arms around him, and braced her against the counter so she could wrap her legs around his waist.

This time, when he lifted her, Parker had no fear that he'd drop her when he turned and headed to the couch. As soon as he sat with her straddling his lap, Parker ended the kiss to stand back up and unbuckle her belt to take her dress off. Gabriel's eyes were on fire as he watched her. He unbuttoned his shorts and lifted his hips off the couch to push the rest of his clothes off.

Parker unclasped her bra as he removed the rest of his clothes, his eyes never leaving her body. His gaze was hot on her, and Parker felt desire fill her to the brim. Her nipples tightened under his gaze. She knew he saw it because he got more aroused. She stood in front of him, with only her underwear on, and slid her fingers under the band. Gabriel watched as she slowly inched them down, but his eyes met hers when she stopped right before they came all the way off. "It's not fair to tease me, Parker."

"I just wanted to know if I had your attention."

"You have the attention of every single cell in my body."

"That's good." Slowly, Parker slid that last piece of clothing off and stood before him.

"I need you back on my lap right now." Gabriel's hands returned to her hips, his thumbs in the crease of each leg. "I need you so badly."

Parker bent a knee and placed it on the couch, her hands on his shoulders, her eyes never leaving his. Gabriel's fingers trailed up and down her thighs, brushing her core. One hand cupped her, teasing and rubbing, stimulating her bud as she kneeled there.

"Now the other, *mon amour*. You tease me too much. I want to feel you slide down me."

Parker put her other knee on the couch and centered herself over him. Gabriel readjusted his body so she could slide down him. Parker's lips hovered over his, and their breaths mingled as he filled her.

"How's that?" she asked as she sank all the way down. Gabriel's eyes had closed at the first feel of her around him.

He moved his hands up her thighs, around her hips, and up her back. Parker knew what he wanted and reached up to take her hair out of the bun. He opened his eyes when her hair fell free. "Everything about you is perfect."

Parker blinked back tears. She wound her arms around his neck as her lips met his. Gabriel gripped her hips as their lips melted together, and Parker moved on him. His lips trailed down her neck as Parker's head went back. She closed her eyes at the feeling of him deep inside her. She arched her back and grabbed his hair, drawing his mouth to her breast. He braced her back as he took her tight nipple in his mouth like she wanted. Her breathing got heavy as her hips continued to rock on him. Gabriel switched to the other breast, and she fisted her hands in his hair.

"Gabriel," she drew out his name.

Gabriel's hands tightened as she continued to ride him. One hand slid between them so he could stimulate her. His fingers found her core nerves, circling her slowly. "I love to hear you purr my name."

Parker wrapped her arms around his neck again, as she rode him, his fingers working magic. Her mouth was right by his ear. Every moan was directed there, and goosebumps rose on his skin at the sound. She ground down on him as her body convulsed. The climax traveled through her body, and her arms tightened.

"I love you." The words came from deep in her soul.

Gabriel placed his forehead on Charles's door and stood there, not actually able to believe those words had come from her. It hit him differently with every incarnation, but this time, tears ran down his cheeks at her words. He'd buried his face in her neck, but it hadn't mattered, she'd felt them anyway.

"Gabriel, what is it?" She hadn't expected that reaction from him.

"I just—" Gabriel paused, and his arms tightened more. "I just never thought I'd hear those words again."

"Is that a good thing or a bad thing?"

"*Mon amour*, it is the best thing." Parker leaned back, and Gabriel placed his hands on her cheeks, wanting her to see the love in his own eyes. "Parker, I love you as well, with all my heart."

She lowered her gaze from his at those words, and he dipped his head down so their eyes could meet again. "You believe me?"

"Yes." Parker set her hands on his face and kissed him gently.

Gabriel didn't let her move away. He deepened her kiss, pulling her closer. His hands slid back into her hair, and he tilted her head to the side as their tongues met again. Parker, still straddling his lap, felt him getting aroused again. "Tell me, my love." Gabriel's lips trailed down her neck, licking the spot where her shoulder and neck met. "How much time do you have before more cooking needs to be done?"

Parker threw her head back when he kissed her in the

hollow of her throat. "That depends on when you want to eat." She was already breathless. "My dad might be upset if I don't give his potato salad the proper time it needs."

Gabriel had just dragged his tongue across to the other side of her neck when her words sank in. "You're making me your dad's potato salad?" Gabriel stopped what he was doing. Not only was she cooking for him, but she was making him a special recipe from one of her parents.

"It's my mom's fried chicken recipe."

"And the strawberry shortcake?" Gabriel ran his hands down her back and cupped her behind. him.

"I know you saw the box of Bisquick in the cart." Parker leaned back so she could look at him.

"So, you're cheating on dessert?"

"That's okay, we can skip it," Parker unwound her arms from around his neck.

"Oh, no you don't." He put his hands on her back again. "That won't work. We're making that dessert. I didn't sacrifice whipped cream foreplay for nothing."

Parker's arms returned to his neck. "I liked your hands better where they were a minute ago."

"I'll be happy to run them all over your body later." Gabriel couldn't resist and kissed her neck again. "After you shower"—his tongue ran over the curve of a breast—"and you cover yourself in lotion." He tipped her back far enough to run his tongue over a nipple. "Except tonight, it will be my hands instead of yours."

"Gabriel…"

"If you keep purring my name like that, there will be no dinner made. Then what will I tell your parents when I meet them?"

Parker's hips had started moving on him again, her breathing heavy, her hands running through his hair. "Then stop teasing me," she ground out.

Gabriel's answer was to grab her hips and pull her in tight to him.

Parker dressed in a pair of shorts and a tank top she had in the bottom of her bag. Normally, she wouldn't be walking around in this little clothing, especially with no bra or underwear on, but she figured what the hell at this point. She also collected their dirty laundry and found the washer and dryer Gabriel said was in the hall closet. He stood in the kitchen in a pair of those jogging pants, cleaning and dicing potatoes. She shoved all their laundry in, poured in detergent, flipped it to cold, and prayed he didn't care.

He was done cutting the potatoes when she got to the kitchen, and she heard the gas burner come on. She'd been surprised to find an entire cookware set in one of the cabinets. Gabriel had winked at her, saying at some point, he'd tried to cook, but he didn't have the patience. Parker had looked him up and down, wondering how he stayed so fit if he didn't eat properly. He'd seen her look, and his eyes had darkened as he started for her. But she had retreated around the kitchen island because no food was about to be made if that happened again.

Parker walked into the kitchen after the washer started, opened the fridge, and took out the strawberries. She turned to put them on the island and caught Gabriel looking at her like she was the tasty snack this time. "What is it?" She popped the container open, pulled the cutting board toward her, and flipped it.

"How do you expect me to keep my hands to myself when you're walking around looking like that?"

"Looking like what?" She had to turn around and reach into a cupboard for another small bowl to put her cut strawberries in. When she faced forward, it appeared as though all the blood had drained from his face.

His eyes met hers again. "Do you really have no idea?"

"You mean this tank top?" Parker asked, slicing strawberries. "I'm not sure why I packed it. Maybe to wear it under something."

"Right now, I'm hoping one of those beautiful breasts you have falls out the side."

Parker stopped slicing and met his eyes again.

"I swear on all that's holy, Parker, if he said something about your breasts, don't tell me. I might have to learn how to teleport myself and murder him." Parker said nothing and went back to slicing her strawberries. It was a good thing for her ex that he'd made that vow and hadn't killed a mortal in almost four hundred years. She'd have been treated better by a psychopath.

They continued to make dinner together. Parker commented on how nicely he'd diced the potatoes. "You have good knife skills for someone who doesn't cook," she said, not understanding the look that went across his face. He helped her scoop the biscuit dough onto a sheet and watched as she seasoned her flour for the chicken. Everything about this ordinary situation hit Gabriel in the guts. He'd had to sit on one of the stools he had. He watched her mix her ingredients for the potato salad, her tongue sticking out a bit. The concentration on her face meant so much to him. When she was done mixing it together, she tasted it with her eyes closed, Gabriel had never wished to be a simple, mortal man again more in his life.

He wanted to grow old with her. He had no desire to live without her.

Parker had tried to cook this very meal for Max once. She'd gone out and bought everything she'd needed and spent a good part of the day prepping it. He'd said they could cook it together when he got there, but he'd never shown up. Parker had called and texted him, but he hadn't responded. She'd just gone to bed and cried herself to sleep. She didn't understand why she'd allowed him to treat her that way. The next day, he'd finally gotten back to her, saying something about his phone dying and car problems and whatever. Parker was so numb to it by then. That had been two weeks before she left for New Orleans. Looking back on it now, it almost did seem like Max wouldn't be happy until he'd driven her so low that she did commit suicide.

Wait, did that make Gabriel a rebound? Parker looked at him across the kitchen as she prepped the chicken to be breaded. He sat on one of the bar stools, his chin in his hand, staring at her with his cute little one-sided smile. Parker's heart fluttered again, and she realized she'd been hoping for someone who made her heart flutter. She remembered thinking that on the bus ride down from the airport, which was only a few days ago but felt like centuries.

No, he was no rebound. Parker had known nothing but relief when she'd finally broken it off with Max, not heartbreak. Now, if anything happened and she and Gabriel split, she would stay single the rest of whatever life she had because nothing would ever compare. Parker was about to start breading the chicken when her phone rang. She turned and saw it across the kitchen island, sitting right in front of Gabriel. He picked it up and brought it to her, "It's your mother." He slid the button to answer it before he put it up to her ear.

Parker tucked the phone between her ear and shoulder with the one hand that hadn't been touching chicken. "Hey, Mom." She kept her eyes on Gabriel's. "No, I'm fine. The bachelorette thing was as atrocious as I thought it would be." Parker pointed at Gabriel and then at the chicken. "I haven't made any plans yet. I was kind of planning to stay here in New Orleans a bit longer."

Gabriel followed her silent instructions and picked up a piece of chicken and placed it in the flour so she could bread it with her free hand before placing it in the hot oil. "Forget about Max. I broke it off with him."

Gabriel heard the relief in her mother's voice. If he wanted to, he could hear what she was saying, but he wouldn't do that to Parker.

She pointed to another piece of chicken. "Listen, Mom, can I call you back later? I'm making fried chicken right now."

Parker's mother cut her off when she said that.

Parker mouthed a curse word. "Yes. I'm making it right now."

Gabriel heard her mother ask who it was for.

"Someone I met. No, he's standing right here. No, he's definitely the opposite of Max." Parker flipped the chicken in the oil. "Mom, he's standing here breading chicken with me, okay? Just like Dad does. Of course, it's your recipe, you think I could make this up on my own? You know making up food isn't my strong point." Parker stopped talking for a second. "Okay, yes, I'm also making Dad's potato salad." Parker listened for a moment, and he swore her face went red. "As soon as we can, okay? Mom, please, I have to go or I'm going to drop my phone in hot oil. Yes, I'll call you back. I love you too." Parker hung up her phone and tossed it on the island.

"So," Gabriel said as he breaded the last piece of chicken. "When am I expected to present myself to your parents?" He handed her the leg so she could pop it in the oil after she took out another piece.

"As soon as possible," Parker answered, fishing out a piece of chicken so she could put the last piece in the oil. She bent down to put the baking pan in the hot oven to finish the chicken and turned to wash her hands in the sink.

Gabriel was right there with her, using the same water as her and his hand caught hers. Parker turned to him, embarrassed about the conversation with her mother, and his hand was behind her head and his lips were on hers. Parker opened her lips for him. She closed her eyes at the feeling of him against her body. He kissed her like she was the most precious gift in his life.

"I can't wait." He'd had to force himself away from her, otherwise, he wouldn't be eating this, apparently quite special, meal she was making for him.

But Parker didn't let him go far. she'd wound her arm around him. "The chicken has about twenty minutes," she murmured against his lips.

"That's so very tempting," Gabriel responded, sliding

his free hand up her side, his fingertips light over the skin peeking out from the side of the tank top. "But I think for the next time, I'll need at least an hour."

"An hour?"

"Or three." His hand went under the tank top strap, running over the top of her breast and dipping down to brush her hard nipple.

"So many things could happen in three hours." She slid her hand down his chest and toward the waistband of his pants, gliding over his hard length.

"That's really the plan." Gabriel sucked in a breath when her hand closed around him, caressing him through his clothing.

"I'm glad we have the same plan." She squeezed him.

"You're a wicked little morsel, aren't you?"

"I'll take that as a compliment." She lifted her hand only as far as his waistband before slipping her fingers under it, touching as lightly as he was.

"It was meant to be taken that way." Gabriel was two seconds away from saying screw it and carrying her to bed when the piece of chicken left in the oil popped and they both jumped.

"Oh, no, turn it off, turn it off," she yelled. They both reached for the knob at the same time. Parker burst out laughing when they both tried to turn it. She got the tongs and fished the piece out, opening the oven door to put it on the rack. It looked a bit browner than the other pieces. "That one's for Charles." She laughed as she closed the oven door and turned to him again.

"You planned to make him a plate too?"

"Of course. You said he feeds you all the time, however reluctantly. I figured I'd return the favor, to thank him for keeping you alive."

Gabriel put her hand on his chest over his heart again. "I'm sure he'll appreciate it."

Parker finished making the food and made a plate for Charles. She made his strawberry shortcake in a separate dish and stared Gabriel in the eyes as she squirted some whipped cream on the side. "Tsk, tsk, *mon amour*. That look in your eyes gives me so many more ideas. I might have to add an hour."

"Take these down to Charles and then get back up here." Parker held the plate and bowl out to him. Gabriel took them from her, kissing her at the same time. When he got to Charles's door, he knocked with the plate and the other man gave him a strange look when he opened the door.

Gabriel held the food out to him. "Parker made dinner and wanted to share with you. She said thanks for feeding me and keeping me alive."

Charles took the plate and bowl out of Gabriel's hands without thinking. "Is this for real?"

"You better eat it," Gabriel said as he turned away and took the stairs by twos.

Parker was nervous when she sat next to Gabriel to eat dinner. What if he didn't like it? What if she made it wrong? She held her breath when he took his first bite of the potato salad. Gabriel turned to her when he heard her intake of breath. "*Mon amour*, your dinner is delicious. You can breathe."

Parker expelled the breath she'd been holding in.

CHAPTER SEVEN

Gabriel brought out his laptop after he helped Parker clean up the kitchen. They ate the strawberry shortcake while looking at properties in Chicago. He emailed a few different realtors who had several listings before closing the laptop again. Parker looked at some social media on her phone, and he tucked a curl behind her ear, letting his finger trail down her ear, then down her shoulder and her upper arm. When he reached her elbow, Parker set her phone down. Gabriel's finger lightly brushed the sensitive skin of her inner arm. "Thank you," Gabriel whispered, "for making me dinner. You'll never know how much that meant to me."

"You're welcome," Parker whispered back. "Thank you"—she turned on the stool to face him—"for showing me what love really is."

"Parker, I haven't even begun to show you anything yet."

"You mean there's more?"

"We haven't even scratched the surface, my love."

"How could there possibly be more?" Parker had a hard time believing there could be more.

Gabriel took her by the hand and led her toward the bedroom, turning off the lights as they went. He drew her to him as he shut the bedroom door, kissing her with all the love and passion he felt. Tonight, he would pretend like he was a normal man, like theirs was a normal marriage. He would pretend he wore her ring around his finger, as a matter of fact, he drew the shadows there, so he could feel it as he held her. He kissed her with his hands in her hair, running through every beautiful, beloved curl. Her hands slid down his chest and around his back, her arms holding him closer as he kissed her.

He pulled that damn tank top off so he could feel her skin. Gabriel had nearly had a heart attack when she'd walked out in just those skimpy clothes. Watching her bend and reach all evening had driven him mad. He hadn't been lying when he'd said he was hoping a breast would fall out the side. The look on her face told him he didn't want to know what she'd been told about them before. He drew his hands over those beautiful globes, brushing his palms over each tight nipple. He trailed his hands down her stomach, her skin so soft under his fingers, until he reached the waistband of her shorts. Gabriel's tongue met hers at the same time his hands pushed those shorts down and cupped her behind.

Gabriel reached behind her and flipped on the bathroom light. Parker pulled back from him, realizing they'd kissed across the room. "I promised you these hands would be all over your body," he told her. "I just wish I had a shower big enough for the two of us."

"You want me to shower right now?"

"Yes." He squeezed her behind while he brought his other hand up her back again. "I want you to shower and I'll fantasize about the water running down you, about you sliding your hands over your body, all soapy and slippery." He moved her further into the bathroom. "And when you're done, I want you to come out here to me, dripping wet," he enunciated certain words and let her mind do what it would with them. Gabriel brushed an errant curl off her face. "Then I'll dry you off, lay you down, and have the pleasure of rubbing that lotion all over you. I'm just sad it's almost gone."

"I have thirteen more at home," Parker said, already breathless. "They're all different."

"I can't wait to smell every single one of them on you." His nose was in her neck as he said that. That was when Parker bumped into the shower stall. "It seems, *mon amour*, that we've come to the end of the road." His voice reverberated on the sensitive skin of her neck and Parker's body tightened.

"Are you sure this is what you want tonight?" Parker asked him.

"Let my fantasy play out, Parker." He never knew how long it would be before they started hunting her again. Last time, they'd given him two glorious months with her before he started sniffing The Fold around town. He'd killed so many of them after the last time that he couldn't believe any were left.

Parker ran her fingers through his hair, his nose still in her neck. "Okay, *mon coeur*, but in order to do that, you have to let me go."

In response, Gabriel tightened his arms around her. "That'll never happen."

"Then I guess I'll have to find room for you in the shower." Parker felt his tongue run down the sensitive cord of her neck, and her knees became weak.

Gabriel unwound himself from her, kissing her one more time before he backed out of the bathroom and into the darkened bedroom. He listened as Parker started the shower and slid the door shut. In his mind, he watched her soap herself as he pulled back the blanket over his bed. He didn't need that much light to see. His eyes pierced the darkness around him as he reached for the bottle of lotion she'd set on the dresser. He wished she would unpack her bag. Maybe tomorrow he'd slip it into conversation.

The shower stopped and Gabriel heard the door open, smelling her soap as she stepped out. He was right there then, at the bathroom door, a towel in his hands, and he wrapped it around her, kissing her as she dried, moving her toward the bed. Parker took the towel off her body and wrapped it around her hair, "It'll get the bed all wet," she said at his frown.

"I'm perfectly fine with you getting the bed all wet." His tone was wickedly erotic and even the darkness couldn't hide the blush that rose on her cheeks. Gabriel pulled his pants off before he laid her on her stomach on the bed and took the towel out of her hair anyway. He squirted some of that deep, sensual lotion in his hand and started at her feet, using a lot of pressure on the arch of her foot. His hands moved up her legs, over her calves, applying lotion as he went. When he reached her thighs, Gabriel fanned out his hands, encompassing her entire leg area. He kneeled between her legs, his hands dipping, his fingers running over her core from behind. Parker moaned and flipped her head to the other cheek, her hips swaying slightly. Gabriel let his hands run up over her behind, his thumbs coming last as they dragged across her core.

"Gabriel," she drew out his name.

"Don't start purring yet, my love, we've just started."

Gabriel moved over her behind and up her back. At this point, he was leaning so far over her, his hands on her shoulders, his hard, hot, length on her, rubbing across her skin. Without thought, his knees opened wider, spreading her legs out more. Gabriel's heart pounded at the position, and his hands were almost rough as he gripped her hips. He couldn't stop himself from rubbing against her wet core. "Parker," he said, his voice cracking.

"Please, Gabriel."

That was all he needed to hear. Gabriel hauled her up by her hips until she was on her knees and brought her straight back onto him. She grabbed the headboard to push back on him as he moved her with her hips. He buried himself in her, that shadow ring on his finger glinting in the darkness of the room.

It was late and dark before Gabriel unwound himself from Parker's arms again and rose out of bed. Gabriel dressed in the dark, pulling on a shirt and another pair of jogging pants. He had no need for a suit of shadows tonight. His bare feet were silent as he grabbed his phone, in case Parker woke up and she texted him, and he exited his apartment by the inner back door. Gabriel made his way downstairs and knocked on Charles's door.

Gabriel placed his forehead on Charles's door and stood there, not actually able to believe yet that those words had come from her. It hit him differently with every incarnation, but this time, this time, tears had run down his cheeks at her words. He'd buried his face in her neck, but it hadn't mattered, she'd felt them anyway.

Gabriel's forehead was still on Charles's door when the other man opened it. Charles stepped back to let him in, and Gabriel practically fell into his apartment. Gabriel made it far enough in that Charles was able to close the door before he fell to his knees and folded his hands before him. "Charles." Tears already fell from his eyes. "I can't lose her again."

Gabriel, on his knees in Charles's apartment, knew the tears streamed down his face, but he didn't care. "I can't do it again, especially not after today."

"What, particularly, happened today? Aside from her wonderful dinner."

"She told me that she loves me."

"Oh." Charles moved away from the door and toward the desk in his living room. "That does make it worse."

Gabriel remained on his knees, but his eyes dried. He had to remember who he was talking to. "Yes," Gabriel agreed, rising to his feet, "it does."

"Tell me, Gabriel, how do you think members of The Fold would react had they seen you on your knees?"

Gabriel felt all his senses tighten at the other man's words. "I don't know, Charles. I've killed enough of them and their demon friends over the last four hundred years that their first reaction should still be fear."

"Someone has spent a lot of time trying to own your soul. The most prolific assassin, gone rogue."

Gabriel said nothing, but his eyes went dark. Charles should have noticed and known when to stop, after all the centuries he'd been around him. "And yet you've once again left her alone, this woman who can bring you to your knees."

Charles was barely able to finish the statement before Gabriel was on him. The assassin had moved so fast. One hand was on the other man's throat, the dagger that appeared in his other hand piercing the skin of his cheek. Charles hadn't seen him move. Gabriel had turned and held the man against the wall. "Watch yourself, Fallen One. Don't forget, my mercy is the only reason you're alive right now. As far as I'm concerned, threats made against her are punishable by death."

"You misunderstood my words," Charles ground out, his eyes showing fear.

"No," Gabriel replied, his voice going quiet. "I don't think I misunderstood."

"I cannot harm her."

"That's right, you can't, because I wouldn't hesitate to kill you." The blade in Gabriel's hand grew and the hand around Charles's throat tightened. "This is the second time I've had you in my grasp, Charles. It's curious how we haven't seemed to be able to find the one responsible yet, almost as if he could be hiding in plain sight."

"Are you suggesting I've put this price on your soul?" Charles barely got the words out.

"You do have a lot to gain. You'll either appease the darkness by handing me over to them in chains, or you'll succeed in regaining favor and no longer be fallen by handing in my captured soul. All the while they've been fighting over me, centuries now, if they had just left me in peace, I would have never killed again."

"After all this time you still don't trust me?"

"When it comes to her, you know I don't." Gabriel moved in closer and watched the blood run down his cheek. The wound would heal. "Do you really think I would leave her alone without some sort of protection? I would know if anyone even breathed on my door right now."

"There could be another shadow walker out there."

"There isn't. If there was, they wouldn't be so interested in me."

"Gabriel," Charles choked out. "I mean her no harm, and I never did. Please, release me. I have nothing to gain. There is no regaining favor, you know that." Charles hauled in a breath. "As soon as they sent you after me, I knew there was no going back."

Like he did the first time he'd had him in his grasp, Gabriel released Charles and stepped back. Charles bent at the waist. His hands went to his knees, the only thing keeping him upright was sheer force of will. Charles refused to fall to his knees before Gabriel again. When Charles looked up at him, he was surprised that black dagger was still in Gabriel's hand. He understood that meant the assassin still saw him as an immediate threat to Parker.

Gabriel watched the other man straighten, his hand shaking as he stepped toward his desk and pulled out his chair. This time, Charles collapsed as he sat and left the blood running down his face. Those daggers were lethally sharp. "Can I respectfully ask how you were able to make her your wife?" Charles dared to look up at him. Gabriel's eyes were still dark as night.

"Voodoo," was all Gabriel said.

"Ah," Charles replied, giving in and running his hand along his neck, even though it would reveal his weakness to the hunter before him. "That wasn't an avenue we considered."

"Another detail I'm surprised you didn't uncover."

"Why would I consider a pagan belief?"

"Because." Gabriel dropped his voice to a whisper again. "God lives everywhere, does he not? And you should know that having once been a revered angel yourself."

Theresa looked up at the building, hoping it was the right one. The sign in the window was flipped to open, so she took a deep breath and made her way to the door. No lie, she was still afraid of Gabriel, even after he saved her life, considering he'd been intent on killing her too. He was a legendary assassin. Theresa pushed open the door to the shop and heard a little bell over the door ring. As soon as the door shut and she took a breath, her heart dropped. She heard a man walk out of a back room. "What are you doing here, Angel?"

Theresa turned to the man, wondering how many more legends she'd see come to life this trip. "Fallen, you are still alive. How did I not know this?"

"I'll thank you to keep that information to yourself." Theresa watched Charles run his fingers over a spot on his cheek. "And I know how to hide my identity." "I am hidden as well."

Charles seemed confused at her words, and she saw him look above her head where he could see the bright light of her halo. "You don't appear to be fallen."

"I said hidden," Theresa replied, "not fallen."

"Why are you here?" His words were clipped.

"I'm here to see Parker."

Life surely can't get any better than this, Parker thought, her head resting on Gabriel's chest, her arm around his waist. The light through the window was bright, but it didn't seem like there was any rush to get out of bed. Gabriel's arm tightened around her as he stretched and woke up. His hand came up and brushed her hair back. "No early morning for you today, *mon amour*?"

Parker snuggled in closer to his side. "Not today. It seems I was extra tired and slept in this morning."

"Me too. My old body can't handle so many late nights in a row."

Parker looked up at him and saw he was smiling. "Maybe you should take naps," she teased.

Gabriel did some sort of tuck-and-roll thing. Before she knew it, he was lying on her body, his hips nestled between hers, his head resting on a bent arm. "Lucky for you, I already went to the bathroom, Sir Bladder Crusher." She wrapped her arms around his neck.

"That is good news for me. And how could I nap when I have all this to distract me?"

"I'm sure you'll get tired of me." Parker was half joking. If she kept it in the back of her mind that there was a chance they wouldn't last, maybe it wouldn't hurt so much when it happened.

"Not a chance, Parker. That will never happen. Don't you understand how I feel about you yet? My life is nothing without you. My soul belongs to you, and only you. I give it to you freely." His eyes were so dark and serious. She felt something zip up her spine and settle across the crown of her head.

"I thought this kind of thing was only in romance novels," Parker whispered. Everything inside her had tightened at his words. Her heart felt like it would explode.

"What kind of thing is that?" he asked, his thumb gliding down her cheek and over her lips.

As usual, his fingers found one of her curls, like he couldn't resist touching them.

"You know." Parker cleared her throat. "Their eyes met across the square, and she knew she'd met her destiny. That type of thing."

"If I remember correctly, you approached me."

"And thank God I found the strength of will to do so."

Gabriel looked in her eyes then, his gaze having been on the curl around his finger.

"Yes," he said, his lips inching toward hers, "thank God you did."

Gabriel's lips had just met hers when she felt his body stiffen. A tremor ran down his back. Her arms tightened around him, and her knees bent more, her hips unconsciously shifting to settle him on her better. And that was when the doorbell rang and the screen on his phone lit up with a notification from the doorbell camera. Reluctantly, even though he already knew who it was thanks to the protections he'd set up around his apartment, Gabriel reached for his phone while he continued to kiss her.

"Tell whoever it is to go away," Parker said. The arms she had around his neck tightened, and her fingers ran through his hair. She didn't know it, but Gabriel could see how dark her own eyes were. He pressed the notification button and showed her the picture of the person standing outside his door. "What the hell is Theresa doing here? I thought she left town yesterday." Parker looked at him, confused.

"*Je ne sais pas, mon amour.* I don't know. Do you still want me to send her away?"

"How did she even know where I was?"

"They all watched you leave with me, Parker. Google my name and this gallery pops up. I'm sure Charles is downstairs puttering around and told her where my door was. Besides that, he did pick up your stuff, remember? Two plus two equals you're at my place."

"Oh, right." She squirmed under him. Gabriel just lay there, not moving, his head in his hand, the phone held out for Parker to see. He knew Theresa wouldn't leave, no matter how long it took to answer. She probably wanted to see Parker, and this was the only way to get past his defenses. Angels could be stubborn. "No, don't tell her to leave. I want to know why she's still here. Why didn't she call me? Where's my phone?"

"You left it on the kitchen counter," Gabriel said before he pressed another button on his phone and told Theresa he'd be there in a minute.

"Can you please go let her in while I get dressed? You know how hot it is out there."

"You realize, of course, that I'm also completely nude,

right?"

"No, I had *no* idea that's what I was feeling."

"So sassy." Gabriel laid his full weight on her. "I like it."

"Gabriel..."

He fisted his hand in her hair and lightly tugged, drawing her head back for a kiss. He watched her eyes get darker and her lips part. Gabriel shifted slightly so his hard length was poised, ready to enter her. He could tell she was ready. "I can see some from your eyes that some rougher play may be called for sometimes," he whispered, his teeth running down her neck. "Your eyes got dark, and that turns me on. Tell me, how quickly do you think I could get you to climax right now?" Gabriel's eyes never left hers as he slowly inched inside her.

Parker's breath caught when he was buried in her, his hand fisted in her hair. One of her knees came up higher, and he felt her nails dig into his shoulders. He placed his free arm behind her knee before he withdrew and slid back hard. His knees came up so he had more leverage over her.

"How long do I have before I can hear you sobbing my name, Parker?" He ground into her, pulling her knee higher so he could get deeper. Her eyes closed. Gabriel pushed himself upright then, kneeling between her legs and grasping her hips before he moved in her hard again.

Parker didn't know what to do with her hands as she threw her head back. With the feel of Gabriel moving fast and hard inside her, she forgot about Theresa standing at the door. She'd already been slightly turned on from him lying on her, the skin-to-skin feeling she loved. When he'd tugged her hair, something primal happened inside her and she wanted him. Finally, she reached and grasped the headboard to hang on because she was pretty sure she would explode in fifteen seconds. The moans coming from her mouth matched the beat of his skin against hers, and his pace quickened. "Oh, God, Gabriel," she ground out, her toes curling. He reached up with one hand and grabbed the headboard, his other hand staying on her hip. Gabriel drove himself into her even harder. Both of her hands were on his chest then, her nails digging in his skin, and it only took three more hard thrusts for him to push her over the edge.

Ten minutes after he told her he'd be a minute, Gabriel opened the front door and stepped back. Never, in the history of their time together, had he taken Parker like that, and he already couldn't wait to do it again. "Parker wants you to wait inside while she gets dressed," he told her. "So you don't get too hot." Of course, Parker wouldn't know angels could regulate their body temperature.

Theresa looked him up and down. He only had a pair of those jogging pants on, his chest bare. The angel saw the red marks there before she met his eyes. "I see you didn't bother getting dressed," she said as she stepped in. She wasn't stupid. She knew why it had taken him so long to answer. She also knew he'd answered the door without a shirt on so she could see the fresh marks on him. Gabriel wanted her to see how easily he could distract her, how Parker would choose him over her. He'd probably hidden the marks from Parker's view because Theresa would bet money Parker would have made him put a shirt on had she seen them.

"Considering you interrupted us, you're lucky I have these on." Gabriel closed the door behind her. "The only reason I let you in was because Parker said she wanted to see you."

As hard as she tried not to, Theresa couldn't stop the angel part of her personality from wrinkling her nose. "Let's be honest, I clearly didn't stop you from doing what you wanted." She looked him in the eyes, so he'd know she understood what he was doing without a shirt on. "And it smells like sin in here."

"A lot of it too. Earth shattering, mind-blowing, sin," Gabriel said as he headed to the other side of the kitchen island to put as much distance as he could between the two of them.

"You could at least spray an air freshener."

"Don't come in here with your goddamn self-righteous

attitude, angel." He looked back at her.

Theresa was glad he'd put the kitchen island between them. His eyes had gone black. "Like I said, we both know she's the only reason I let you in. I don't give a damn who you are or what you think about me, you will not judge her. *No one* will judge her."

Theresa took a breath to answer when they both heard the bedroom door open, and Gabriel's eyes returned to their normal deep-blue color. What he didn't need to add was that Parker was the only reason she was still alive. It didn't matter to him that Theresa had been Parker's guardian angel at one time, because, in his mind, she'd also failed Parker's every single incarnation. And done nothing about it then.

It only mattered that Parker considered her a friend now.

Theresa didn't get to say what she'd wanted. She didn't get to say that she would never judge Parker, and hadn't meant to say any of that, but it was too late now.

Parker stepped out of the bedroom, with one of those t-shirt dresses on, pulling her hair up into a ponytail. "I got her safely inside, *mon amour*, no need to worry," Gabriel professed softly when she stopped next to him. "I'll go finish getting dressed now." He placed his hand on Parker's cheek and gently turned her to him to give her a kiss. Parker blushed and her gaze flicked toward Theresa. The angel, meanwhile, had a hard time remembering the part she was supposed to be playing when she saw what was around the crown of Parker's head. Her shocked eyes met Gabriel's, and the look in his dared her to say something about the halo his freely given soul was making there.

Gabriel's immortal soul now belonged to a mortal woman.

It belonged to Parker.

But Theresa thought the exchange of souls could only happen in a blessed marriage union. It was something only whispered about in lore, she'd never seen it. Had she missed something? When did this happen?

All of the sudden, Theresa felt sick at the judgment she'd

hurled at him. She knew how many times he'd tried to make Parker his wife. And she'd used the word *sin* to describe what took place between them. Something beautiful and sacred between Gabriel and the woman he'd desired as his wife more than he'd desired anything. The woman he loved. It was something he'd waited centuries for, and she'd stomped on it like it was nothing more than an ant.

No wonder he hated angels.

CHAPTER EIGHT

Parker watched Gabriel walk away. She knew her face was flaming as she turned to Theresa. She hoped she could pull off the lie she was about to tell her friend. "Sorry it took so long to answer the door. I was still sleeping." Parker turned to Theresa. "The heat here got to me, and my body finally realized it's on summer break."

Theresa let the lie slide. "That's okay, it got to me too. At least you didn't walk around half drunk all weekend and add dehydration to your ailments." Theresa stepped up to Parker, and the two women hugged.

"What are you still doing here?" Parker asked when she stepped back. "I thought your flight left yesterday. And why didn't you call me?"

"Girl, I did try to call you last night and this morning. And I texted you." They both turned when Parker's phone beeped on the kitchen island, several notification lights blinking. "I see why you didn't answer."

"Oh, no." Parker raced to the counter, picking up her phone. She hoped her mom hadn't tried to call her back because she'd forgotten to last night. She scrolled through the missed calls and texts, passing Theresa's and several others before she saw two texts from her mother and one from her dad, both asking if she was all right. Her dad's more saying her mother was worried and to please call her back. Both came in last night. Parker took her phone and sat on the couch, her fingers flying on the screen as she texted both her parents back. "I'm such an asshole," she said as she dropped her phone in her lap. Parker pinched the bridge of her nose and tilted her head back on the couch.

"You aren't an asshole." Theresa sat on the couch next to her. She turned so she leaned against the arm rest, facing Parker. Both women heard the shower in Gabriel's room turn on. "My mom probably thought I was dead." Parker raised her head back up and looked at Theresa. Her phone beeped then, and Parker read the message, her face relaxing a bit.

"There, see, no harm no foul. Your parents always were cool."

"Sure, but this is a new situation. I'm almost a thousand miles away, not two hundred. And with someone they don't know…" Parker trailed off, peeking at Theresa.

"Since you brought it up." Theresa bounced a little and opened her eyes wide. "Tell me everything. I almost hyperventilated when he opened that door."

Parker flopped back against the couch and closed her eyes. "Oh my God, Theresa, it's like living in a romance novel with a whole lot of erotica sprinkled in."

"No need to fake it then?" Parker had broken down and told Theresa about her sex life with Max once. She'd needed to talk to someone about it, and Theresa seemed to always know when to call. She knew when Parker was feeling her lowest, like she had a sixth sense about it.

"He makes everything in my body vibrate and stand at attention. I didn't know these types of feelings existed. There is no faking anything."

"Sounds like a nice summer diversion."

"No," Parker admonished, her eyes still closed, shaking her head, "it's so much more than that."

"Are you saying you love him?" Theresa asked. "Already?"

"I don't think that's a strong enough word for what I

feel." Parker felt her cheeks flame again. Was she really telling Theresa this? About someone she'd known for four days? How was she supposed to explain to Theresa that it was more like she'd known him for four hundred years? Both women looked over when the bedroom door opened, and Gabriel walked out. He hadn't put a shirt on, but he'd showered and changed into a pair of shorts. He was on the phone, speaking in what she thought sounded like German as he stepped across the hall and opened the door to his laundry room. Gabriel used his free hand and switched the laundry she'd started last night to the dryer, tossing in a few dryer sheets. He stopped in the hallway after that was done, motioning with his hand and his voice slightly raising. Parker felt his eyes on her then, and her skin got warm when the scent of his cologne reached her. Gabriel walked back into his bedroom and quietly shut the door.

"Okay, so maybe I was wrong and there's definitely something there," Theresa said. "I hope it's not a rebound relationship."

"I was always so envious of your relationship, you know. I wanted someone I could have a life with, grow old with, maybe even see the world with." Parker looked over at Theresa. "I've felt so intimidated by life, so afraid of everything for as long as I can remember. He doesn't care about these ugly scars that I have no idea how I got." Parker pointed at the scar across her jawline. He'd lightly kissed across the entire scar on her jaw last night and she'd felt such deep sadness from him while he did it. In fact, he'd done it with all of them the last few days. Gabriel had loved on every scar she had.

"They shouldn't make a difference."

"They did to Max. He told me once they made it hard for him to be aroused. My body just didn't turn him on."

"Well, we established a long time ago that he was an asshole, and you were better off without him." Theresa hated Max and what he'd done to her already tortured soul. It seemed like his goal had been to end Parker's very life.

"Yeah." Parker readjusted her body and turned toward Theresa. "I needed to find the strength within myself I guess."

"Speaking of my relationship," Theresa said, digging her phone out of her purse and swiping the screen. "Don't be envious because look at these." Theresa handed Parker her phone, and Parker's mouth dropped open as she went through the five pictures. They were pictures of Theresa's fiancé and Emily in some very compromising situations. Sharing an intimate meal. Holding hands while walking down the street. One had her straddling his lap on a park bench.

Parker looked up at Theresa. "What the hell?"

"Yeah, turns out they've been having an affair for a couple of years now. She disappeared after we got back Saturday, packed all her stuff, and left. Found out she'd flown back home, and they took off to L.A., which is why I missed my flight and I'm still here."

"But you're supposed to get married in a month and a half."

"Seems that isn't happening anymore since I broke it off with him as soon as I found out about this. Why someone waited until now to send me these pictures is beyond me but thank goodness they did before I said I do."

"That's complete bullshit." Parker looked at the pictures again and didn't see the look on Theresa's face. She'd only heard Parker curse a handful of times in the ten years she'd been around her, and it was surprising every time. Parker was so gentle and kind. An old soul.

Gabriel came out of his room then, completely dressed in a light-purple shirt and tan shorts. He was buckling the watch he wore around his wrist. He always wore light colors and Parker thought they looked so good on him with his darker skin. She wouldn't know what to think if he wore dark colors. She'd even seen a couple of pink shirts hanging in his closet. God love a man comfortable enough with his own masculinity to wear pink occasionally. He stopped when he reached the loveseat across from the couch and looked up at them, his gaze landing on Parker first. They would always go to Parker first. "I apologize if I'm interrupting, I was hoping I'd given you enough time before I joined the conversation."

"Not at all," Theresa said, "I'm glad you came out to join us." Theresa's throat tightened when his eyes landed on hers again and she could see the deep mistrust he had in her. To him, it was all just the game she was playing for Parker. Gabriel sat on the smaller couch across from them and crossed his ankle over his knee.

Parker resisted the urge to switch couches and sit next to him, but it was exceedingly difficult. "Theresa, this is Gabriel. Gabriel, this is Theresa."

"Nice to meet you."

Gabriel nodded at her greeting.

"I met Theresa in college," Parker continued. "It was her bachelorette party I was here with."

"Congratulations," Gabriel told her. "I hope to get married one day." His eyes landed on Parker again, and she blushed. All she ever did was blush anymore.

Theresa pretended not to notice. "Well, don't hope to have one like mine because I found out Saturday that he and one of my 'best friends' quote unquote, were having an affair for a couple of years. She took off Saturday night after I found out, flew back to Chicago, and they took off to California together."

Gabriel had to give it to her for that story. It was much better than her disappearing into the night, and no police were involved, but he furrowed his brow in pity for the story. "That's terrible. I'm sorry to hear that happened."

Theresa shrugged. "What can you do? There's nothing I can do to change what happened in the past, no matter how much regret there is. All I can do now is look ahead to the future." The angel hoped he would read between the lines. She didn't want this tension between them.

"Parker mentioned you were supposed to leave

yesterday. Did you miss your flight? I only have one bedroom, but I could have offered you a couch at least."

"I appreciate the offer, but I splurged and got myself an expensive hotel room and pampered myself. Honestly, I missed my flight on purpose. I wasn't looking forward to discussing what had happened with the other women on the flight. Sorry if I seemed like a stalker hunting you down, Park," Theresa said, using the nickname she'd given her in college, "I actually am leaving today and I wanted to see you before I left."

"I'm glad you did. I'm sorry I didn't get your call last night."

The two women talked back and forth while Gabriel looked at something on his phone.

"Parker," he said during a lull in their conversation.

Her eyes turned to him, and he smiled. "Parker, have you ever been to Boston?"

"No, why?"

"You did mention a few free weeks for traveling. I have to meet someone in Boston the day after tomorrow. Would you be interested in joining me?" Gabriel could at least put the angel's mind at ease that Parker would be safe with him when she left.

"Oh, my God, Parker, you would love Boston. So many museums and old cathedrals and buildings to look at. I'm jealous." Theresa reached over and slapped Parker on the knee.

"Where would we stay?" she asked.

"I have an apartment in Boston." He looked down at his phone when he said this, typing and scrolling quickly.

"You do?"

"I don't stay here in New Orleans a lot. It was just the best of luck that I happened to be here this past weekend." Gabriel looked up into her eyes. His were filled with every emotion he felt for her.

Parker looked between Gabriel and Theresa and back again. They were both looking at her expectantly, and Parker hated being the center of attention. Gabriel's fingers were poised over his phone, waiting for her response. "The best of luck, huh?" Parker said.

Even if he'd have been halfway across the world, he'd have known when she entered the city. Gabriel would have dropped whatever he was doing and returned home, but thankfully, he'd already been here. "The kind of luck that only gets written about." Parker gave him a little smile.

"Geesh, Park," Theresa injected, "stop torturing the man and just say yes already. That's clearly what he's waiting to hear."

Theresa's voice shook her back to reality. "Yes," she finally said, "I'd love to go."

Gabriel did his one-sided smile and looked back down at his phone, his fingers resuming whatever typing they'd been doing. "When are we leaving?"

"There's a four-thirty flight tonight." He looked up at her. "It will be late when we get in, but that will give us all day tomorrow for sightseeing." Gabriel didn't mind flying, even though he could shadow walk and be there in seconds.

"Wait, you want to go today?"

"R-e-e-d, right?"

"Yes," Theresa said. Gabriel nodded at her.

"Gabriel," Parker started.

"Yes, my love?" Parker stopped because he said it in English this time, and in front of Theresa.

"I—" Parker visibly swallowed. "I can't afford a last-minute flight." She diligently saved in her travel fund all year, but it had to last her for a couple of weeks. She'd already saved some money by staying with him, but it had to last.

"It's already taken care of," he said, pressing on his phone screen one more time before he placed it on the loveseat next to him.

"I can pay you back."

"No, thank you," he replied.

"Parker, let the man spoil you, he clearly wants to."

Theresa shook her head. "And it's about time someone did."

"Yes," Gabriel replied as he looked at Theresa. "I've heard about the ex-boyfriend."

"If only I could commit murder," was her response.

"Lucky for him, there were no available flights to Chicago yesterday."

Parker watched this back and forth between the two of them, not sure if she should be embarrassed or elated. It seemed like they both wanted to protect her. "Gabriel?"

His attention was instantly back on her.

"Can we get clam chowder?"

Sunlight hit her face as Parker stretched and yawned, pulling the blanket back over her naked chest. Yesterday, Theresa had stayed about an hour before she had to leave to catch her flight. The two women had hugged before she left. Parker and Gabriel ate some leftover potato salad and strawberry shortcake, and he kissed her before saying he had to go talk to Charles before they left. Parker had folded the laundry from the dryer and repacked her bag. Since she didn't know how long they'd be gone, she just took everything with her. Gabriel returned and packed his own carry-on, eyeing her bag speculatively.

"What is it?" she asked.

"You're taking everything?"

"I don't know how long we'll be gone or what will happen, so I figured I'd bring everything."

"I have an appointment to look at some property in Chicago in early July."

"Really?" Parker's heart burst with joy.

"I was sort of hoping you'd just stay with me until then."

"I am with you. I don't have a closet full of clothes at my disposal. I have one bag's worth."

Gabriel pulled her close, and Parker leaned back so she could see his eyes. He ran his hand down her cheek again. "We could buy you some stuff." He said that before his lips met hers, his kiss gentle and reverent.

Parker stood there with her eyes closed after Gabriel ended the kiss, savoring the feeling of him so close to her. "I don't need more stuff, *mon coeur*," she whispered, opening her eyes. "I have plenty of stuff at home. You'll see when you come up in July."

"Are you inviting me to stay with you in July?" He'd have to cancel the hotel reservation he already made.

"Now that's a silly question." Parker wound her arms around him. "I need you to stay as close to me as possible. It's only a thirty-minute drive from my house to The Loop neighborhood in downtown Chicago."

"Your bed better be super comfortable," Gabriel teased, using the same words she'd said to him.

"I promise, you won't be disappointed in my bed."

Parker stretched again, her hand landing on empty space next to her instead of Gabriel. He'd had her close her eyes and promise not to open them when he unlocked the door to his apartment last night, leading her through it. She heard the distinctive sound of curtains being drawn back before he pulled her back to his chest and told her to open her eyes. When she did, Parker was looking out the floor-to-ceiling windows of his apartment at the city below, and beyond that, the dark expanse that she knew was the ocean. "Gabriel"—she stepped closer to the windows— "this view is amazing. I can't wait to see it in the morning."

Gabriel stepped up so he was right behind her again and she felt his hands run down her sides, bunching up her dress. His breath was hot on the back of her neck. "Not as amazing as you."

Parker shivered at his touch. "You fly me first class and then bring me to your tenth-floor downtown Boston apartment with a view like this. Are you trying to impress me with your money?"

Gabriel's hands were under the hem of her dress now, splayed across the tops of her thighs. The reflection in the window showed him slowly dragging his tongue across her sensitive neck. Those hands drifted up, lightly brushing her core and making her shiver more until they were on her hips. He drew her back against him. Parker felt how hard he was already. "I wanted to be with you here," he whispered in her ear.

Parker turned in his arms then and his hands now traced down her behind. Gabriel pushed her back against the windows as he kissed her, his fingers running from back to front on her underwear. "Do you want the whole city of Boston to see my ass?" Parker asked as she pulled his shirt over his head. She put her hands in his hair, pulling his mouth back down to hers.

Gabriel broke their kiss and led her across the darkened room. "Not a chance in hell." He turned and sat on his bed, easing her down onto his lap, her legs around him. He hadn't bothered drawing the curtain closed and let the moonlight shine in as their bodies came together.

Which was why the sunlight poured in this morning. She sat up, surveying the room. Aside from the bed, there was a dresser and two bedside tables in the room. Only, it wasn't a full bedroom, there was only a half wall separating this space from the rest of the apartment, and no door. Parker frowned, confused for a minute before she craned her head to look over the wall and discovered this was more of a studio apartment. She saw the living room and, across from that, his kitchen table in front of the small complete kitchenette. It was all one big room, the partial wall being the only separation. Parker heard the shower running and figured Gabriel must be using it, but she was drawn to check out the view from the windows in between the living room and kitchen.

Parker stood, not bothering to find her clothes, and wrapped the blanket around her body so she could walk to the windows and stand in front of them. The view truly was breathtaking. She looked out over the city, but beyond, with the sun rising over it, she saw the harbor, and beyond that, the ocean, glistening in the early morning light. She'd never been to the ocean, and she wanted to touch it. Parker felt a warm hand on her bare shoulder as Gabriel stepped up behind her and gently placed his arm around her from behind. "This view really is amazing," she told him.

"This view is the only reason I bought this place," he responded. "What it lacks in space, it makes up for with this." He spread his hand out to encompass the sight from the windows.

"I don't want to know how much you paid for this place." Parker shuddered at the thought of the price. She bet it was more than the cost of her home in Illinois.

"No, you probably don't. And it wasn't cheap."

"Just so I'm not surprised, do you own any other property? A private jet maybe?" Parker looked at him over her shoulder.

"I actually do own an apartment in Paris…"

"Of course, you do," Parker cut him off.

"But I inherited that, I didn't buy it," he finished. She didn't need to know that he'd inherited the apartment from himself, for so many generations he couldn't remember. "And no jet, I fly commercial."

Parker sighed and looked back out over the ocean. Great, a world traveler.

"What's that sigh for?" He was afraid of that sigh because it sounded like she was about to give up.

"Gabriel, I'm a plain old fifth-grade teacher. I own a little two-bedroom, thousand square foot ranch house in the middle of a suburb. I have student loan debt. I've never seen the ocean. But you, you own property in different cities. A different country even. You can fly off to wherever in the world whenever you want. I have to save all year. You lived and studied abroad. You can spot a fake Monet. Your family name must be as old as time. How can I compare to this?" This time, it was Parker who swept her hand out to encompass the view.

"Parker, I don't care about these properties. If you want

127

me to sell them, I will. I can't help traveling for the work I do. I can't change that, but if you want me to give up everything else, just say the words. Every property I own, anything I have, it means nothing to me without you." Gabriel wound both his arms around her and buried his face in the crook of her neck. "I'll be happier in your little two-bedroom house on the outskirts of Chicago than anywhere else in the world, because I'm with you."

"You can't know that."

"I do know that."

"It's because it's all new and different and the sex is amazing. Sooner or later, it will wear off and then you'll resent me. You'll want to jet off somewhere and I can't go because my life is ruled by school breaks and conferences and lesson plans." The words hurt coming out, but it was a fear she kept in her heart.

"Four hundred years hasn't made me love you less."

"What does that even mean? It's barely been over four days."

"Parker…"

"No, I refuse to get so deep in this and then have my heart ripped out like every other time. I'd rather rip the Band-Aid off now than have it hurt worse later. Trust me, you'll be thanking me for ending this." Parker couldn't stop the tears from flowing. She knew where some of this fear came from, but there was something else, something deeper inside her that cried out in pain. All she became at that moment was a conduit for whatever was inside. "I refuse to lose you again."

"I won't let it happen again." Gabriel's voice was rough.

Parker understood there was a double meaning to his words, but she didn't know what it was. As Gabriel said this, Parker saw darkness start along the edges of her vision. Something in his voice made her go still, but it wasn't in fear. She didn't know what it was, but something in her wanted to hear what he said. "I've hunted and killed almost every being who's ever touched you or had anything to do with it."

And then there was the twenty-first century her that started crying. "Great, I knew it was too good to be true. You're crazy, aren't you? A crazy lunatic. Let me go or I'll scream." Parker tried to extricate herself from his arms, but they tightened around her.

"I'm not letting you go." Gabriel tried to keep the ice out of his voice, but what he needed to do required some of his immortal power to come out. His arms became a vise around her. Parker stopped struggling only because she could no longer move with his grip so tight.

"I need you to listen and listen to me deeply, because I can't let your conscious self remember this conversation, not right now." Gabriel's darkness swirled around them. He was glad she couldn't see how black his eyes had become. "Four hundred years, I have loved you, and six times I've lost you, but never again, Parker, never again. If I must hunt every demon, angel, or member of The Fold in order to secure your life, I will. I've begged God on my knees so many times, for mercy for you. Because love should mean more than my past. All I've wanted was you, for four hundred years. I will crawl through the very fires of Hell if that's what it takes."

This was the first time, in any of her incarnations, that she'd displayed knowledge that she might know what happened to her, even if it was on a subconscious level. The very fact that she'd more than once used the term *again* or *this time* proved it. The room was pitch black, but Gabriel could still see.

Another sob caught in Parker's throat. "You're scaring me, Gabriel."

"I'm so sorry you're scared of me right now, thankfully you won't remember." Gabriel buried his face in her neck. "Parker, every scar on your body reminds me of my failure to you. That I didn't keep you safe. That I underestimated the lengths my enemies would go to. They want to possess me by hurting you. But they can't have what is no longer mine, *ma femme*. For you are now the one who possesses my soul. You are my wife in the eyes of God. Mine. From the very first time I laid eyes on you, it was all I wanted. My soul, I gave it to you freely. It settled about you like a halo, *mon ange*, my angel. My soul shines around your beautiful head. Even Theresa saw it."

"How could Theresa see a soul?" Her voice sounded distant, and he knew the swirling darkness was working on her. It was something he used if a mortal saw him doing his job, to make them forget what they saw. He hated killing and he refused to kill any mortal other than who his soul-contract demanded him to.

"Imagine my surprise when I found out she had been your guardian angel. Not a very good one if you ask me, considering she did nothing to stop what was happening to you." Gabriel snorted. "To claim free will, as if you chose to be murdered. All you did was choose me."

Parker slipped away, her body going limp as the darkness moved through her. Gabriel swept her up before she crumpled to the floor, holding her close to his chest. He turned with her, and the darkness followed as he carried her back to the bed and gently laid her down.

CHAPTER NINE

Penelope rushed through the streets, moving as fast as she could over the heaps of garbage and sewage. Thankfully, she'd hitched her dress up so the hem wouldn't drag in whatever nastiness was on the ground. It had rained last night, so the mire was worse than usual. She had to deliver this bread for her father before making her way to the market square. Once a week, there was an open-air market a few streets over from her father's bakery, and he insisted they be there.

After seven years of marriage, Penelope had found herself back in her father's house, a widow. Her husband, who'd she thought to be gentle and kind, had turned into a cruel, useless man once they'd married. His words would hurt her as his hands would beat her. He'd put her to work at the inn his family owned, carrying and washing tankards, cleaning rooms and bedding. Sometimes, it had seemed like she was the only one who did any work, and she'd barely slept these past seven years. Thank God she'd never conceived his child. Over the years, the strain had started to show on her face and body. Her curls no longer had the bounce they'd once had, and her gray eyes showed the strain and hopelessness she felt. Although short, her body, that had once been plump and full of life, was near skin and bones by the time she fled back to her father's bakery, all thanks to a falling keg of ale.

Penelope didn't know how many times she'd warned her husband and his father that the way they stacked the kegs was a danger and they risked them falling on their heads. The men had scoffed at her. What could a mere woman know? Even now, in the advanced year of sixteen twenty-three, women were still treated as nothing more than property. At least her father had treated her mother well before her death. But, back to her being a stupid woman and knowing nothing, what she'd said would happen had finally happened. One day, while stacking the kegs, they'd toppled over onto her husband's head, nearly crushing it with the weight. Penelope had hoped, even though she'd hated the man, that he'd died quickly and hadn't suffered. As soon as he'd been placed in the ground, Penelope had said a prayer, packed her meager belongings, and fled back to her father in the night.

That had been six months ago.

Her husband's family had come and tried to lay claim to her. She was, after all, one of the only workers at the inn, but her father had refused them entry. Her father may not have been an overly sentimental man, but one look at what his child had become had him fuming. The baker had sent them away and threatened to take it to King Louis himself if they returned. Their son, her husband, was dead, and she had no more ties to that family.

After her race down the street to beat the rising of the sun, Penelope stood at the back door of the large house, trying to catch her breath. She wiped the sweat from her brow, pushing an errant curl back under the scarf she wore over her head. Just then, the sunlight peaked over the rooftops of Paris. Penelope took a moment to again thank God she was back in her father's house. The door in front of her opened, and an older woman peeked out, right on time. "*Bonjour, Madame de la Maison,*" Penelope said, greeting the head mistress of the grand house. She held up the sack of bread and sweets she'd rushed over. "*Pour la Grande Dame de la Maison."* The other woman said nothing as she took the bag from Penelope, tossed her a few coins, and promptly shut the door in her face. It was always the same, even the domestic staff liked to think they were above the bakers, but Penelope knew better. It was why she liked to remind the woman with her sweet greetings that, in the end, she was not the master of that house, her mistress was.

Penelope turned, shaking her head, no longer caring about the house staff, and raced back the way she came. Her father would be loading his cart soon, and he wanted her there to help. A stitch started in her side, and Penelope had to slow her pace, her heart racing in her throat. She slowed to a walk, her breaths heavy against the tight bodice of her dress. How she sometimes wished for the freedom of movement that men had. Since escaping her husband's family, she'd put back on the weight she lost, no longer looking emaciated. The glow had returned to her skin and hair. She finally started to feel more like herself again. What she was afraid of was her father looking for a new husband for her.

After walking a bit, her breathing and heartrate slowed. She was about to quicken her pace when a strange sensation went down her spine and goosebumps raised on her flesh. She passed a dark alley. The rays from the rising sun had not yet made it there, and she swore she saw something move in the shadows. Against her better judgment, considering she was a woman alone, Penelope paused for a moment and looked down the alley, deciding it had been a trick of the light, and continued on her way. After a block, Penelope became aware of light footsteps behind her, and she tried not to panic. More people stirred on the street now, and she didn't want to assume it was someone following her.

Ignoring the beggars crawling toward her, Penelope turned and headed down the street her father's bakery was on. She snuck a glance behind her, and her breath caught. About a dozen paces behind her she could see the outline of a man dressed from head to toe in black. He appeared to be keeping close to the shops on the street, never stepping into the light. When their eyes met across that space, Penelope felt that same sensation run down her spine, and she took off running and didn't stop until she reached the bakery.

Gabriel stepped from the shadows into the alley he knew his prey was heading toward. Just this one last time, and they would set him free, that was the deal. Just one more. The offer did strike him as suspicious, but he wanted to believe that he would be free, that he could do what he wanted. He wanted to believe Charles could find an end to this curse of immortality he'd ended up with. It had been almost five hundred years of this life, and he was tired of it, so tired.

His gaze sharpened, piercing the darkness that encompassed the alley he hid in. At his thought, his sharp, black dagger appeared in his hand, ready to strike down his final victim. He was poised to strike when the woman stepped into view. Gabriel paused, a shiver running down his spine. She stopped at the entrance of the alley, pushing a curl of hair back from her face.

Gabriel had never seen someone more beautiful in his many years of life. He was sure women more beautiful than her had—and did—exist, but, to him, there was no greater beauty. Why had he been sent to kill her? His every human instinct fought against plunging his assassin's blade into her neck.

When she moved on, Gabriel stood in stunned silence for a breath of time before his blade disappeared and he stepped out of the alley, following behind her. He didn't understand what The Fold wanted with the death of this woman; he'd never been sent after a woman. That wasn't to say a woman had never died because of his actions, but never by his hand. Gabriel hadn't heard the call of his soul-contract in many years, and he'd spent that time with Charles, trying to discover a way out of it.

The woman in front of him turned a corner and he

followed her, never losing sight of her simple, brown dress. No rich, genteel lady here, dripping in gold and diamonds, whipping the backs of those beneath her. A simple peasant woman. It didn't make sense. She paused then and looked behind her. Their eyes met across the distance of the street. He wished he could discern the color of her eyes. When she took off running, Gabriel felt no concern, he'd be able to find her anywhere.

After all, she was his prey.

The market day was good, and Penelope's father ran out of bread and sweets by midday. By then, she found herself alone by his stall, wiping her brow, the sun warm in the sky, her father having left her to clean up by herself. It was fine, she didn't mind being alone, especially after the noise and crush of people in the market all morning.

"*Excusez-moi, Madame.*"

Penelope turned at the sound of the deep voice behind her. Her heart caught in her throat. Standing there was the most beautiful man she'd ever seen. He had honey-blond hair pulled back and tied at the nape of his neck, accentuating the angular planes of his face. Penelope didn't consider herself to be an overly dramatic woman, but she'd never seen such lips on a man. "*Oui, Monsieur?* Can I help you?"

"I pray I have not arrived too late to purchase a loaf of bread."

"I'm afraid we have no more to sell, *Monsieur.*" Penelope's heart dropped at the crestfallen look on his face.

"Ah, well, such is my loss then." Gabriel turned to leave.

"Perhaps," Penelope said, not willing to let the man walk away. There was just something about him that had her wanting him to stay. He turned back to her and pinned her in place with his deep-blue eyes. "Perhaps my father has a loaf or two left at his bakery."

The man stepped closer to her, and Penelope's heart fluttered. "Your father, you say?"

"*Oui, Monsieur*, his shop is a mere two blocks away."

"Not your husband, then?" Gabriel wasn't sure why that information made his heart race.

This close, he saw that her eyes were gray.

"No," Penelope whispered as he stepped closer. "My husband is dead."

The man took another step closer. Penelope watched in astonishment as he reached for her left hand and brought it to his lips, kissing her fourth finger. "May I ask what your name is?"

Penelope had to swallow since her throat had become so dry. "Penelope," she said, "my name is Penelope. And what is yours, *Monsieur*?"

"My name is Gabriel."

Two days. It had been two days since he'd met her, and Gabriel couldn't get Penelope's face out of his mind. He didn't understand what was happening or why he'd been sent to assassinate her. When he'd walked with her to her father's bakery, he'd noticed that, with every step, the instincts he'd run on had disappeared. Almost five hundred years as an assassin dissipated with one look from her slate-gray eyes. When they'd arrived at the bakery, he'd followed her inside, unable to stop his eyes from glancing down at the swing of her hips under her dress. The problem came when her father caught his look. Gabriel inclined his head at the man, standing back at the entrance, not wanting to be thrown out of the shop.

"Father," she announced, rounding the counter and stopping beside the man, "do we have a loaf or two of bread left? This gentleman was asking, and I told him you may have one here at the bakery."

"No, *ma fille*, we are out." Her father never took his eyes off Gabriel. Maybe he could sense the danger in Gabriel's stance. Maybe it was the way he held himself, like a soldier, that most mortal men backed away from. But not her father. He stood in challenge to him. He wanted Gabriel to know he wasn't intimidated.

Penelope turned to Gabriel. "I'm very sorry, *Monsieur.*"

"*C'est ne pas problème,*" Gabriel replied. "There is no problem, I can return tomorrow and buy a loaf for my assistant."

"Tomorrow is Sunday," her father replied quickly, drawing himself up to his full height, "we are closed."

"Monday then." Gabriel's eyes narrowed on the man, letting him know he too wouldn't be backing down.

Monday came and Gabriel stood outside the bakery, across the small street, watching through the window while she helped patrons at the counter. He'd felt deeply unsettled ever since he'd met her. Everything he'd been for the last five hundred years no longer had meaning, and neither did the reason behind why he'd done it. Gabriel stared so intently that it took a moment before he realized she had stepped up next to him, a wrapped loaf of bread in her hands. Five hundred years as a soldier, and she'd slipped past his defenses. He hadn't seen her come out the front door, so she must have exited through a side door down the alley beside the bakery. "Good morning, *Monsieur.*"

Gabriel turned to her, and they got lost in each other's eyes. "Gabriel," he reminded her. "Please, call me Gabriel."

"Then I also insist that you call me Penelope." She smiled slightly at him. Penelope held up the bread. "*Le pain pour vous, Monsieur*, I mean, Gabriel." It was the first time she had said his name, and chills ran down his spine.

"Thank you, Penelope." Gabriel took the loaf from her, and his fingers brushed hers. Penelope's cheeks flushed and her heart raced at the contact. Wasn't she too old to feel this way? She was a widow, not a virgin. But her deceased husband had never made her heart flutter, even when he'd been so sweet while he courted her. "I was going to come in and purchase it." His words snapped her mind back to reality.

Penelope's gaze slid to the window of the bakery. Her father stared at them out of it. "I thought it best you did not."

"I take it I did not make a good first impression on your father."

"He's been quite overprotective since I returned from my late husband's home in such a state. He did not realize what they were doing with me..." Penelope's voice trailed off at the sudden look in Gabriel's eyes, like they had turned into blocks of ice.

Sudden rage clouded his vision, and his body tensed at the thoughts her sentence brought to his mind. "What did they do to you, Penelope?" The question was no more than a whisper. He might make an exception on not killing unless he had to, depending on what her answer was.

Penelope took a tiny step back. "It no longer matters, he is dead." Penelope looked over and saw her father was still staring at them, his other assistant working around him. "I should go back." Her eyes met his again, and this time, they were back to that deep-blue color, looking at her with such warmth.

"I still owe you money for the bread." Gabriel reached into the pocket of the vest he was wearing.

Penelope held her hands up. "Please, it is nothing. Consider it a gift. Maybe you will like it so much that you return and buy more."

"I would come every day and buy everything, without even trying it, if it meant I could see you again." Gabriel brought her hand to his lips, and Penelope's knees went weak at the feel of his lips on her skin.

"I like to walk along the river in the afternoon," she said breathlessly.

"What a coincidence, so do I. God willing, I will see you while I do so."

"There's a lovely park, not too far from here, where I like to sit and watch the water.

Perhaps you should visit it today while on your walk."

Four weeks. Four wonderful, divine weeks. That first

day, when he'd met her at her favorite park, Penelope knew she was in trouble. She knew that if he showed up, it wouldn't take long to fall in love with him. And it hadn't.

Every morning, he came into the bakery and bought his loaf of bread, nodding to her father, his fingers skimming hers when he placed his coin there. And every afternoon, he'd meet her by the river. She'd seen him, that first time, sitting on a park bench, his long, lean body appearing so relaxed. The urge to reach out and touch him had been so strong that she'd had to clench her fists. He'd turned to her, as if he'd felt her presence, and smiled a little half smile.

Yes, she was hooked that quickly.

He'd held her hand as they walked, the heat from his palm racing up her arm. How could that simple touch cause her heart to go so frantic? They talked over these weeks, and Penelope had finally opened up to him about her late husband, about how that family had treated her. She told him about how guilty she felt to be thankful he'd died, and how she prayed to God for forgiveness for those thoughts. Gabriel told her about his life as a soldier and how it affected him, and about his life as a merchant now. Penelope had nothing but sympathy when he'd told her that he had no family left in the world. The only person left in his life was his assistant, Charles.

That first time, when the sun started dipping lower in the sky, Penelope knew it was time to head back. He'd pulled her to him and kissed her. His first kiss had been nothing more than a light touch of their lips, but Penelope had wound her hand around the back of his neck and pulled him back to her. That second kiss, Penelope got lost in. She'd taken off the scarf she wore while working, and one of his hands went to her hair while the other one went around her back, holding her to him. There was no way this was real; she'd never felt a kiss like this before. The way his lips seemed to devour hers, as if he was a man dying of thirst and she the water. Penelope felt it to her toes. Gabriel ended the kiss but didn't move away, placing his forehead against hers, their breath mingling.

Gabriel had brushed her hair back from her face. "Who knew a loaf of bread would bring me to you?" He kissed the end of her pert nose. "How am I to leave you, even until tomorrow morning?"

"You are coming back in the morning?" Penelope placed her hands on his arms.

"I told you I would be back every morning, just to see you."

Four weeks.

She knew after four days that she loved him. Her father said nothing to her about it, but she knew he didn't approve. Why, she didn't know. Gabriel was a perfectly fine suitor for her. And she craved his touch. From the very first time his fingertips had skimmed over her skin, she'd wanted more. She wanted to lie on a bed with him and feel his body next to hers, skin to skin. She wanted to live in those arms. The closest they'd come to that was when he'd rented a horse and carriage and they'd escaped the city for a few hours. Gabriel had made a bed of hay and blankets as comfortable as he could, and he'd held her close as their bodies strained together. He'd given her pleasure and release for the first time. Penelope could never have dreamed of what she'd been missing. She wanted to fall asleep in his arms every night and wake up next to him every morning. Penelope knew he wanted that too. His own protestations of love had come before hers.

But every morning, when he came in to buy a loaf of bread, he would nod at her father and the man would turn his back to him. Penelope didn't understand it. Didn't he want her to be happy? Couldn't her father see he was breaking her heart? But now, as of this afternoon, she knew why, and her feet couldn't fly fast enough to Gabriel.

"Gabriel," she cried out when she saw him. He turned and caught her in his arms. Penelope could no longer keep the hot tears from falling.

"What is it, *ma chérie*?" He'd stepped back from her and

taken her face in his hands, brushing away her tears with his thumbs.

"My father," she gulped around the lump in her throat. "My father told me today that he found me another husband."

"He did what?"

"He said I'm to marry within the week, Gabriel." Penelope fell back into his arms. They went around her, but even that didn't comfort her today.

"I don't understand why he'd do this to you. He knows how much we love each other."

"He said only a man of his choosing would do, one who didn't lead me to temptation and sin. My first husband was of his choosing and look how that turned out."

"Marry me, Penelope." Penelope stilled in his arms. "Come with me, be my wife. All I want is you by my side. We'll find someone to marry us."

Penelope stepped back from him. "You wish to marry me?"

"There's nothing I want more in this life, Penelope. Say you will. We'll leave tonight. We'll find someone who will marry us tomorrow."

Penelope threw herself back into his arms. "Yes, Gabriel. I want to be with you forever." "Can you get out of the house tonight? Meet me back here at the midnight hour. Your father should be well asleep by then. Bring only what you can carry. I am more than capable of buying you whatever you need."

Penelope had returned to her father's shortly after because she didn't want him to be suspicious. She suffered through a dinner with her potential new husband and excused herself early, feigning a headache. She packed what few belongings she wanted to take with her in a sheet and hid it under her bed in case her father came into the room. Eventually, the house went quiet, and Penelope heard the church bells ring eleven times before she got nervous. What if she fell asleep and didn't leave on time? Would she miss the chance to leave with Gabriel? Penelope didn't wait any longer and snuck out of her father's house.

Gabriel had a bad feeling the closer he got to the meeting spot. He was nervous about having Penelope waiting for him in the dark. Any number of predators waited out at night. So, he'd left his apartment early, stepping from the shadows well away from the park in case she was already there. He didn't want to scare her by appearing in front of her. However, his feelings got worse the closer he neared her, and he'd learned to never dismiss his feelings. Gabriel started running, his heart pounding. When he was a hundred yards away, something put him on high alert. A smell in the air made the hair on his arms stand on end.

It smelled like The Fold.

"Penelope!" Gabriel yelled her name the closer he got to the park. "Penelope, are you here?" His senses tightened when he stopped at the beginning of the park. One of his daggers appeared in his hand. The unmistakable smell of The Fold permeated the air here. His eyes pierced the darkness, and Gabriel stopped moving forward. "I can smell the five of you."

The church bell rang twelve times before a man stepped from behind a tree, Penelope in his grasp, his hand over her mouth, his dagger across her throat. "Right on time. You don't disappoint, Crusader."

"Let her go, Maximus, and I won't be forced to kill you."

"I'm not surprised you couldn't kill her, Crusader. After all, she is your soulmate."

Gabriel heard the four other Fold members circling him. "Let her go," he said before turning and shoving his dagger into the heart of the man who'd tried to rush him from behind. Gabriel pulled his dagger free and kicked the man back, where he fell to the ground, dead. "I have no problem killing the rest of you," Gabriel growled. Another dagger appeared in his left hand while the one in his right grew to the size of a sword.

"We really don't want to kill you, Crusader. You aren't the target. This one though," Maximus pulled Penelope's head back so more of her neck was displayed. "As long as she is alive, she's a distraction to you. I may as well tell you this. It was a trap from the beginning. They have no plans to set you free."

"Let her go."

Maximus continued as if Gabriel had said nothing. "Your agreed contract is to kill your soulmate, and your own soul is then set free. But if you don't complete your contract, your soul is theirs forever. It's diabolical." Maximus ran the flat part of his blade across her neck. He leaned down so he could whisper in Penelope's ear, his eyes never leaving Gabriel. "It's the perfect plan, and he walked right into it."

Gabriel rushed the man on his left, moving so quickly that he didn't know Gabriel had moved until his dagger was embedded in his neck. Gabriel pulled it free and turned to engage the other man, pushing his sword into the other man's stomach before lifting him and flipping him over his shoulder, his sword nearly severing the man. Darkness swirled in Gabriel's eyes as he looked at Maximus again. "It's like your men aren't even trying, Maximus."

"Crusader, you should know what a distraction looks like by now." A portal opened behind Maximus. "Before I go, I'll share one bit of good news for you. Your darling soulmate, she has six more lives to go. Six more opportunities for you to fulfill your contract before we do it for you." At that, Maximus flipped his dagger and pulled it across her neck before stepping into the portal and it closed around him.

"No!" The word was torn from him. Gabriel watched as she fell to the ground, her blood streaming from the slash across her neck. The last man left tried to stop him. This time, Gabriel opened his hands, his weapons disappearing back into his darkness, before he grabbed his head and broke the man's neck. Gabriel was at Penelope's side before the dead man landed in the grass. "Penelope, no."

He watched life leave her eyes as her blood drained onto the ground. Gabriel brushed her hair back before he leaned over her, his forehead touching the ground on the other side of her. "Please, God, no."

That was the moment Gabriel felt her body shudder one last time, and he screamed into the ground, his fists clenching. This couldn't be happening. She couldn't be dead.

Because of him.

"Gabriel," a voice said before a hand touched his back. Gabriel sprang up, his dagger in hand, ready to strike. "Gabriel, it's me, Charles."

"They killed her, Charles."

"I heard everything. I followed you. We must go. The guard will be here soon."

"I can't leave her like this."

"There's nothing you can do, Gabriel. At least now we know what you're up against." Charles put his arm through Gabriel's and gently pulled him away from her.

Gabriel let the older man pull him away while he watched his very heart bleed into the ground.

CHAPTER TEN

Parker stretched as the sun streaked across her face. Her arm came down on the empty side of the bed, searching for Gabriel. She stretched again and smelled the unmistakable aroma of coffee. "Gabriel?"

Gabriel leaned over the partial wall, shirtless and his hair damp from a shower. "About time you woke up, sleepyhead."

Parker looked up at him. "When did you take a shower?"

"While you were still snoring," he said as he turned away and walked back to the kitchenette.

"I don't snore," Parker huffed, rising on her elbows.

"Tell that to the neighbors."

Parker watched as Gabriel carried a tray around the partial wall and into the room. He only had on a pair of the boxer briefs he liked to wear. Parker rubbed her feet across the bed under the blanket. "Are you breakfast?" Parker licked her lips as she stared at his chest before looking up and catching his eye.

Gabriel's eyes got dark as he stood at the end of the bed. "You're making my whole breakfast-in-bed surprise very difficult to accomplish with that look, *mon ange*."

"Do you mean difficult as in hard?" Parker bent her knees and started swaying slowly back and forth. She leaned back on her elbows, the blanket barely covering her breasts, and she let her eyes slide down his torso. He happened to be holding the tray right over his groin and Parker frowned at him because she couldn't see it.

"Eyes up here, lady."

"I'm pretty sure I'm not wearing underwear," she declared coyly as her eyes met his again.

"Do you like cream or sugar in your coffee?"

"Sugar and cream." Parker drew the last letter out a little too much.

"That's it," Gabriel muttered, giving in. He set the tray on the ledge the partial wall made before lifting the blanket she was under from the end of the bed and crawling in with her. Parker laughed as he tickled her on his way up, but her laughter turned to a gasp, which turned to moans when he stopped halfway up her body. Hopefully, the walls weren't that thin because she wasn't that quiet.

"This coffee is cold," Parker said half an hour later.

Gabriel looked up at her while he continued to spread cream cheese on a toasted bagel, lounging across the bed, back in nothing but his boxer briefs. She had a towel wrapped around her body and one around her hair after her shower, leaning back against the wall.

"It wouldn't be cold if you'd have let me serve it to you like thirty-ish minutes ago." He held the bagel out to her.

"It's not my fault you're hot," she said as she took the bagel from him.

"Flattery will get you everything, except sympathy for your cold coffee."

"Why are you so mean to me?" Parker licked some cream cheese off the bagel.

"Do you want to leave this apartment today?" Gabriel asked as he picked up one of the strawberries on the tray. "Because the way you're going, you won't even be getting dressed." He popped the strawberry in his mouth.

"Is that supposed to be a threat? Because it doesn't sound like one." Parker took a bite of the bagel.

"Sounds more like a fantasy come true to me," was Gabriel's reply.

"Haven't we already fulfilled that fantasy?"

"Not in Boston."

"Guess there's nothing to argue about then."

"Were we arguing?" Gabriel popped another strawberry in his mouth. "Sounded more like agreeing." This was a better way to start this day than the other one that happened. Gabriel felt guilty about erasing her memory, but everything had come too close to the surface.

And he wasn't ready to have that conversation with her yet. He didn't care how selfish that statement sounded.

Parker stopped with the bagel halfway to her mouth and gave it a strange look. She then looked over at the tray that had more strawberries and bagels on it, before looking at Gabriel, spreading cream cheese on his own bagel. "Wait, where did this stuff come from?"

The knife in his hand stilled as he cautiously met her gaze again. "The grocery store, I assume."

"But how did it get here? I don't remember anyone coming to the door. You must have just gotten out of the shower right before I woke up."

"Ok," he exhaled, "this property has a service. If you know you're coming in late or if you need something, they will get it for you. I emailed yesterday and asked for a few things," Gabriel motioned to the tray. "I knew it would be late when we got in and we'd be hungry when we woke up. All we had was those sandwiches at the airport."

"So, this is more than just an 'apartment building.'" Parker stuck the bagel in her mouth and did finger quotes after those words. "There's no normal apartment building with a concierge service. That sounds way too high-end."

Did God hate him? Was he destined to have this conversation with her today? He didn't want to erase her memory again. It didn't make time stop. "What's upsetting you about it?" Maybe a different approach would work.

"How much did this place cost you?"

"Too much." He set the knife on the tray. "I'm thinking about selling it. I don't really come here often enough to justify the cost." He was in Boston a lot more than he'd tell her right now. Gabriel took a bite of his bagel, praying this conversation would go better than the other one had.

Parker straightened her spine and leaned over. From this angle, she was able to see the windows over the partial wall. The sky looked blue and clear. She'd wanted to see the sunrise, but she must have slept through it. Or had she? Parker cocked her head at some weird memory or dream at the back of her mind. "Did you tell me something about Paris?"

Gabriel nearly choked on the bite of food he was swallowing. "Paris?"

"Are you okay?" she asked him. When he nodded, Parker shook her head. "Maybe it was a dream, but I swear you told me about an apartment in Paris." After another moment, Parker shrugged her shoulders. "Maybe you could list this on Airbnb. I bet you could charge at least three hundred dollars a night for this place. Especially with that view I want to see after I get dressed."

"You think I want strangers sleeping on my bed? No, thank you, ma'am. The only woman I want naked and climaxing in any of my beds is you."

"What about the bed in my house?" Parker smiled at him.

"Not my bed, but I want you naked and climaxing in that one too. Multiple times in the same night preferably."

This time, Parker leaned toward him. "How about in a sleeping bag, in a tent, on the ground, in the middle of a forest."

"Is this a test? I want you there too. Sleeping bags are slidey though, so you'll have to be on top so I can grab hold of your fabulous hips. I know how much you like it when I do that. The end result is still the same." Gabriel picked up a strawberry and held it up to her mouth. His skin tightened when she took a bite and sucked the juice back in her mouth. "I see my sweet little morsel is feeling extra naughty today."

"Must be getting close to my period. I always turn into a hornball right before." Parker leaned over and ate the rest of the strawberry he held, sucking on his finger for good measure.

"A hornball?" Gabriel's finger, amongst other body parts, tingled.

"Which sucked for me, being in a relationship with someone who couldn't give me what I needed." Parker unwound the towel from her hair and tossed it on the floor before taking the tray off the bed and setting it on the floor too. She turned back to Gabriel. He still lounged across the bed, seemingly relaxed, but his eyes had gone dark again. "So, I had to take care of myself, if you understand what I mean." Parker shifted her weight and slid her hand down his chest.

"And here I thought it was me."

Parker turned so she faced him fully. Gabriel sat up and pulled her mouth to his. She untucked the towel from around her body and tossed that to the floor as well, and Gabriel's lips left hers to start kissing down her body. "Believe me, it's about ninety-five percent you right now, and a hundred percent you the rest of the time." Parker moaned when her nipple ended up in his mouth and his teeth scraped against it. She fisted her hands in his hair, and she lightly tugged his head back so she could look in his eyes. "Please take your boxers off so I can climb on you."

She brought her mouth back to his as she felt him hurriedly comply with his free hand. This time, she was the one who kissed down his neck until she reached his chest and ran her tongue over his nipples. His groan made her even hotter for him. "I want you, right now," she demanded.

With those words uttered, Gabriel sat up and dragged her over him, so she was right where she wanted to be.

Parker smiled up at Gabriel when he held the door to the restaurant open for her. It was almost two in the afternoon. The lunch rush was over, so there was no one around to see her run her hand across his stomach as she passed. "Careful, *mon ange*, we've only just left the apartment," Gabriel nearly growled in her ear as he followed her in. "I would hate for you to miss something while we're here."

Parker was saved from answering when the waitress welcomed them to the restaurant. Parker watched as the young girl blushed lightly and, probably unknowingly, fluttered her eyelashes at Gabriel. To his credit, Gabriel pretended not to notice as he placed a hand in the small of Parker's back while they followed the hostess to their table. She left menus on the table and rushed off. Parker picked up the menu. "The Union Oyster House."

"You wanted clam chowder, *mon ange*, and this is where you get it. The oldest continuously run restaurant in Boston."

"And after this?" Parker perused the menu.

"A simple walk down the street and you'll find history."

"And after that?"

Gabriel looked at her over the top of his menu. "Grocery store. Whipped cream. Snacks."

Parker smiled at him over her menu. The waitress came, and they placed their order, both getting a bowl of clam chowder and some cornbread. Gabriel also ordered their Boston baked beans to try. Parker took a sip of her water. "Sorry if my comment earlier about my period embarrassed you."

"Why would it embarrass me? I'm well aware of how the female body works." Gabriel reached across the table and ran his fingers over the knuckles of her hand sitting on the table.

"Some guys don't like to hear about it, much less talk about it."

"I am not some guy. It's not something I'm embarrassed

to talk about. I want you to feel comfortable enough to talk to me about anything. Stomachache. Cramps. Migraine. Kids drove you crazy at school. I pissed you off, let me know. You want sex, just tell me. Need me to stop at the store to get you tampons, send a text. You can talk to me about anything."

"Anything?"

"Anything."

The waitress arrived with their order, so they both leaned back so she could put it on the table. They thanked her without breaking eye contact with each other.

"What if I call you…" Parker started.

"I will always answer."

"Any you're in Germany," she continued.

"My phone works everywhere."

"And it's three in the morning."

"Guess who's going to be awake, talking to his angel when she needs him." Gabriel leaned over the table a bit. "And if you should call or text me and I can't get to you right then, it will be the first thing I do when I can. Trust me."

"Will you always let me know when you land safely?"

"The very second."

Parker looked down at her bowl of clam chowder because the intensity in his eyes was becoming too much for her. She must be hormonal because she was so close to tears. When she looked back up, he was still gazing at her intently. Neither of them had taken a bite of food yet. "The same goes for you. I want you to be able to talk to me too. To trust me."

"I do trust you," he said.

"Because I'm not letting you go."

The sun had just started to rise the next morning when Gabriel woke up with Parker's arm over his chest and her head on his shoulder. They'd left the restaurant after lunch and walked across the street to the Holocaust Memorial.

Parker held his hand tightly while they walked through those glass spires, moved to tears. It wasn't really a spot meant for light conversation. Gabriel had seen so much tragedy he'd thought himself nearly immune to it by now. But seeing this memorial with Parker made it all real to him again, from the Crusades until now. Gabriel didn't want to think about that right now. If he let his mind wander about everything he'd seen and been through, he was sure he'd go crazy himself.

He walked her down Congress Street then toward the Old State House, and he marveled at how much joy she found in even walking down the busy streets. She would point out everything that caught her eye, from a manhole cover on the ground to the spires on top of a building. They stopped at the Old State House, where the Boston Massacre happened, before continuing around the corner and down a set of steps. They walked together until they found a large ground sign that said Boston, and Parker took out her phone to snap a few selfies of them together. Gabriel couldn't honestly remember when he'd felt as close to her as he did this time.

If it was possible, he loved her even more.

After some sightseeing, he'd done exactly what he'd said they were going to do and stopped by a grocery store. He'd enjoyed the cute little blush on her cheeks when he picked out a can of whipped cream. Gabriel wasn't letting the fantasy go this time. He bought some more easy snacks and drove them back to the apartment building. They were the only two in the elevator, and Gabriel backed her up against the wall, not stopping until his body was flush with hers. He saw her heartbeat in her neck, and he planted feather-light kisses there before moving up to kiss her lips just as gently. When her lips melted to his, he brought one hand up to cup her cheek, his touch still so light when he curled his fingers and ran them across her cheek.

It wasn't lost on him how hard she pressed her hands against the wall of the elevator, as if she might slide off the world if she let go. When the elevator binged at the tenth floor, Gabriel stepped back and took her by the hand, drawing her with him to his door. No words passed between them as Gabriel led her inside. He didn't turn any lights on, and he didn't let her think about anything as he put the grocery bag on the kitchen table and drew her to him again. The whipped cream could come later. Right now, he wanted this softness, this intimacy, with her. He craved her, like the very air he breathed. He'd thought he couldn't love her more than he had the first time he'd met her, but he was wrong.

She owned his soul.

He wanted to worship her.

So, that was what he did, throughout the night. He made love to her body, wanting to reach back in time and heal every hurt in her lives. Gabriel laid his soul at her feet to pay penance for loving him. His guilt at not being able to stay away from her a tangible pain in his chest. But how could he when she was the other half of his soul?

He ordered food at some point, and they sat at the kitchen table, totally nude, the lights of the city shining behind her. Only then, when he felt he'd paid his dues to her, that he deserved her, did he grab the whipped cream out of the fridge.

Because I'm not letting you go.

Now, in the early morning light, with Parker nestled up to him, he let himself think about what she'd said. How she'd said the same words back to him. The words he'd said to her yesterday morning. Was it possible that conversation was still in her subconscious? Not to mention when she'd asked him about Paris, he'd nearly choked on his bagel. He wanted to ask Charles what he thought, but he wasn't sure how much he trusted the fallen angel. Too many roads seemed to point back to him. Of course, it was also possible that was another trick by his enemy, to make him distrust Charles. That was a trick The Fold would employ, planting the seed of doubt. The other man had never told him how he had fallen from grace, just that he had. Charles had been his partner for almost five hundred years.

Parker stirred next to him, and he pulled her closer. He was supposed to be meeting someone at the Boston Museum of Fine Arts today, and he hoped she wanted to come with him. Gabriel hated the very idea of even a few hours away from her. When he looked down at her in the early morning light, Parker's eyes had just opened, and she gave him a shy smile. "Good morning, *mon ange*. How are you feeling?" Gabriel turned onto his side, so he faced her.

"Hmmm." Parker smiled wider at him as she snuggled into his chest. "Is this to be your usual morning question after playing my body like a fiddle?"

"Just a single fiddle? I'm clearly off my game since I was going for the whole Boston Orchestra."

Parker chuckled as she turned on her side to face him as well. "You're right." She ran a finger down his cheek. "It was the whole orchestra."

"What kind of man would I be if I let my lady walk around all hornbally?"

A laugh escaped Parker as she buried her face in his chest.

"Oh," Gabriel said, placing his finger under her chin and tipping her face up to meet his eyes. "Are we being shy this morning, *mon ange*? This is a bit different than yesterday."

Parker stared into his deep-blue eyes, her breath catching at the love and amusement she saw there. It was different than yesterday. Yesterday, he hadn't spent the night before basically worshiping her very existence. He hadn't made her feel like she was on a pedestal somewhere and he'd never be able to reach her. Even with his finger tilting her face up, she lowered her eyes so she wasn't looking into his anymore. Some of the insecurities she'd lived with her entire life crept in, no matter how hard she tried. Parker felt her face flush in embarrassment again. "Gabriel, I just... I don't know how to handle all this."

"Just go with it, Parker," Gabriel said, and she laughed at him. He pulled himself over her and settled on her body, his favorite place, and propped his head on his hand. "I have to meet someone at the museum today, and I would like you to join me."

"Mixing business and pleasure?" She arched an eyebrow at him.

"I don't want to be away from you for even a moment, *mon ange*, not until I have to. When do you go back to school?"

"End of August."

"That's only two months to spend every day with you."

"Gabriel," Parker started, wincing, "I would love to come with you today, but right now you're crushing my bladder."

Gabriel climbed out of the Uber, bent low, and held his hand out to Parker. The smile she gave him when she slid out of the car toward him made his heart melt more. He thought she looked especially delicious today, and he wished he didn't have this meeting to go to. A week with her wouldn't make a dent in the hunger he'd developed after the last hundred years without her. Were it up to him, she wouldn't leave his bed for the next month. Even then it wouldn't be enough. "Do you enjoy museums, *mon ange*?"

Parker wound her arm through Gabriel's and smiled up at him. Even to come to the museum, he dressed the same as he did most days. "I very much do. I try to plan at least one trip to the Field Museum for my students every year."

"Hmmm, I would very much like to join your class for that day." The couple leisurely made their way up the steps of the large columned building. When they reached the top, Gabriel held the door open for her and winked at her as she passed. For some reason, that wink made her blush today. She didn't believe this would last, but she'd enjoy every moment of it while she could.

There was a short line, and Gabriel settled his body behind hers, his arms around her shoulders. Parker was too nervous to look around and see what kind of looks they were getting from the others wandering around the atrium. The high windows kept this area well lit, and sound carried because of the high ceilings. When it was their turn, Gabriel pulled out his wallet and bought two tickets for them. The girl behind the counter looked Gabriel up and down before Parker watched her eyes rove over her. *I know girl*, Parker thought, *I don't understand it either.*

Gabriel turned after he was handed the tickets and grasped Parker's hand, waving off the map because he knew his way around this museum. "Follow me, *mon ange*. There's something I want you to see." He didn't let go of her hand as he led her up two flights of stairs and through a few different galleries before he turned and smiled at her again. Parker would never get enough of those smiles. "This is the Monet – Rodin gallery."

Parker looked around as he led her in. On one side were many Monet paintings, and on the other was art work by Rodin. "Didn't Rodin sculpt the Thinker?"

"*Oui, mon ange*, he did. Rodin has a particular sculpture I'm quite fond of, but the original is at the *Musée Rodin* in Paris." Gabriel led her to a set of benches set up in the center of the room. Parker sat on the padded bench and tucked the purple dress under her thighs. Gabriel sat next to her and leaned close. *"I hope to be able to take you there very soon, my love."* Parker's skin pebbled because he spoke in French in her ear.

"I very much want to visit there," Parker responded in French.

"*Le Baiser*, The Kiss," he continued, the rest he spoke in French. "There is a replica in the Rodin Museum in Philadelphia, but I prefer to see the originals. However, since it's not here to look at, I guess we'll have to recreate it. Have you seen it before?"

Parker had to clear her throat before she could answer him. Even now, even after the night they'd had, his proximity made her heart flutter. He was close enough that she felt his breath across her cheek. "No… no I haven't."

"Well, in the sculpture, the man and woman are nude, but we won't be doing that in public.

The last thing I want is some other man's eyes on your skin."

"Not that they'd want to see it," Parker responded with an eye roll.

"You're very wrong about that, but I'm not going to argue with you about it. Now, we're recreating my favorite sculpture. I sit next to you, which I already am, and you place this leg over mine." Gabriel picked up the leg closest to him and placed it over his own.

"Um, Gabriel…" Parker looked around them and could see a few other people roaming around the gallery.

"Next," Gabriel continued, ignoring everyone else in the room. "You take this arm and wrap it around my neck." Gabriel braced his arm against the back of the bench. "This other arm of mine." Gabriel held up the one not behind her. "Goes on your hip, like this." Gabriel placed his hand on her hip and moved closer. "Can you see why I love this sculpture yet? So, here we are, close, and your arm around my neck, but we aren't quite done yet. After all, it is called The Kiss. Can you guess what comes next?" Every word, every word he'd spoken, had been in French. Parker had watched a couple of women walk by and their eyes and ears had been on Gabriel and the words coming out of his mouth. A beautiful language from a beautiful man.

"The kissing part?" Parker asked.

"See how smart you are? That's one reason why I love you so much." That was when Gabriel closed the small distance between them and placed his lips on hers. Of course, here in the middle of the museum, he wasn't going to kiss her the way he wanted, but this kiss would do for now. Parker's arm tightened around his neck, and the hand on her hip gripped harder. Gabriel's hand had just tangled in Parker's hair, turning her head to deepen the kiss, because he couldn't resist her.

"Ah," they heard from behind them. "The Kiss.

Masterfully recreated." Parker and Gabriel both turned to the voice at the same time. The only difference was that Gabriel smiled at the man standing behind them, and Parker's face flamed.

"Mack," Gabriel said, rising to his feet and bringing Parker up with him. What she really wanted to do was go hide somewhere. Instead, she found herself standing in front of a stranger who'd seen her kissing Gabriel. He was an older man, with gray hair and smooth cheeks. His blue eyes were shining as they bounced between the two of them. He only stood about five inches taller than Parker, which meant he was a few inches shorter than Gabriel. When they made it around the bench, Gabriel had his hand out. The two men shook hands before Gabriel drew Parker next to him.

"Mack, can I introduce the love of my life, Parker Reed."

"It is lovely to meet you, young lady," Mack said as he held out his hand to her. Parker extended her hand to the man and decided she liked him. Instead of shaking her hand, he merely enfolded hers into his and smiled at her for a moment, then let go.

"No Susan today?" As soon as Gabriel asked the question, a tall, thin, beautiful blonde woman walked through the gallery door. She was wearing a tight gray pencil skirt with a flowing white shirt tucked into it. Her hair was beautifully coiffed, and her heels clicked on the floor. She was exactly the type of woman that Parker thought Gabriel should be with. Parker wanted to shrink away, and she started to move behind Gabriel's back to hide.

Naturally, he would have none of that and he placed his arm around her shoulders and brought her back to stand next to him. "Here she is," Mack waved toward Susan.

"I apologize for being late," Susan announced when she arrived. *Shit*, Parker thought, *even her voice is cool and cultured.* Susan's eyes had barely left Gabriel since she walked into the room. Parker briefly wondered if they'd had a sexual relationship in the past. She'd bet Susan's legs didn't end until her armpits and the woman wanted them wrapped around Gabriel's face and body. "It's no worry," Gabriel told her. "I was just explaining to Parker about my favorite Rodin sculpture."

"They were recreating 'The Kiss' to be exact," Mack added, winking at Parker. Parker's face flamed, and that was the first time Susan's eyes had left Gabriel. She looked Parker up and down and immediately dismissed her as no competition.

"I trust your flight went well," Susan said. "Also, please tell me you did not pay the entrance fee."

"Of course, I did. Two of them to be exact." Gabriel let his hand leave Parker's shoulder and trailed down her back.

"We've told you before it's not necessary." Susan looked like she was about to explode.

"Please." Gabriel's hand slashed the air, cutting her off. "Every museum I walk into I pay the entrance fee, because that fee keeps the museums open."

"Very well." Susan sniffed, clearly realizing there was no point in arguing with him. "If you want to follow us, Mack and I will show you the painting in question." Susan turned to leave, but Mack stayed where he'd been. Gabriel turned to Parker and placed his hand on her cheek, just as he'd done when Theresa came over.

"Hopefully, I won't be more than a half hour, *mon ange*. I will call you to see where you are when I'm done."

"Take your time," Parker told him. "I'm sure there's a lot to look at."

"You're the only one I take my time on, Parker." He whispered the words in her ear, again in French, before he softly kissed her on the lips. Parker quickly glanced at Mack and Susan, the latter of which had turned around and was tapping her foot. Mack, however, looked extremely pleased with how Gabriel was acting toward Parker. Gabriel stepped away from her and joined Mack, the older man slapping Gabriel on the back as they walked away. Susan did not look at all pleased with the interaction.

Parker watched the trio walk away, hoping this was a forever thing. The way he made her feel sent her head into the clouds. Parker sighed, deciding she should at least look around the galleries. She wandered aimlessly, losing track of time, until she found herself in a gallery with a lot of religious artworks in it. Damn, she'd been hoping to find the gallery with the mummy, so she could take some pictures for her class, to show them when she taught about ancient Egypt, but she didn't have a map. There weren't too many people in this gallery, so she decided to take a quick walk through.

Parker had almost finished her circuit when a smaller painting caught her eye. She moved closer for a look at it. She guessed the picture depicted a battle that had taken place during one of the crusades considering one force wore robes and armor with a large cross, and the other side wore the flowing robes of ancient Middle East. Parker's head tilted, and a shiver ran down her spine. "Gruesome, isn't it?"

Parker was startled by the voice so close to her. She took a step to the side and checked who it was. Standing there was a dark-haired man, dressed in black from head to toe. His skin was pale, and a feeling of unease rolled down her back. This man exuded a feeling of fear and danger, and Parker grew nervous. She took another step to the side. The man's gaze hadn't left the small painting. "Yes," Parker finally answered, "quite gruesome."

That was when the man fully turned to Parker, and she took another step away. His eyes were such a pale, ice blue it was like they had no color. His smile was predatory. "I saw you in the other gallery. You and your partner looked quite cozy. Precious."

Everything in Parker's soul told her to get away from this man immediately. "Excuse me, I have to go." Parker turned to hurry away from the man when she felt him grab her by the arm.

Her heartbeat accelerated and panic set in as soon as his fingers touched her arm. A scream was about to leave her lips as his hand curled around her elbow. She needed to get away. His touch was like ice against her skin. Like death.

"Ah, Miss Reed," she heard from in front of her, "here you are." Mack stood at the gallery door, looking at the man behind her. The hand fell from her arm, and Parker took the opportunity to get away from the scary man. She didn't stop until she was behind Mack. Parker still felt his fingers on her skin. Mack stood tall as a shield between her and the threat that man's presence presented. "The General won't like this at all," Mack told the other man.

"The Crusader's time is about up; I was simply hurrying along the process. His soul will belong to us. I do not fear him."

"You should. I'll be sure to tell the General who is next on his list," Mack said this before he turned to Parker. "Miss Reed, if you would please proceed me down the hallway." Mack waved his hand to Parker, showing her the way to go. Parker looked over Mack's shoulder, and her eyes caught those soulless, ice blue eyes. "Come, Miss Reed," Mack said as he placed a hand on her back, "pay no attention to the interloper."

The desire to run was strong. Her heart rate was still racing, and she didn't understand what was going on. "Who was that?" She turned to Mack, looking behind the man but no longer seeing the devil in disguise.

"Gabriel can explain it better than I."

They came to another set of hallways, and Mack directed her to the left. Ahead of them was a set of doors. Mack reached out and swiped a badge to open the door when they reached it.

Five minutes after he'd left her, Gabriel realized his mistake in doing so and had pulled Mack to the side to ask him to find Parker. He never should have left her alone, especially away from his home. Gabriel didn't know what was taking so long, and he was getting nervous. What if something happened to her?

"Why are you so nervous, Gabriel?" Susan asked him,

innately perceptive. He knew she wanted him, but he'd never entertained the idea, even when he was waiting for Parker to return. Ignoring her question, Gabriel continued to review the painting. They'd asked him to authenticate it as an independent expert. The painting was authentic, he knew it because he'd visited the artist when he'd been painting it, and Gabriel placed his mark in the corner. But Susan was a mere mortal and unlikely to take his opinion if he didn't appear to go over it.

"I am not nervous, Susan."

Susan stopped behind him, placed her hands on his shoulders, and started massaging them.

Gabriel stiffened. "Please remove your hands from my body." His voice was hard and that was when the woman pulled her hands from him and backed away. He turned on the stool he'd been sitting on and met the woman's gaze. "I know you saw the woman I was with."

"Really, Gabriel? Her? She's not your type. I expect she must have good bedroom moves to keep you interested..."

"Don't." Gabriel rose to his feet, his voice low. Susan took two steps back because his eyes went black before he could stop them. "Don't ever say another word about her. Don't even breathe her name. She is worth more to me than you'll ever know. Than you *ever* will. This painting is authentic," Gabriel uttered before he walked away. If he didn't get away from her, he was afraid his knives would come out. He stalked into the adjoining room; his hands clasped behind his back. Where were Mack and Parker? Gabriel got impatient and paced the room while he waited. Wisely, Susan had remained in the other room, no doubt filling out the paperwork he'd need to sign with his official assessment.

Moments before Gabriel's patience wore out, the door opened. Parker walked in, followed by Mack. Her face was pale, and he saw the fear in her eyes when their gazes caught. Gabriel's nostrils flared at the scent around her.

She smelled like The Fold.

CHAPTER ELEVEN

Parker gasped when Gabriel's eyes went black.

"Who touched her?" The words were no more than a growl.

"It was Antony, General. She was trying to escape his company when I intervened. He had his hand around her arm."

"Gabriel, what's going on?" Parker questioned, looking between the two men. His eyes were freaking her out, and she had a nagging déjà vu moment.

"It is too dangerous for you to remain with her in Boston, General."

"It's dangerous for her no matter where we go." Gabriel didn't move a muscle. Parker was too afraid to budge.

"That's true, but I feel you are better able to protect her at home."

"Take care of Susan," Gabriel told the older man, his eyes never leaving Parker. It sounded like an order, and Mack jumped to obey it. Meanwhile, Parker couldn't take her eyes off Gabriel. Fear clogged her throat again, and she flinched at the tiny sound made when Mack closed the door to the room.

"Gabriel…" She backed up and only stopped when she bumped into a desk behind her. Something was there, something in her memories, about the blackness now filling the space around her. Parker's heart was lodged in her throat, and she wondered why she wasn't running scared.

"What did he say to you?" Gabriel asked her as he approached. He didn't want to do this. He didn't want to alter her memories again. What if her brain turned to mush? What if he went too far and she forgot about being in the gallery with him? What if he erased the memory of that kiss? Gabriel didn't want to. He wanted her to keep it.

"What... what did who say to me?" Her heart raced, and she started to sweat. Right now, Gabriel looked like a predator coming toward her.

"The man in the museum, *ma femme*." My wife, that was what those words meant. My woman, my wife, it was all the same. "Tell me every word he said to you." Darkness gathered at their feet. It was like her feet were cemented to the floor. She couldn't leave, she didn't want to leave. Why was this familiar?

"I was in a different gallery. A painting caught my eye. I believe it was a depiction of the crusades." Parker swallowed as she remembered the painting. Even though it had been small, it had been full of blood and gore. That darkness was at her knees now, and Gabriel was only inches from her. "Why are you doing this to me again?"

Gabriel's heart stopped at her words. "*Je suis desolee, mon ange*. I am very sorry, but I have no choice. Tell me what Antony said to you."

"Who is Antony?"

"An enemy of mine from a long time ago. What did he say to you?"

The darkness swirled at her thighs. She pulled her hands up so she wouldn't accidentally touch it, pretty sure she was about to die, but a strange, calming sensation had pulsed out of the darkness at her. "He said the painting looked gruesome, then he turned to me. I couldn't believe how light blue his eyes were. Like ice. I agreed with what he said."

The darkness was at her waist now, like water filling a tub. She dared a look past Gabriel at the rest of the room.

Surprisingly, the darkness only extended a few inches beyond where they stood. The rest of the room remained bright under the fluorescent lights.

"Was there anything else, Parker? It is important you tell me everything."

"He said… he said he saw us in the other gallery. He said we looked quite cozy."

"Goddammit." How had Antony been there, and he not smelled him? This whole situation

had been a ploy to let Gabriel know they'd discovered a way to disguise themselves from him, even if it was only for a short time.

"My gut told me to get away from him. When I turned to leave, he reached out and grabbed me. I was afraid."

"You were right to trust your instincts." Parker's eyes had glazed over, the darkness swirling around them was up to her chest. Gabriel moved closer to her until their bodies touched. Parker's eyes closed at his proximity.

Then, her eyes popped back open, that strange glaze over them. "Are you going to let us die again?" Behind her eyes, he saw every incarnation staring back at him. Every part of her he'd loved for four hundred years. Her voice, the voice of her seven lives.

"You will not be taken from me this time, Parker. I won't allow it." He looked above her head, at his soul still shining there. Clearly, Antony had not seen that, and maybe they couldn't. Maybe only he could see it because it was his. Maybe Theresa could see it because she was an angel and that was what they dealt with. *Give your soul freely*, the voodoo priestess had said, so that was what he did. Every time he saw it there, his heart felt lighter knowing the only woman he'd ever loved carried it for him and The Fold would never get it, even if they killed him. "I wish I did not have to erase your memory, my love." The French came naturally from his lips, for her ears, the language of her birth.

"Why must you, Gabriel?" His eyes closed as her seven voices washed over him and crashed around his heart. They were totally encased in his darkness now. His hand cupped her cheek, and he felt every incarnation lean into his touch.

"Can you imagine if your conscious mind remembered everything that had happened? Your head would explode. I just can't have that, *ma femme*. I like your head as it is much too much."

"Tell us, Gabriel." They said his name in the way Parker purred it.

"That's not fair, *ma femme*. You know it's difficult for me to resist when you say my name like that. Especially when it's all of you. And I will tell you, but not here, it is too dangerous for you here."

"We're afraid, Gabriel. We don't want to live without you."

"I know, *mon ange*, I know. I don't want to live without you either. This time, we will figure out the way."

"We want to be your wife forever." Parker placed her hand on his cheek, just as he did to her. Gabriel swallowed past the lump in his throat and placed his forehead on hers.

"I love you," Gabriel whispered before he set his lips on hers and kissed her.

"Ah," they heard from behind them. "The Kiss. Masterfully recreated."

Parker and Gabriel both turned to the voice at the same time. The only difference was that Gabriel smiled at the man standing behind them and Parker's face flamed.

Wait. Parker's eyebrows pulled together, and she looked around. Why did this seem so familiar?

"Mack." Gabriel rose to his feet, bringing Parker up with him. She had wordlessly spoken Mack's name at the same time Gabriel had said it out loud. Then, she stood in front of a stranger that had just seen her kissing Gabriel again. Again? Was he a stranger? Why did it seem like they'd met before? He was an older man, with gray hair and smooth cheeks, his blue eyes shining as they bounced between the two of them. When Parker and Mack's eyes locked, her brows drew together more. He only stood about five inches taller than Parker, which meant he was a few inches shorter than Gabriel. When they made it around the bench, Gabriel had his hand out. The two men shook hands before Gabriel drew Parker next to him.

"Mack, can I introduce the love of my life, Parker Reed."

"It is lovely to meet you, young lady," Mack said.

"Susan is late," Parker muttered, rubbing her forehead, and both men froze as they looked at her. Just then, a tall, thin, beautiful blonde woman walked through the gallery door. "She's sorry for being late and hopes your flight went well." Not another soul dared move while Parker said that, except for Susan, who looked at Parker in confusion. "Also, she says you shouldn't pay the entrance fee, but I like that you still do." Parker turned to Gabriel, her head spinning, and she reached out for him.

"Parker…"

"I think I'm going to pass out now."

Gabriel sat on Mack's office couch with Parker across his lap. Mack had taken the seat opposite him. "What does it mean, General?"

Gabriel ran his finger through another of Parker's thick curls. "I wish I knew, Mack." Mack had been his personal advisor for nearly a thousand years. He'd been his second in command during the Crusades. He was the one person Gabriel trusted with his life. After death, Mack had also been pulled into service, not as an assassin, but as a member of the Archangel Michael's counsel. He wasn't an angel, but he became immortal like Gabriel.

Funny how everything circled back around to the Archangel Michael in some way.

"May I ask, General, how many times have you altered her memories?"

"That was the second time. And she's made comments that lead me to believe she remembers the conversation that led to me doing it the first time."

"Interesting," Mack said as he leaned back in his chair

and watched Gabriel run his fingers through another curl.

"They all spoke to me, Mack. I heard every one of her incarnations before I altered her mind." Gabriel looked up at Mack again.

"It is the end of her lives, General."

"As Charles likes to continually remind me." Gabriel couldn't help it and ran his whole hand through her hair. If he didn't figure out a way to keep her alive this time, The Fold might as well kill him with her. Even now, after these many centuries, he didn't understand why they'd sent him after her because what if he'd never met her on his own? There was always a chance he wouldn't have, so why set him on this path? To simply torture him? To break his mind?

"I do not trust the fallen one, General."

"I know you don't, Mack. But tell me why God would allow this to keep happening to her."

"Tell me in what way the fallen has prevented it? How he always knows to follow you when it happens."

"All questions I've been asking myself as well. But maybe there is no answer, Mack. Maybe this is punishment for the crimes I committed during the Crusades. For all the families I tore apart." Gabriel lightly ran his hand over her cheek. So many centuries of guilt lay buried in his soul.

"It was war, General. And I will remind you, again, that you did not start the war, you merely believed in what your church taught you."

"And look where it landed me, Mack. Nine hundred years later, my soul almost a prisoner, a bargaining chip, forced to kill at the behest of who and what?"

"You believe the Archangel Michael did not want you in his army? He did, he just didn't get to you first."

"What does it matter in the long run, Mack?" Gabriel asked while looking in his counsel's eyes. "Angels, demons, The Fold. In the long run, I'm still just a pawn, an assassin, a killer." Gabriel's eyes softened then when he looked down at Parker. "With her, I am different, someone different. In me, she sees love. A future. They should have left me as dead as my body at the gates of Jerusalem, Mack."

"Blasphemy."

"Is it though? Have you forgotten the crimes we committed?" Gabriel's voice became steel, his eyes focused on the past.

"I have forgotten nothing, General. I have especially not forgotten how many innocent people you did *not* kill, even when given the order to do so. Besides," he said, pointing to Parker, "where would she be without you?"

Gabriel ran his hand over Parker's hair again. Her head was in his lap, her body in the fetal position next to him. He'd caught her as she collapsed and swept her up in his arms. What did it mean that she remembered what had happened previously? "I don't know, Mack. Perhaps my incarnation would have been a better man."

"Or perhaps you are your only incarnation and she'd have spent these lives unfulfilled, without you."

"But alive."

"Tell me, General, how is life without love?"

Gabriel's gaze landed on Parker. He could attest to the fact that there really was no life without love. Parker stirred. Her body stretched, and her eyes slowly opened. She smiled when she met Gabriel's eyes before confusion dropped over her face and she rose on her elbow, looking around the office.

"Where am I?"

"In my office," Mack said. Parker turned and spied the other man over her shoulder.

"What happened? How did I get here?"

"You passed out, *mon ange*," Gabriel said as he brushed her hair back. "Do you remember?"

"No," Parker said as she furrowed her brow. "No, I don't remember past that kiss." She blushed and looked over at Mack. "I do remember meeting you, and then there is nothing."

"Let me take you home, Parker, now that you're awake. In case you feel sick again."

"But what about whatever it is you have to do here? I don't feel sick."

"It's not as important as you, Parker," Mack told her. "He can come back at any time to authenticate the painting. It does my heart good to see him fuss over you."

"He does like to fuss," Parker said as she looked over at Gabriel. He leaned over and kissed her as he handed Parker her glasses. They'd slipped off her nose when she'd collapsed. Gabriel rose with her. Mack accompanied them through the museum. Parker paid little attention to their conversation, and she stopped short at the entrance to a gallery that was filled with religious art.

That was when Parker let go of Gabriel's hand and entered the gallery, the two men close behind her. She didn't understand why she was drawn to the end of the hall, toward a small painting in the corner. Parker recoiled when she stopped in front of it, the sight of blood almost too much to handle. It was a painting of Crusaders and Middle Easterners engaged in a ferocious battle.

Something was familiar about this painting. Parker's vision went blurry and didn't snap back into focus until she felt Gabriel's hand on the nape of her neck. "Gruesome, isn't it?" she asked.

"What drew you to this painting, *mon ange?*"

"I don't know, just something about it I guess." Parker couldn't take her eyes off the painting.

Gabriel put his arm around her shoulder. "Come, Parker, let's get you home. I'm worried that you collapsed."

"Sure, okay," Parker said to him, because honestly, she wasn't sure she wanted to stay here at the museum anymore. Why did her brain feel so fuzzy? What happened? Why did she pass out? And why did she remember Gabriel's eyes being black?

In the darkest part of the night, Gabriel once again slid his body out from under Parker's and rose. After returning from the museum they had a late lunch. Parker had a nap, claiming extreme fatigue. What she didn't know was that Gabriel was the one pumping the fatigue into the air of his apartment. Tonight, he had a score to settle, and the last thing he wanted was Parker to wake up to an empty apartment. He'd worked the afternoon away on his laptop while she napped and eased on the fatigue pheromones when she woke in the late afternoon. Together, they ate dinner and showered before Gabriel laid her out on his bed and blew her mind again and again.

His hunger for her still twisted his gut. Almost as much as the fear and anger.

He'd started to wonder if he hadn't landed in some twisted game of cosmic tug of war. A tug of war with two different warring sides and his unknowing soul in the middle. He'd told Mack the truth. They really should have left him dead at the gates of Jerusalem. Every sin committed, every life taken, weighed on his soul, even to this day. He'd followed his church and his leader with a zealousness and belief that bordered on insanity. After the first two years at war, his fervency had dimmed to nonexistent. The only reason he stayed was a sense of duty to his king and country.

Now, Gabriel eased himself out of bed and gathered the shadows around him. Tonight, he was going hunting. With one final look at Parker and the lightest brush of his lips to her temple, Gabriel melted into a shadow, his mind on the colorless face of Antony.

Gabriel wasn't surprised when he stepped out of the shadows in a darkened hallway at the back of a club. At the mouth of the hallway, he saw strobes of light flashing red, blue, and white. Gabriel stalked forward, the beat of the song pounding on the walls of the club. When he reached the end of the hall, Gabriel stepped back when a woman, wearing only some tight spandex shorts and a sports bra, walked by with a tray in her hands. As soon as he could, Gabriel spied the stage and saw four different women dancing on stripper poles, each one completely naked except for a tiny thong.

Of course, this was where Antony would be. He was one who'd enjoyed the spoils of war way too much. Right now, Gabriel wished he'd killed him a thousand years ago.

He scanned the crowd, his vision piercing the darkness and blocking out the light distraction. There, in a corner booth, his eyes glued to one woman in particular dancing on stage, was Antony. Curious, Gabriel shifted his eyes to see which woman had Antony's attention, and his stomach heaved when he saw her. She was shorter than all the other women, a bit plumper. A strobe of white light hit her, and her brown hair shone.

The woman looked amazingly like Parker.

Gabriel's eyes narrowed and rage coursed through him. All these centuries Antony had been hunting Parker along with Maximus, taking sick pleasure in killing her, and now this? Did he lust after Gabriel's soulmate? Was killing her not enough, he also wanted to possess her body?

Good thing the other man would die tonight.

Slinking from shadow to shadow, Gabriel made his way around the club, ensuring Antony was the only Fold member present before sinking into darkness again. When he reappeared, Gabriel sat in the booth right behind an unsuspecting Antony. Gabriel's dagger appeared in his hand while he watched the other man swallow the last of his drink and set the glass on the table. His eyes remained on the girl who looked like Parker. Silent death filled Gabriel's soul as he wound his arm around Antony's neck and dragged him further into the booth, his dagger sliding between spine, organs, and ribs. Antony made a strangled sound and grasped at Gabriel's arm while he waited for death to take the other man.

"Do you come here and watch her, wishing she was the one I claim as mine?" Gabriel whispered in Antony's ear.

"Crusader…"

"You'll never have her." Gabriel pushed his blade farther. Antony's body arched.

"Did Maximus tell you to touch her, or was that your own stupidity? You should have known that would bring me right to you." Gabriel's voice was as hard as steel. He'd been a hunter for over a thousand years. Antony had made it too easy on him.

"Did you think I wouldn't kill you if you were among all these mortals?" His blade tipped up, and Gabriel heard it piercing Antony's heart as the man gurgled blood. "You knew you were dead as soon as you did it."

"Distraction…" That was the last word Antony managed before he expelled his last breath. When Gabriel opened his hand, the dagger disappeared. He melted back into the seat cushion as Antony's body fell back.

"Maximus used you," Gabriel whispered to the dead man. "The question is why."

The next time Gabriel stepped from the shadows; he stood outside his apartment building. He blocked off every sound that came from the city, no cars, no horns, no air traffic, and expanded his hearing. Before his mortal death, this wasn't something Gabriel could do. Since then, since being forced into service with The Fold, it became like second nature.

There, off to the left, came the faintest scrape of a shoe on concrete. Gabriel backed into a shadow, melting into the dark, his senses reaching out and perceiving the threat. He stopped outside a circle of light from a streetlamp and opened his fist only to close it again on the black shadow dagger. "You can't hide in the shadows from me, Maximus."

From the other side of the light, a large, blonde-haired man stepped away from the building.

"Crusader, it's been a long time."

"Only because you've been hiding from me for four hundred years, coward." Gabriel moved into a fighter's stance when Maximus halted in the circle of light. Behind him, more footsteps stopped, surrounding him.

"Do you mean to kill us all, Crusader?"

"One by one, until you're gone." Gabriel held his

shadow sword up and pointed it at Maximus. "Ending with you."

Maximus stood in the circle of light and folded his hands behind his back. "You fail to see the bigger picture here don't you, Crusader?"

"There is no bigger picture to me. I'll kill every one of you until she's safe. I would burn this world to the ground for her."

Maximus paced, two steps left, before turning and doing the same to the right, his brow furrowed. "Honestly, Crusader." Maximus stopped and shrugged his shoulders. "I didn't expect you to hold on this long."

"You, and The Fold, have only yourselves to blame. You're the ones who brought her to my attention. Had you not done that." Gabriel shrugged. "Who knows what may have happened?"

"Perhaps," Maximus uttered that word as if even the slightest agreement with Gabriel

pained his soul. Maximus stopped pacing and stood in front of Gabriel, completely still. "Tell me,

Crusader, the killing. Did you enjoy it? For the glory of God?"

"The only men I've enjoyed killing at any point in history are yours, Maximus." Gabriel lowered his arm as if he were letting down his guard. He heard the other assassins accompanying Maximus close in on him. "Curiously though, what did Antony do to deserve such a fate?"

Maximus sighed and shook his head. "He was so sloppy, Crusader, nothing like you. How many of my men have you taken out in the last four hundred years?"

"Innumerable, Maximus. But you should know by now her life is worth more to me than your men, worth more than my own life, so I'll continue to take them out, one by one. Is this how you test new recruits? Have them try to take down the rogue assassin? How long have they been dead?"

After saying that, Gabriel flipped a dagger toward the man who'd crept the closest to him. Without him taking his eyes off Maximus, the dagger found its mark in the man's throat and then disappeared as he crumpled to the ground.

"What you fail to understand is that we don't want *you* dead, Crusader."

"I give less than a goddamn what *you* want, Maximus." Gabriel dropped into a fighting stance again. It made no sense that Maximus would take the time to stand here and talk to him like this. Gabriel let his mind check the security he'd put in place around his apartment and Parker. No disturbance. Parker was still sleeping. "*I* want you dead. You put that in motion the first time you held her body to you and slit her throat in front of me."

Maximus sighed again and dropped his shoulders. "Maybe this wasn't handled properly in the beginning, but in the end, it will be the same. Your soul will be tied to The Fold, and there's nothing to be done about it."

"My soul will never belong to you, or The Fold, Maximus. It was never something I wanted. My mortal body was dead. My soul should have been allowed to pass on and face judgment."

"It's a shame you died at the very gates of Jerusalem, Crusader," Maximus stopped all movement to stand in front of Gabriel. Gabriel's body tensed. No other man had dared step forward since he'd dropped the one without looking. "To miss the glory of that…" Maximus closed his eyes and lifted his face to the Boston sky, a small smile on his lips. As if he was reliving the beauty of the past slaughter.

Gabriel nearly took the man's immortal life right then, to suggest he'd missed out on his soul's calling. "You're right, Maximus, it is too bad, because maybe I could have defended some of the innocent lives slaughtered when that gate went down." Thousands of innocent Muslims and Jews were slaughtered once the crusading army passed into Jerusalem, for no other reason than being present. The very fact that Maximus had carried that feeling of glorified killing with him for nearly a millennium showed what a twisted soul he was.

The idea of the slaughter caved Gabriel's chest. Sure, it was war and, right or wrong, too many lives had been taken, but Gabriel had never participated in needless slaughter. His men had been trained to not participate as well. Any soldier under his command that was caught raping, pillaging, or needlessly killing was dealt with swiftly.

"How do you think your little woman will react when she finds out the truth, Crusader?" A gleam in Maximus's eye caught Gabriel by surprise and gave him pause. "This time around, I'll let her know the whole truth before I end her last life. Since I took her first, I want to take her last."

Gabriel's fury broke free. He stepped deeper into a shadow and appeared behind one of the three men left circling him. He drove a dagger into the man's neck, just like he'd done when he killed Emily. As the man fell, Gabriel moved to the next one, who only had a moment to react before Gabriel's blade sliced him from stomach to sternum. That left only one man besides Maximus, who still stood in the streetlight, watching the situation play out.

This time, The Fold member had enough time to draw his own weapon, his eyes nervously on Gabriel, but not enough time to use it. Perhaps, at one time, when he'd started hunting those responsible for Parker's death, Gabriel would have enjoyed taunting the man. Not anymore. Now, he handed out swift justice, like he had to his troops if they dared to disobey his direct order. Gabriel straightened to his full height and opened his fist to close it on another shadow sword. The other man's face blanched when Gabriel slipped into a shadow. He didn't have the chance to react when Gabriel materialized behind him, placed his neck between the two blades, and sliced off the man's head. One more shadow slip had Gabriel standing directly behind Maximus, and he parried Gabriel's sword, only a moment to spare.

Maximus stepped further into the light, his blade glinting in the brightness. Gabriel remained in the shadow, letting the man think he wouldn't follow. "What a mess for the authorities to clean up later." Maximus motioned to the four bodies laid out in a semicircle.

Gabriel was thankful it was the middle of the night and no pedestrians or vehicles had gone by. Maximus took another step back, and Gabriel stalked forward into the light. He let the sword in his hand go, and Maximus's reaction told him all he needed to know. Clearly, the other man thought he needed the darkness to call forth his weapon, but that was furthest from the truth. The only thing he needed the dark for was to move through shadows. The rest came from inside. From that dark place in his soul where the pain of his past sins lay. From the blackness of the fury he lived with.

"Finally, just the two of us," Gabriel taunted as he continued to step closer to Maximus.

The other man flicked his sword with his wrist, as if to remind Gabriel of its existence.

"Do you think killing me will stop whatever the monsters we serve have already set in motion, Crusader?"

"So, you finally agree that they are monsters, Maximus? To hold us in this static place and not allow our souls to move on?"

"Not all of us welcome death."

"It's fear that keeps you here then?" Gabriel circled Maximus, stepping sideways, keeping his hands closed so no blade appeared. "Fear of God's judgment."

"It's you they favor above all others; you have to know that." Maximus moved in the same pattern as Gabriel, sidestepping each other around the ring of light.

"Once again, I give less than a damn. Once I get through you, I'll find the bastards responsible for this assassin's league and kill them too. Never again will these bastards control another soul. Even you must see how insane this is."

"How does this differ from what the angels presume to do? Pulling your soul into service.

It's the same." The hand around Maximus's sword grip tightened.

"It is the same, but you seem a bit upset about not being wanted by the angels." Gabriel taunted the other man, wanting to get him angry, to slip up. This had gone on for too long. Gabriel was ready to finish it. Maximus lurched forward, bringing his sword up, and Gabriel lifted his hand for his sword to appear. Maximus stopped short.

Like he was now afraid to continue.

"You aren't in the shadows."

"What an amazing assumption I let you create for yourself, Maximus." For the first time, Gabriel saw fear enter the other man's eyes. Only then, when Maximus realized the circle of light wouldn't save him, did a portal open behind him. Quickly, before he could get away, Gabriel hurtled a dagger at the other man, hoping to bury it in his throat like he had the other member. Maximus turned slightly at the blade, and Gabriel watched it sink into Maximus's shoulder before the portal closed around him.

Gabriel heaved out the breath he'd been holding, hating that he'd missed his mark, and slowly let the sounds of the city back in. There, in the background, he heard police sirens. He returned to the shadows and stepped out of them back into his apartment. Moments later, standing at his window, Gabriel saw the red and blue flashing lights and only then realized the whole confrontation had taken place directly under his window. Gabriel watched as the police secured the scene. He squinted his eyes at the police helicopter searchlight that went past.

"Gabriel?" Parker's voice came to him through the darkness, and he shed the suit of shadows until he stood in nothing but his boxers. "What's going on?" She stepped up beside him with his blanket wrapped around her body again.

"I'm not sure, *mon ange*, but something bad must have happened." Gabriel pointed to the numerous police cars and several vans that were now down below. He placed his arm around her shoulders and pulled her close, kissing her temple as they stood there and watched the commotion. "Is the door locked?" Parker asked him, turning her head to look in that direction. The room was still dark, so she couldn't see it clearly.

"I'm fairly certain it is, but I'll double-check to be sure." Gabriel pulled the curtains closed, encasing them fully in the dark, and turned her back to the bed. "Come, you lay your delicious little body back down while I check the lock." Gabriel flipped the lock back and forth, so Parker could hear it was set, before making his way back to bed. It was adorable how she'd worried about the door, not realizing he was more than capable of protecting her. Much less that he was the reason the police were here in the first place. Gabriel climbed under the covers with Parker and pulled her close again. "The door is locked, *ma petite*. Nothing to worry about."

"That's a lot of police. Of course, I'm going to worry." Parker snuggled back into him. "Maybe we should leave tomorrow. That makes me nervous."

"If that will put your mind at ease, then of course we will go."

"I don't want anything to happen to you, Gabriel," Parker whispered into the dark. His arms drew her closer.

"I'll protect you with my life, Parker."

CHAPTER TWELVE

"General, I've assembled your men as you instructed."

"Thank you, Mack." Gabriel turned to the man, his face and clothing dusty and torn. He would never know why the man had decided on that title for him. At the beginning of this war, he was hardly a knight. But, with morale sinking the longer this siege lasted, Gabriel would forgive his men much.

Except for what had occurred last night.

The crusading army had arrived outside Jerusalem in early June to find the wells had been poisoned and any surrounding forest cut back by the Fatimid Governor in charge of the defense of Jerusalem. For over a month now, they'd been slowly chipping away at the walls and defenses of the city. Gabriel had managed to keep his small attachment of men in line. They were all dusty, thirsty, and hot. Disillusioned by the war and the call to the glory of God and the Holy Pope.

After the nine-month siege of Antioch, and subsequent march on Jerusalem, Gabriel had lost his way. This no longer felt like a holy war to him. He'd questioned the zealousness that drove the crusading army and their utter belief in the rightness of this war. Was God really looking down on them in favor? Did he, Gabriel, have the same belief in the cause as he had two years ago? This seemed all wrong. God wouldn't want them to fight and force another to his word. It went against everything he'd thought he'd known his whole life.

Gabriel slowed his steps and let Mack catch up to him, the dust of the Earth kicking up under his feet. "I bring news, Mack."

At some point during this war, Gabriel and Mack had been brought together. Mack had become an important addition to his men. Gabriel found the man to be smart, loyal, and honest, three qualities he favored above others. "Have our leaders stopped squabbling long enough to work together?"

Gabriel had joined the army of Tancred of Hauteville and followed him, a loyal knight to the end. He stopped walking, and Mack stopped with him, both men seeking the small amount of shade they found. Looking out over the land, Gabriel knew what was currently happening not too far off. "Reinforcements have come from the sea." Gabriel and his men had been part of Tancred's party that rode down to Bethlehem and drove up livestock for the army, since most of the livestock outside the walls of Jerusalem had been slaughtered before their arrival. They were now situated along the northwest corner of the walls. The constant noise of bombardment rang in Gabriel's ears.

He just wanted peace.

Every night, he prayed to God for an end to this war.

Gabriel no longer flinched at the sound of the catapult hurling debris at the ancient city walls. "Do you still believe in this cause, Mack?" Gabriel's eyes bored into the older man.

"It does not matter what we think, General."

"Doesn't it? When did our opinions come to mean so little?"

"We are but knights who serve our leaders."

"Why would God look favorably on this slaughter?" Gabriel threw his arm back to encompass the city walls. "Would God be proud of what two of my men did last night? Good men once, driven mad by this crusade and endless siege. By the death and carnage."

"We will all sit upon judgment for our sins one day, General." Mack's eyes softened on Gabriel.

"You know what I must do, Mack. You know that I must now judge them and mete out punishment." Gabriel gestured off to the far side of his camp where two men were tied to a pole, their heads hanging low in shame.

"You are but judging them on their actions, not on their souls. That is not your place."

Gabriel stopped walking and turned to the other man, the cloak he wore swirling around his legs. From this position, he saw the two men clearly as they sat, tied to a post, both heads down, in shame or sleep. He wasn't sure which one. "Is there really a difference, Mack? And what are we doing?" He gestured toward the walls the crusading army tried to breach. "Are we not just as guilty? Judging others for their beliefs? Beliefs that don't align with our own?"

"General." Mack placed his hand on Gabriel's shoulder. "I understand your words. And your struggle, but these men"—he gestured to the men behind them—"they do not deserve your compassion. Do not give them a piece of your soul. Their acts were depraved and caused the ruination and death of a young girl. Do not blame the war for what they did. That type of evil lives in men's souls. It is not a compulsion that started with the Crusades. If they haven't done so before, they would again." Mack's hand tightened on Gabriel's shoulder. "Give them nothing of you. Hide your pain away. Do not grieve for them."

A shutter slammed in Gabriel's mind at those words. In the end, he knew what needed to be done, and he turned his body fully toward the men imprisoned in his camp. In this, in the disciplining of his troops, Tancred, his leader, did not interfere. Gabriel's entire body tightened with the first step toward the men. His jaw was hard as he approached and pulled his sword. Until then, the men had looks that spoke of their desire to plead their case, to try to make sense to

Gabriel what they'd done. How finding, defiling, and ultimately, killing a young girl, no more than ten, was some God-given right as a crusader. Gabriel watched all these thoughts travel across the eyes of the two men as they scrambled to their feet, pulling on the ropes that bound them.

"God alone will judge you, not I," Gabriel told one before driving his sword into the heart of the man. Normally, he would give the men time to plead their case, but not this time. This time, Gabriel had enough. Enough of this war. Of these acts of viciousness. Of the hunger and thirst. Of watching innocent lives lost. "And you." Gabriel turned to the other man after pulling his blade from the first man's chest cavity. The mouth of the man opened as if to speak when Gabriel drove his sword into his body, this time to the hilt. Gabriel drove the man back into the post and watched as the life drained out of him. "Your words mean nothing to me, just like that young girl's life meant nothing to you."

For the space of heartbeats, Gabriel stood over the two dead men at his feet before turning to face his remaining troops. Maybe two hundred now. So many lives were lost, on both sides. "Would any other man care to step forward and meet my sword?" Gabriel flicked said sword, and blood droplets flew from the tip. "We are supposed to be basking in the glory of God." Gabriel's eyes scanned the men assembled. "Not raping and murdering children." He spat the words. "Innocent lives we do not take. Any man who feels differently may step up to me now." He pointed to the ground in front of himself.

Not a single man stepped up to him.

"Nearly a month ago," Gabriel said, "reinforcements came through the port city of Jaffa. Since then, siege towers have been built. Tomorrow, we prepare for an assault. I expect every man here to pray and receive penance when offered. Pray for our very souls. Within the next few days, these walls will come down and we will take Jerusalem."

The men didn't cheer at his words, their bodies barely shifting at the announcement. All of them, like Gabriel himself, were dirty, tired, and thirsty. He suspected most of them were also tired of the war and wanted to go home. Desertion was rampant among the troops. Those who fought against his restrictions on raping, pillaging, and taking innocent lives had joined with other leaders who turned a blind eye to such things. Gabriel could care less. Right now, what he cared about was bringing an end to this war and returning home where he would never take another blade of green grass for granted again. Perhaps he'd finally be able to take possession of the home awarded to him as a knight. Perhaps find a wife, have some children, fade into normalcy. Take care of his land and people.

Something slow, simple, and easy. A life that hadn't appealed to him fifteen years ago. A life that he could now taste with a passion he no longer had for battles and war. The next opportunity he had, Gabriel would write to his father and ask him to search for a bride for him. This would be his final battle of the Crusade.

Hours later, when the priests came through the camp, Gabriel fell to his knees, folded his hands together, and lowered his head. Next to him, Mack took the same position. Gabriel didn't know how many of his men took to their knees to receive penance. At this point, he didn't care. Gabriel prayed for forgiveness. He prayed for God to absolve him of the guilt he had and the sins he'd now felt he'd committed in God's good name. He prayed for the hearts of all men to be filled with the love and light Gabriel had once felt at the thought of God's holy grace. On his knees, he prayed for Mack and for the woman who would someday become his bride. For her, he asked God to wrap her in his light, strength, and protection.

At that moment, on his knees in the soil of the Holy Land, Gabriel allowed his mind to wander over the thought of his future bride. What would she look like? He prayed for strong and healthy. For a long life of happiness together. He tried to imagine what she may look like, this future woman of his. In his mind's eye, he could see the roundness of a cheek, the bounce of a curl, the softness of a smile.

Surviving this war and finding the wife he wanted now became the driving force behind everything Gabriel did. To feel that round cheek and place his palm around it pushed him through.

That night, after the siege towers had been rolled into place and the bloody fight began, all he thought about was the bounce of a curl. Somewhere in his future, the woman who belonged to those small parts would be revealed to him and she would be his. Gabriel believed, with all his heart, that God had shown him his future bride. He'd hold those few short glimpses close to his heart.

The night turned into day, and Gabriel led his men away from the fighting to rest and drink what they could. How many of them remained? Less than half now? Gabriel, like his men, was injured, bloody, and exhausted. A film of sweat and dirt mixed with the blood on his skin. He wished for nothing more than a cool stream to wash in. Around him, the cacophony of war continued. Men's shouts of victory and screams of death. The never-ending pounding of rocks against the walls of the city.

Gabriel lost track of time and most of his men after that. All he knew was that Mack continued to fight by his side. Minutes bled into hours which bled into night. The next time he gathered his men, only fifty remained. He wanted this to be over, done, just as he was with this war. Two nights and a day of fighting before they breached the city and the gates of Jerusalem fell to the Crusaders. Elation surged through Gabriel and the thought that the battle would soon be over, that they'd take the city, and he could leave this dry, dusty place. He fought the soldiers who attacked him, ignoring the women and children running around in the confusion.

Inside the gate, the scream of a woman caught his attention. Gabriel turned his body and started toward it.

There, he could see three Crusaders surrounding a woman and two young children. The woman had the children behind her back, pressing them against the wall of the city, brandishing a dagger at the three men. Gabriel knew she was no match for the three because he was sure bloodlust had set in and all they saw was an infidel conquest to rape and murder. In a coordinated move that told Gabriel these men had done this before, one man disarmed the woman, one took possession of her body, and the other held the children in place.

The children, a boy who looked to be around twelve, and a girl, who was perhaps a year or two younger, fought against the crazed crusader. Their mother, in the arms of another, kicked and screamed, trying to release herself. Gabriel watched in slow motion as the boy removed a hidden dagger from his vest, drew his hand back, and stabbed the man standing close to them in his side.

Gabriel had already moved closer to the situation and was screaming at the three men to stop when the unoccupied man whipped out his sword and sliced open the boy. The three men watched as his blood and guts spilled out and the child fell face first to the ground. Laughing. Enjoying the screams of the boy's mother. At that point, Gabriel wasn't sure if the roar from his mouth had any sound when he launched himself at the Crusader who killed the child, pushing him back from the scene. Mack's words ran through his mind when his attack was parried, and he refused to give these men a piece of himself. The only thing they deserved was to stand before the gates of heaven and explain their actions to God. He would not stand around and watch them rape and murder an innocent woman and her children.

Gabriel wanted their deaths on his blade. Wanted it with an amount of bloodthirst that frightened him. If he had to carry the sin before God, so be it, it was worth it for the lives of these innocents. What he didn't expect was the attack from behind. He felt no pain as he stared down in disbelief at the sword thrust through his back and exiting his belly. Gabriel's bloody sword slipped from his hand, landing in the dirt, his eyes on the man standing in front of him. Ice-blue eyes. When the crusader behind him pulled his sword free, Gabriel staggered back, his eyes wide, until he slammed into the city wall. Looking down, he watched his blood run like a river, pooling at his feet. He held his hands up, now red and shaking. Covered in his own blood. A scream came from a distance, and his eyes focused on the scene he'd encountered, the men now returning to their sick, perverted game with the two living females. Gabriel watched, falling to his knees, unable to do more, unable to save them, as his life drained from his body into the holy soil of Jerusalem. The last thing he saw before darkness took his vision was a soft smile on a plump cheek, a curl of hair blowing in the breeze.

"Rise, Crusader."

Gabriel stared in confusion at the environment surrounding him. Still on his knees, but the city of Jerusalem and the surrounding hues of brown were gone. No dry, hot breeze. No sand stinging his skin. All that was before him was white so blinding it should have hurt his eyes but did not. Gabriel blinked again, trying to remember where he'd last been before waking here.

"Rise, Crusader."

Gabriel lifted his head. "Do I kneel before the gates of heaven?" He remembered now. The blade through his back. The betrayal of his brethren. That innocent boy, dead on the ground, defending his family. The woman… The girl…

Rage started then. Though he was on his knees, rage boiled up from his feet, tightened his thighs, and clenched in his belly. Gabriel slid a hand across his belly, no longer feeling the slippery blood that had covered him. When he looked down, his clothes were free of any tears, dirt, or debris. He wore the clothing he'd been in when the attack on Jerusalem happened, but the longer the rage rose, the blacker they became. Finally, when he was encompassed with a burning fury, darkness settled around him like a shield. Gabriel knew this was not heaven. "So, 'tis the gates of hell then." Around him was the white nothing, the only color the darkness of the shadows around him.

"This is neither heaven nor hell, Crusader." The voice came from around him, battering him from all sides. Gabriel swayed on his knees and looked down again, expecting to see his blood in the sand.

Nothing.

"Where am I?"

"I had to fight to get your soul the moment your last breath escaped your lips, Crusader."

"Who are you?" Gabriel saw no one.

"Did you have any idea of how closely you were watched?"

"Show yourself!" Gabriel jumped to his feet, his hand opening involuntarily and closing on a sword that formed from the shadows surrounding him.

"What a treasure you're turning out to be, Crusader."

Gabriel couldn't tell, but it almost sounded like giddy pleasure escaped from that voice.

"I'm ready to stand before God's judgment."

"God can't touch you here, Crusader. Your soul belongs to me now."

Gabriel gathered the shadows closer to him, the field of white seeming to shimmer. Before him, starting hazy but coming into clearer focus, was a dusty lane winding through a valley. In the distance, Gabriel saw a village. Dirt lane and squat, wooden structures. Spread out behind the village were rolling hills of green, a color he hadn't set eyes on in many years. Beyond those hills, mountains rose, greens and browns rising to the white summit. The sky so blue it hurt his eyes.

The scene moved forward until Gabriel stood in an alley off the town square. He heard it now, the sounds of the village. The rolling of wagon wheels and the clip clop of horse's hooves. Somewhere, the bleating of goats. People speaking in a language he didn't know but understood all the same. A breeze came, and Gabriel's eyes closed at the clean, crisp scent of it, a hint of snow and sunshine. When had he last felt a cooling breeze?

"Is this heaven?" Gabriel prayed that this was because he never wanted to leave the village he saw beyond this room of white nothing.

"The time has come to fulfill your first contract, Crusader. An easy one for your first." At those words, knowledge of who he was to kill flooded Gabriel's mind. For a moment, his rage had been soothed by the view before him, but it returned with the knowledge now pumping in his head.

"I will not."

"The choice is not yours, Crusader. God has forsaken you. Had he wanted you, he would have been quicker to you. Your soul belongs to me until I deem you no longer necessary. Fulfill your contract, and I'll grant you a reprieve."

Gabriel straightened then, his conscious mind trying to grasp the knowledge flooding his brain. It seemed nearly two centuries had passed since his mortal death, even though it felt like mere moments to him. What he also now had was the knowledge of who owned his soul, of the assassin's league who imprisoned him. Rage continued to fester deep as he took that first step through the portal into that village nestled in the northwestern part of Burgundy.

Gabriel pressed himself against the side of the wooden building he'd entered by, hiding in the shadows cast by the sun. Again, that cool breeze blew by, and he shivered, not remembering the last time he'd felt anything like cold. Shadows gathered around him, and a cloak appeared around his shoulders. Finally, the knowledge bombarding his brain trickled to a stop and Gabriel marveled at everything that had happened in the last two hundred years.

What the knowledge didn't do was dampen his anger at

the one now holding his soul hostage but also at God for forsaking him. Was this to be his punishment for sins he'd committed during the Crusades? To live this eternal life in the service of another? He'd have rather taken judgment upon himself than be cursed to this life.

A tug on his consciousness happened when the man he recognized from the information poured into his brain crossed the mouth of the alley he hid in. At that, Gabriel gathered the shadows around him and stepped from between the wooden frames, keeping his quarry in sight.

CHAPTER THIRTEEN

Gabriel smiled at Parker, reaching for her hand across the space of the table between them. "Why are you so far from me, *mon ange*? Sit here." He patted the seat next to him. Parker's cheeks flushed, and she picked up her coffee and beignet before moving to sit in the chair next to Gabriel. God only knew why she'd decided to sit in the chair across from him. They'd taken the earliest flight out of Boston that they could and returned to New Orleans late yesterday afternoon. Parker wasn't sure what it had been, seeing all those police cars in the street below Gabriel's apartment. An irrational fear had gripped her tight, and all she could think about was getting out of there.

For the last two nights, almost since they'd landed in Boston, Parker had been having strange dreams. Each dream had Gabriel and herself in it, but each dream happened during a different time period. Parker couldn't make sense of them and hadn't shared the information with Gabriel because... well, because she didn't want him to think she was crazy. Or know how insecure she was about this whole relationship. The reality was that it felt like a fantasy that would come crashing to an end before she knew it. And it was nothing Gabriel had done or not done. From the very moment she'd met him, he'd acted like his whole body and soul was committed to this relationship. It was only Parker's insecurities that had her believing it was a nice, summer diversion that would end the second he left Chicago in July. That even though they had both said words of love, she was the only one who really felt them.

But, looking at Gabriel now, the way his eyes lit up when she changed chairs and sat next to him, her heart squeezed and rejected her insecurities. When she took a bite of her beignet from Café Beignet, his mouth quirked up in a half smile. He always seemed to enjoy watching her eat and discovering new tastes. It was as if her enjoyment and enthusiasm was his as well. Parker's heart fluttered again when he reached out with his thumb and wiped powdered sugar off the side of her lip.

Her lady parts clenched when he stuck that thumb in his mouth and sucked the sugar off. Wait, did she just call them her lady parts? Parker swiped a hand over her brow. Maybe the heat was getting to her because she'd never, in her twenty-eight years, used the term *lady parts* when referring to her body. Parker winced.

"What is that face for, *mon ange*?" Gabriel brought her hand to his lips and kissed her ring finger. Then he flipped her hand and kissed her palm before also kissing the pulse point in her wrist. His kissing her wrist made her think about what he'd done to her last night. How he'd picked her up and carried her to his room after they got back from Boston. How he'd laid her out on his bed and used lips and tongue and fingers on her. Her face flamed. She clenched her thighs together. Gabriel's eyes darkened and his nostrils flared.

Parker cleared her throat. "Just something I was thinking about."

"What would that something be, *ma petite*?" With his hand encircling her wrist, he drew her closer. By now, Gabriel felt that he knew all her looks, and the expression on her face went from embarrassment to desire in the blink of her eyes. Since he knew her so well, he looked away from her for as long as it took him to sip his coffee, giving her the time she needed to pull her emotions back together. By the time he looked back at her, Parker's expression had settled on neutrality. He hated that look of neutrality and the thoughts that probably led to it. He hated that she questioned his love for her, that she couldn't believe how tightly he was wrapped around her fingers.

Gabriel had been around long enough to know what some men would call him if they knew how dedicated he was to her. How he'd do anything to make her happy. There was less than a damn in his soul to give to people who would dare poke fun at his love for her. He was a slave to her. To her eyes. To her mind. To the curve of her plump cheek. To her soft smile. To the bounce of her glorious curls.

For the first time in centuries, Gabriel's breath caught as a memory raced through his brain. One he'd nearly forgotten in the last thousand years. Of kneeling on the ground of Jerusalem. Praying to God for the life of his future bride. His heart stuttered as he watched Parker sip her coffee, letting his mind open to the faith he'd once had. To the unbelievable that he hadn't recognized until this moment.

That, a thousand years ago, God had shown him his future wife, and it had been Parker he'd seen.

"You're staring at me." Her perfect round cheek turned pink, and everything in Gabriel went hard as a rock at the realization he'd had.

"Why wouldn't I, *ma femme?*" It was the first time he'd called her that when she'd consciously remember it.

Parker's eyebrow raised. "*Votre femme?*"

"*Oui, ma femme. Je t'aime.*" Gabriel reached out and wound his hand around the back of her neck, tangling his fingers in the thick, gloriously curly mass of hair she'd left down this morning. He'd almost dragged her back into his apartment when he'd realized it was staying down. Not caring one bit for the people walking by the little sidewalk café they were sitting at, Gabriel yanked her closer to him until her lips were a mere breath from his. "You are everything good and beautiful in my life, Parker."

Parker sucked in a breath and her eyes closed. She licked her lips, waiting for him to close the distance between them and kiss her. Gabriel stared at her lips for a heartbeat longer before he moved his head in. At that moment, a prickle of a warning skated across the nape of his neck. He raised his eyes to the street in time to haul Parker to her feet with the hand around her neck. Parker gasped as Gabriel pulled her up, his chair flying as he kicked it to the side. Their little café table crashed to the ground, coffee spreading across the concrete. He pushed her behind him and jammed her into the corner of the café between the brick façade and the window. Gabriel spread one arm out to cover Parker should her side be exposed and pushed her back with his other side. He heard the gasp from her lips when his shadow sword appeared in his right hand.

"Lucky for her you have such good reflexes, Crusader." There, standing behind the chair Parker had been sitting in only moments ago, was Maximus, a dagger in his grip. He'd swiftly run up behind her and swung his dagger to plunge it into Parker's neck. Now, it was lodged in the wooden awning beam of the café. Maximus took a moment to pull it out of the wood. "or she'd be dead yet again." Maximus ran his finger over the blade of his dagger, a faint line of blood appearing.

"You dare try to attack her on the street, in front of my own eyes?" Instinctively, Gabriel moved back farther, covering as much of Parker's body with his as he could. People on the street made a wide berth around them. The remains of their coffee strewn across the ground. Chairs were tilted onto their sides. On the street, out of Gabriel's reach, Maximus stood alone. At this time, Maximus would be secure in his safety, knowing Gabriel wouldn't leave Parker unprotected.

"I grow weary of the wait, Crusader." Maximus sighed and shook his head. "The time grows short."

"I should have killed you in Boston as well, Maximus."

"That's true, Crusader, you should have." Gabriel felt

Parker shift behind him, and he knew the moment Maximus's eyes also tracked her movement. Without thought, Gabriel brought his sword up and let it grow another inch. The group of mortals gawking on the street had grown. Gabriel was afraid Maximus would try to take out his anger on one of them. "I will not be free until this is over."

"M-Max?" Parker said from behind Gabriel.

His whole body stiffened because there should be no reason Parker would know this killer's name. "What are you doing here?" A sly smile spread across Max's face the tighter Gabriel's body became.

"Ah, Parker, I told you I would come down here and find you, my dear."

It felt like someone poured ice water over his head. Everything in Gabriel slowed, and his eyes zeroed in on Maximus and the shit-eating grin spreading across his face. The realization of what Parker said hit him in the solar plexus. The same rage he'd felt when he'd first been awakened built again. "You son of a whore." The insult came out of Gabriel's clenched teeth.

"Come now, Crusader. No need to insult my dear mother." Maximus chuckled and stretched out his arms in a wide arch. It was then that five more Fold members crept around until they had surrounded Gabriel and Parker in a semi-circle. "You can't deny me the brilliance of my plan. Not sure why I never thought of it before now, or why you never tried to find her yourself. How does it feel to know I had her before you in this life? I must say, amongst the many women I've had over the last millennia, she doesn't rank very high."

"I'll enjoy draining the blood from your body, you psychopathic bastard."

"Gabriel," Parker whispered from behind him. "What is he talking about?" Fear like she'd never known coursed through her body. None of what was going on made any sense to her. Yet she felt like she'd encountered this situation before. How did Gabriel know Max? And how had Max found her?

"Find her. Endear her to me. Lead her to her own destruction before you know she's alive. It ranks up there with sending you to kill your own soulmate."

Gabriel pushed Parker back as far as he could, watching as the Fold members inched forward. Why had none of these mortals called the police? Not that it would matter. Looking around, Gabriel could see no way to escape. Maximus and his men had them trapped against this storefront. If he attacked them, he left her unguarded, then one of them would go after Parker and he had no doubt the job would be finished this time. As soon as Gabriel's body was no longer in front of hers, Maximus would launch his knife at her, taking her last life. Their only way out was through the shadows, but Gabriel didn't know if he could take her. He'd never tried to bring another with him. At least, not one who was alive and mortal. "The last thing I'll be doing is praising you, Maximus. I will, however, enjoy carving your body into bits and feeding it to the alligators, just like I did to Emily."

"How very grotesque, Crusader. I like it."

Gabriel heard it then, the wailing of police sirens. Felt Parker's fingers tangling in his shirt. The shadows gathered around him, twining in and out of Parker's limbs, around her torso, connecting her to him. Inextricably linking them together. A thousand years of rage was the only comfort he had.

Until Parker.

"Come now, Crusader. I hear the authorities approaching. Give me the girl." Now, Maximus's teeth were clenched, his men drawing closer.

"Over my dead body, Maximus. You'll take my immortal life before I give her to you."

"Give her to me, so I can be free!" The anger and frustration exploded out of Maximus.

Spittle from his outburst ran down his chin. For the first

time, Gabriel heard the whispers of the shadows. Heard the promise in them. He let go of his sword and turned to Parker, holding her body to his as he pushed her into the darkness.

Who is that screaming?

"How could he have found her, Charles!"

Does no one else hear those screams?

"You brought her through the shadows?"

Was she hearing that screaming with her ears or just in her mind?

"Goddamn Maximus and his whole bloodline! I'll hunt them down if it's the last thing I do!"

Is it only in my mind? That screaming?

"Gabriel, you cannot leave, what if she wakes up?"

Gabriel? Why was that so familiar?

"I need Mack here, now, Charles!"

He is our soulmate.

"I'm here, General. How long has it been?"

"Gabriel..." The name barely escaped her lips, more of an exhale of breath than an actual sound.

"He got to her, Mack! How did he find her before I did?"

"Gabriel..." Louder this time, and it sounded like a chorus of voices behind hers. Her eyes refused to open. "Gabriel..."

"General..."

"Gabriel..." The soft curl of the French *r* rolled off her tongue with an echoing sigh. *"Nous avons besoin de toi."*

A hand went to her cheek, brushing her hair back. Her eyes, refusing to open and yet seeing him in her mind. "I'm here, *mon ange*. Parker, I'm here."

"Gabriel, nous avons besoin de toi. We need you."

A different man in her mind's eye. Older. Hair and eyes the color of hers. Arms heavy with muscle. "I have found you another husband, Penelope. You will marry within the week." His eyes met hers across the table.

"Father, no!"

"You will marry who I say, Penelope." His hand came down on the table and rattled the plates. "One who will not lead you to temptation!"

"Like the last one you chose for me! Who used me as nothing more than a slave?"

"You think I don't know what you've been doing?" The man stood to his full height and leaned over the table toward her. "How you've been spreading your legs for that merchant like a whore. You'll marry who *I* say. You're lucky anyone wants you at your age. A widowed farmer with five children to care for is the best I could find."

"I hate you," she gritted out between her clenched teeth. The man merely resumed his seat and continued with his meal as she turned and ran from the room.

"Gabriel…"

"Hello." She looked up from the book she'd been reading, placing her hand over her eyes to block out the sun. Standing before her was the same man she'd spotted standing near the cathedral when she was here the day before. Jackson Square had been her destination with the Lamont children yesterday, the twins enjoying the long walk after their morning studies. Now, it was Saturday, and she'd returned to the square, found a bench, and opened a book. She tried to convince her brain she was submersing herself in the culture of the city she now called home, but she knew it was mostly a lie.

She'd come back here hoping to see the same man as yesterday.

"Good morning," she returned after tearing her tongue off the roof of her mouth, unable to believe he was here. The man was absolutely, breathtakingly, handsome. Honey-blond hair. Deep blue eyes. He held out a hand to her, his fingers long and strong. Mouth open, she didn't hesitate to place her hand in his own.

"My name is Gabriel. May I ask what your name is?" His eyes never left hers.

"Pippa." She watched in fascination as he raised her

hand to his lips and kissed her ring finger. "My name is Pippa..." Her voice ended in a whisper at the softness of his lips on her finger.

"Gabriel... nous avons besoin de toi."

Parker stumbled her way back to bed. She'd gotten up to use the bathroom, her eyes still half-closed with sleep. She hadn't turned the lights on. The light through the window blinds was weak and pale, like the early-morning light. Her entire body was sore, but it was such a delicious soreness that Parker didn't mind. Parker was sure she and Gabriel had sex more times since she landed in New Orleans than she and Max did the entire two years of their relationship. Max had told her once that the way her body looked, especially the scars, made it difficult for him to get aroused, but he still loved her despite it.

That one had hurt. It had brought her so low that she was barely able to get out of bed and go to work for weeks. The kids in her class had noticed. She'd never told anyone, but she'd started feeling so depressed, looking back on her life, seeing what she thought were failures, that she'd thought about just ending it. Parker had sat down and started drafting a letter to her parents.

But, when she pulled the blanket back over her and snuggled down into Gabriel's bed, which was super comfortable, his arm went around her, and he pulled her body into his. He didn't seem to have a single issue with the way her body looked. When his arm wrapped around her, she wrapped her arms around his, hugging it to her. His palm ended up laying on the scar over her heart. "*Mon amour*, it is very early, I'm surprised you're awake."

"My body must not realize it no longer has to get up for school." Parker said as she snuggled back deeper into Gabriel's chest. A shiver of cold recognition slithered down her spine. A tremor racked her body, strong enough that Gabriel's head rose off the pillow. "That's weird," Parker uttered with a sigh. "It's almost like déjà vu."

"What do you mean?" Gabriel's finger rubbed the scar over her heart, as if he could caress away the indentation on her skin.

"I don't know." Parker shrugged. "It just feels like this situation happened before, I guess."

"You mean the one with your body under this tongue?" Gabriel ran said tongue up the

curve of her neck to her ear, filling his palm with her breast at the same time. "I can't wait for that to happen again." Gabriel brought his leg over hers and inserted it between her thighs, opening her body for him. He let his hand lightly glide down her body, her heart racing under the palm covering her breast.

When he reached her center, Gabriel buried his face in her neck the same moment his fingers buried themselves in her body. He teased her, drawing his fingers in and out, rolling her bud in his fingers before delving back in. Parker pushed her hips back against him, and one hand gripped his wrist while the other one wrapped around his neck. Scooting as close as he could, Gabriel hooked his fingers inside her, pressing on her g-spot and her bud at the same time. God, the way she sounded, he'd never get enough of hearing it.

"Gabriel, j'ai besoin de toi."

Everything in Gabriel stopped at her words. "What did you say?"

Parker arched against him, unaware of his question, able to feel nothing more than what he was doing to her body. *"S'il vous plait, Gabriel."* Her arm tightened around his neck. "Please," she pleaded. "I need you."

"Parker…" Her name gasped out of Gabriel's mouth. He knew, at that moment, he knew there was no erasing what had happened anymore. Very soon, he would have to face the reality of telling Parker everything. Her former incarnations would no longer be denied.

"Gabriel…" Parker purred his name, the French even more erotic to his ears. Gabriel knew the very second her

conscious mind lost to the bombardment of her former lives. Knew when she let her fear and insecurity go because she melted into him. Four hundred years of loving the same woman over and over and finally having all of her accept him drove him to an almost animalistic height.

"Do you know how long I waited for you this time?" Gabriel pressed deeper inside her, half turning her body, so his chest covered hers. In her eyes he saw them all. Saw *it* all. The passion. The love. The pain. Everything she'd felt for four hundred years.

"Mon mari." Parker's back and neck arched as her arms went around his neck. The explosion of her orgasm raced through her, and Gabriel soaked in each cry. Before the tremors of that orgasm had finished, he wedged himself between her thighs and slid his aching length in her.

Gabriel kneeled between her thighs, crushing her body into his so she could feel every hard thrust he gave her. One hand tangled in her hair and pulled her head back, so their lips were inches apart. "A hundred goddamn years I waited this time, and you think I'd be tired of you in a week? The heavens will crumble, God will be forgotten, and I'll still never get enough of you."

"Plus dur, Gabriel." Parker reached up and grabbed the headboard with one hand, the other tangling in his hair while she urged him to take her harder. *"Prends-nous plus fort."*

Take us harder.

All Gabriel was capable of was smashing his lips to hers and drinking in every moan while his body slammed into hers. When he felt her second orgasm start, he reached for the headboard, leveraging himself into her harder, just as she demanded. Her hips tilted to meet his, her legs clenched around his waist. Parker's nipples hardened against his chest while she spasmed until he couldn't hold back anymore and followed her over the edge.

They lay there for some time, arms and legs wrapped around each other, hearts beating a matching rhythm. Gabriel's face remained buried in Parker's neck. *"Je t'aime aussi, Gabriel. Mon mari."*

Gabriel shivered when Parker ran her fingers through his hair. He lifted his head to steal a kiss. When she pushed on his chest, he flipped over onto his back, his breathing still heavy. His eyes closed for only a moment before they flew open when Parker straddled him. *"Encore, Gabriel. Nous avons besoin de toi."*

CHAPTER FOURTEEN

Pippa blew a curl out of her eyes as the book she was reading plopped into her lap with a sigh. She'd been trying to read the same passage for the past ten minutes, but her neighbor wanted to turn the volume up on her record player. She knew, as soon as she'd seen Mary's male friend lug it into her room, that her quiet, peaceful nights were over. Not that she'd come to New Orleans for quiet and peaceful, but it had been nice for the first couple of weeks.

Now, a week into her position as tutor to the Lamont twins, she knew her nights were about to be sleepless because of that record player. Not a good thing considering the twins were entirely too rambunctious and demanded all her attention during lessons. The last thing she needed was Louis to get Camille going, then there would be no end in sight to their pranks and giggles.

At only ten years old, keeping the Lamont twins in line was, at times, harder than a full classroom of children.

Sighing again, Pippa placed her book on the bedside table and stood, smoothing the wrinkles out of her dress, and patting down her curls. Before leaving Chicago, to fight the heat of Louisiana, Pippa had taken scissors to her hair and cut several inches off. Regret had stabbed her immediately, looking at the curls in her bathroom sink, until she'd spied herself in the mirror. With the extra length taken off, her hair had bounced up to brush her shoulders, the fat curls of her hair framing her face in a way they hadn't when she'd worn it long. If she wanted, she could tame and smooth them with hair gel, pin them back in a sophisticated way, or leave them bouncy and natural. Right now, as she was preparing for bed and the last day of her work week, Pippa had a handkerchief tied around them to preserve the style she had for one more day. Truly, she'd been about to change and climb in bed before she heard the scratching sound of the needle across a record. Now, Mary's room was filled with the sounds of jazz trumpets and giggles. Normally, she wouldn't be so forward, but tonight, she needed sleep, so Pippa slipped her house shoes on and exited her bedroom to knock on Mary's door.

Pippa blushed and dropped her eyes when Mary's male friend opened the door, his shirt untucked, and all the buttons undone. It fluttered in the breeze he created opening the door and gave Pippa an eyeful of his chest hair and pectorals. Never, in her twenty-eight years of life, had Pippa viewed a man's entire naked body. Not that he was naked, even if his trouser button was also undone. A twenty-eight-year-old virgin, in the age of the sophisticated nineteen twenties, was nearly unheard of, but here she was. "Oh, um…" Pippa took a step back from the door.

"Hey there, sweet little mama," the man said right before swigging a drink from a bottle. "You interested?" He motioned to the room behind him, and Pippa raised her eyes to see Mary dancing in nothing more than her robe. Pippa watched Mary take a swig of liquor from her bottle before her dancing turned her toward the door and she saw Pippa standing there.

"Hey, Pippa, what's catching tonight?" Mary danced and rocked her hips toward the door, stopping next to her boyfriend and placing her arm around him. "Harry, this is my roommate, Pippa."

"The pleasure is mine," Harry replied with a wink and another swallow of alcohol. Even now, years into the

Prohibition, it amazed Pippa how easy it was for some to get their hands on alcohol. Pippa, feeling flustered, took another step back from the couple. She assumed that Mary would be upset with Harry's obvious flirtation, but when she flicked her eyes to the other woman, Pippa detected no jealousy in her gaze.

Pippa had been lucky to find a room in this boarding house before moving down here. There were five bedrooms, not including the room for the woman who lived here fulltime and ran the house. It was an older Victorian home that had been built in the late eighteen-eighties here in the Garden District of New Orleans. All the women who rented the rooms upstairs had to share a single bathroom, but it was right across from Pippa's room, so she was closest to it. She'd been given the last room in the hallway, and she was surprised when she'd seen the double bed and dresser in there. Buying any furniture hadn't been in her budget, so she was thankful for what she was given. Pippa had left Chicago with only two trunks of belongings, leaving some with friends and donating the rest.

At that moment, Pippa realized she'd been standing in the hall staring at Mary and Harry without answering their questions. "The music," Pippa squeaked out. "Could I bother you to turn it down some? I still have work tomorrow." Pippa felt her cheeks heat with embarrassment, and she took another step back, hoping Mary wouldn't think her a prude and hate her.

"Sorry, Pippa," Mary told her as she spun to the player and turned it down. When she looked back at Pippa, she smiled and winked. "We were just about to head out to go dancing. Want to come?" Mary took another drink from her flask when she stopped next to Harry. Pippa eyed the two of them and didn't mistake the gleam in Harry's eyes. Pippa may have never been with a man, but she wasn't clueless about what went on. She had read plenty of stories about more than two people having sex with each other at one time. That was what the look in Harry's eyes said, that he'd like to have both the women in his bed with him.

"Thank you for the invite." Pippa took another step back and ran her shaking hand over the handkerchief protecting her hair. "Like I said, I have the children to tutor tomorrow. Another time." Quickly, because she could feel the embarrassment climbing up her cheeks, Pippa scooted away and softly closed her bedroom door, leaning against it and blowing out the breath she hadn't realized she was holding.

The next morning, at exactly eight in the morning, Pippa was outside, waiting on the streetcar that ran on the street one block down from the boardinghouse she was living in. This time of the morning, the streetcar was packed with people. Pippa found herself smashed into the railing, hanging on for dear life. More than once, she'd felt a hand wander down her back inappropriately.

Six stops from when she hopped on, Pippa was hopping off, continuing her three-block trek to the Lamont house, a large, three-story house built in the popular way most homes were in this area. Each level of the house had its own veranda running the entire length of the house, and the maids were fond of keeping all the French doors open to catch the breeze. As it was only the beginning of June and Pippa already had sweat dripping down her back, she was very grateful for whatever breeze she could get.

After arriving at the house, Pippa found the twins already in the schoolroom on the first floor, thankful this room looked out over the courtyard in the middle of the house instead of the street. "Come now, children." Pippa clapped her hands together, so they'd know it was time to get started. "Our first lesson today will be French."

Louis and Camille both groaned at her comment. "Do we have to, Miss Pippa?" Camille smiled at Pippa, trying to use her 'good girl' look on her.

"Your father insists you learn, so yes, you must. But…" Pippa let the word trail off, her heart melting when both children's faces creased in a frown. "How about a walk to the square after our lesson?" Both children cheered at her statement, and Pippa knew she'd get about an hour of undisturbed work from the children. At this point, she'd take what she could get.

As expected, Louis started getting restless first, and Pippa knew that was her cue. She may have only been their tutor for a week, but Pippa knew children and when Camille also started squirming, she knew it was time to go. The trio stopped by the kitchen and asked the cook for a mid-morning snack and then started on their journey.

It was a three-block walk from the Lamont home to the French Quarter and Pippa used that time to continue her French lesson. *"Il y a l'église,"* Pippa said as she pointed to the St. Louis Cathedral. *"La cathédrale Saint-Louis."* Unfortunately, the children were beyond listening to her as they veered toward a man selling candied pecans. They had no desire to look at the St. Louis Cathedral. Churches did not excite children. Candies and toys and piano playing monkeys excited the children. Pippa sighed as the twins pointed and laughed, wishing she'd known that there was a festival happening before coming down here.

"Miss Pippa! Miss Pippa!" Camille went running back toward Pippa, the young girl's dress flapping around her knees. "That man has taffy. Can we get some, please?" Camille folded her hands under her chin and batted her eyelashes at her. Right before they left the Lamont house, Pippa had grabbed the small bag she was to carry with them in case the children wanted to buy anything while they were out.

"Lunch first, Camille, then treats."

Pippa led the children a bit farther down Decatur Street to a small grocery store she'd heard a few of the women who lived in the boardinghouse with her talk about. She ordered two muffuletta sandwiches she'd been curious about, gave a math lesson as she counted change, and sat with the children under a tree by the river to eat.

The twins, free of the restrictions they lived with at

home, chased each other through the park, their laughter making Pippa smile. She led them back toward Jackson Square and the promise of candy, letting them both fill a small bag to take home. Since they were there, Pippa managed to get the children to pause for fifteen seconds to view the church. Not able to contain her smile, Pippa looked around the church, turning to gaze into Jackson Square before looking back.

Her eyes halted when she spied a man in the shadows watching her. His gaze was intense and direct, and that would normally make her uncomfortable, but this time, it made her blush.

Gabriel had been following her for the past two weeks. Every morning when she left the boardinghouse to walk to the Lamont's, and every afternoon when she left to walk back. He was surprised she hadn't spied him by then. Each day that passed, it became harder and harder to resist approaching her, even though he knew he shouldn't. So far, he'd yet to sniff any members of The Fold, but he knew they would arrive sooner or later.

For now, he would maintain his distance and watch her from afar, mostly so he wouldn't scare the children in her charge. Gabriel's body tensed when she paused and looked his way, their eyes finally meeting after so many years apart. Once again, his heart started thumping for her. All he wanted was to cross the square and pull her into his arms. As he watched, a blush crept up her cheeks, and she brushed a curl behind an ear before bobbing her head and looking down. Gabriel remained standing where he was, his hands in the pockets of his trousers, his eyes on her and no one else. Another shy glance from her before the two children she was with drew her attention away. She had to pull them back from the curb before they got hit by an automobile.

"What do you think her name is this time around, Charles?" Gabriel had sensed the fallen angel walking up to him from behind.

"How long has she been here?" The question was spoken in Latin.

"Two weeks now," Gabriel responded, his eyes remaining on the trio until they walked out of sight.

"How have you managed to stay away?"

"Sheer force of will, Charles, and nothing else."

"Have you forgotten…"

"No, Charles, I have not." Gabriel said the words while rounding on the angel, his eyes going black. "I have forgotten nothing." Gabriel knew he had to get out of there before the shadows swirled around him. There were too many people about for him to be able to hide anything. Gabriel turned his back to the fallen angel and took off in the direction his love and the children had gone. Gabriel spent that night patrolling the area around the boardinghouse she was staying in.

Just as he did every night. Lately, he'd discovered how easily his temper would rise, how quickly his shadows would gather. The closer it came to the end of her lives, the less Gabriel was able to control his emotions, and the shadows were directly tied to them.

At the corner, a few houses down from where she was staying, Gabriel leaned against a tree and settled into the shadow. From here, he could see the deep porch of the house, the white columns holding up the roof over the porch. Several times over the last two weeks, he'd been rewarded when she had stepped out of the house and sat on the porch after the sun sank into the horizon. Both times, she'd fanned her dress over her legs, holding it up over her knees, allowing whatever breeze there was to cool her down. Those times, Gabriel had needed to dig his fingers into the tree to keep him rooted there and not walk up on her. The last thing he wanted was to scare her. The *only* thing he wanted was to love her, hold her.

Keep her forever.

The next morning, Gabriel returned after a few hours of rest in time to watch her leave the house with a book wrapped in her arms. Curious, he followed her until she caught the streetcar heading into the French Quarter. Relying on instinct, Gabriel stepped back into the shadow of the tree and exited in the shadow along the side of St. Louis Cathedral. Minutes later, the streetcar she'd been on stopped at the corner. Gabriel watched as she hopped down, smoothed her dress, and headed toward Jackson Square.

He could no longer resist the pull toward her. Fourteen nights he'd stood outside where she stayed and stared up at her window. Fifteen days he'd followed her. Protected her. Watched over her after waiting so many years to hold her in his arms again. This existence was never one that he wanted. His life as a killer wasn't meant to be permanent. All he'd wanted was to survive the Crusade, return home, and settle into a life of obscurity. With a wife, children even, the blessings of the church upon his home.

She'd settled now on a bench under the shade of one of the many trees in the square. Her hair, much shorter in this life than she'd ever worn it, danced in the breeze until she tucked the curls behind an ear. Gabriel's hands clenched and he shoved them in his pockets, wishing for nothing more than to twirl those curls around his fingers. She looked around, pushing her glasses back up after they slid down her nose, the action so achingly familiar that it hurt. Only minutes passed before Gabriel started toward her, his willpower gone. He needed to get close to her. Touch her. Find out her name.

"Hello," he said, his shadow falling across her bowed head. When she looked up, he was caught again by those slate-gray eyes. The eyes that had been haunting his dreams for almost fifty years.

"Good morning," she replied. Gabriel watched a beautiful pink blush creep up her cheeks as she tucked another curl behind her ear. He reached out his hand toward her and she slowly placed hers in his. Slowly, so he could savor it, and not scare her, Gabriel brought her hand to his lips.

"My name is Gabriel. May I ask what your name is?"

"Pippa."

Gabriel finished the motion, his lips ghosting over the spot on her ring finger where he'd wanted to place a ring for centuries.

"My name is Pippa." Her voice ended in a whisper.

"Pippa," Gabriel repeated her name, tasted it on his tongue. "That is a beautiful name."

And it was. They always were. It was the only thing about her that had ever changed.

"Thank you." Pippa blushed again and lowered her eyes to the hand he continued to hold in his own. Gabriel couldn't let go. Didn't want to let go. Wanted to raise it to his lips and taste her skin again. "Have we met before?"

"Would you like to walk with me?" Gabriel asked, gesturing along the square and up the street. "Or perhaps a beignet?" Café du Monde was across the street and the line for the pastry wasn't quite that long yet.

Pippa looked around, breathing through her nervousness before meeting Gabriel's beautiful blue eyes again. Eyes that hadn't wavered from hers, despite the group of beautiful women that had passed them by. "Yes," Pippa answered, allowing him to help her up and shaking out the skirt of her dress. She felt no fear or trepidation when she answered. "Yes, I would love to walk with you."

Pippa knew it was a silly reason, but she wanted to visit Jackson Square one more time before the wedding. The place where all her dreams had come true. The place where she'd met the love of her life.

The last two months had sped past. Every day she'd spent with Gabriel in some capacity. The first day, after enjoying beignets, they'd walked around the French Quarter for hours, talking about their lives. She'd told him about being a schoolteacher and moving down here to tutor the Lamont children. Pippa spoke for the first time of the fire that took the lives of both her parents. Of how she'd had to get away from the city she'd grown up in. Pippa had fallen fast and hard, quite sure she was in love with Gabriel before that first weekend was over.

And he had no qualms with telling her exactly how he felt about her. Gabriel held her hand as they walked. Listened when she spoke. Told her how beautiful she was. And his kisses, God, his kisses.

Like sweet torture.

She'd never experienced such kisses before. How he pulled her close and used his whole body to kiss.

They did everything together after her work with the children was over. After a week, she could no longer keep her emotions inside and let words of love burst from her. All Gabriel had done was pull her close, his mouth on her skin when his own love confessions also poured forth.

A week later, after another toe-curling goodnight kiss, Pippa had brought Gabriel into the boarding house and up to her room. "Are you sure about this, *ma petite*?" he'd asked her, holding her body close to his just inside the door to her bedroom.

"Yes, Gabriel," she whispered as she quietly closed her bedroom door. "I want it to be you."

The next day, Gabriel had dropped to one knee and asked her to marry him. He'd wanted to head directly to a judge to have it done that week, but Pippa had convinced him to wait until the Lamonts left for a month. They were taking the children with them while Mr. Lamont had business in London and were paying Pippa for the time off. "Then," she told him while they were lying in her bed one night. "Then, I can spend the first month of our marriage in your bed."

Gabriel growled as he rolled onto her body, settling himself between her thighs. "At least the first twenty-four hours, *mon amour*."

Now, mere hours before their vows, Pippa stepped off the early morning streetcar and walked the last few blocks to Jackson Square and the Saint-Louis Cathedral. A pull on her consciousness had her coming here so early, wanting to light a candle of thanks in the cathedral before a moment of reflection in the square.

She entered the square from Decatur Street and slowly made her way across the square, a wistful smile on her face. Pippa followed the path the long way around, enjoying this early morning time before the sun rose and bathed the city in light and heat. A sudden flash of blue light had Pippa stopping in her tracks, a sizzle of fear running down her spine.

"Here she is," a raspy voice said, "soul number six." A chorus of laughter rang out, and Pippa found herself unable to move.

"This has never been right."

"It doesn't matter what we think." The voice moved closer to her. "I don't want this to be my eternity." By the time Pippa's flight response caught up to her body, she was surrounded by five men dressed in black.

"Pl-please don't hurt me." Tears fell down her cheeks. Fear made her heart race. "I'm supposed to get married." The statement ended with a sob.

"You understand this is nothing personal, right?"

Pippa couldn't move, couldn't turn to the voice that spoke to her. She maintained eye contact with the man in front of her and looked at none of the others. His eyes were the coldest blue she'd ever seen. "This is the Crusader's fault, precious."

Pippa didn't understand what she felt at first, what that sudden pain in her side had been. Then another across her stomach. Too late, Pippa's hands rose to protect her body. "Gabriel!" The screams also came too late. The knives continued to slash at her before stabbing deep. Pippa turned, trying to escape, unable to fight her way free. The screams rose from her throat, pleas for her life, begging for Gabriel to save her. One more time, Pippa turned before a knife was driven deep in her chest, right into her heart.

Everything stopped.

"No!" she heard as the men stepped back from her, retreating into that blue light as she collapsed to the ground. "No, please, God no." Strong arms went around her, comforting her as her final breath left her body, the scent of Gabriel's soap in her nose.

The last sound she heard was a cry of complete anguish.

CHAPTER FIFTEEN

Parker awoke with a start and shot up in bed, the sound of that anguished scream still in her mind. She was confused at first, until her breathing slowed, her heart rate eased, and she realized she was in Gabriel's bedroom. What she didn't remember was how she got there. What did she remember?

Parker felt her facial expression scrunch in confusion, and she looked around the room, hoping something would jog her memories. It was dark and the shades drawn, so she had no idea if the sun was out or not. Parker rose and headed to the bathroom, flipping on the light and leaning her hands on the bathroom counter. She leaned toward the mirror, taking in the paleness of her cheeks and the dark bags under her eyes. Had she been sick? Why couldn't she remember anything?

She used the toilet, washed her hands and face, and brushed her teeth before once again leaning on the bathroom counter. Parker slanted toward the mirror, as far as she could go, until she was on her tiptoes and inches from the glass. In her eyes, she could see the confusion, but she continued to stare. Nothing, no memories. Until… Wait…

What was that?

May I ask what your name is?

Her lips formed Parker, but her mind said Pippa. Was that a dream?

217

Parker stumbled back onto her feet and rushed out of the bathroom, her escalating heartrate chasing after her. She had no idea why it was so high. Why she was so confused. Why she couldn't remember how she got here. At the bedroom door, she paused and pressed her ear to the wood, hearing low murmuring from the kitchen. Slowly, so the door made no noise, Parker opened it and peeked out into the other room. Another few inches of space and she saw the island in Gabriel's kitchen. She recognized Gabriel on one side of it, his arms locked straight as he leaned on the counter, his head bowed.

Next to Gabriel, on the other side of the square island, Charles stood, his arms crossed, spectacles on his head. He looked down his nose at the other man standing on the side of the island across from Gabriel. The man was older, shorter than Gabriel, his hair completely gray. Parker squinted her eyes because something about the man was remarkably familiar to her.

"Where is the angel, Mack?" The words heaved out of Gabriel.

Mack, Parker said to herself. In her mind's eye, a painting of a bloody crusade-era battle.

"Any moment now, General, she will arrive."

"What is the point of waiting for the angel?" Charles asked, crossing his arms over his chest.

"Because she *was* her goddamned guardian angel, Charles." That voice, coming from Gabriel, was more of a growl than actual words. Guardian angel? What was going on? Had she stepped into the middle of the twilight zone? Parker readjusted her body, hoping the floor didn't squeak. A silent gasp left her lips when Gabriel became obscured by a dark shadow. One second, he was at the kitchen island, and the next, he was opening the apartment door, Theresa's hand still poised to knock.

"*Was* is exactly the right word," Charles responded, his eyes rolling to the ceiling.

Parker, standing in the shadow of the bedroom door, felt

her whole body freeze when she saw Theresa. What the hell was she doing here?

"I don't appreciate being summoned, assassin," Theresa said as she walked through the door.

"I don't really give a damn about what you appreciate or don't, angel," was Gabriel's response.

At that sentence, Parker nearly gave herself away when a streak of jealousy fired up her spine at him calling her angel. Theresa settled herself on the side of the kitchen island that was free. Gabriel returned to his spot, once again leaning his locked arms on the counter.

"Why are we all here?" Theresa asked, motioning in a circle to encompass them.

"Because of Parker," Gabriel responded, his head remaining bowed, his eyes closed.

"What did you do?" Theresa asked, facing him, her face turning red with anger.

"The General would never cause harm to Parker," Mack admonished. "This you know." A shudder ran down Theresa's back before she turned her attention to Mack. "Who are you?"

"That is unimportant," Charles said. A look of pure disgust crossed Theresa's features.

"I took her through the shadows." The words were no more than a whisper from Gabriel. "To escape Maximus of Cordova."

Four sets of eyes turned to Parker when she gasped.

Give her to me so I can be free!

Gabriel's arms caught her before she hit the floor.

Gabriel looked around at the strange group surrounding him. Like the last time she'd fainted, he'd caught her and swung her up in his arms before sitting on the couch with her in his lap. Mack chose to sit on the coffee table right in front of him, hands clasped between his knees, head bowed. Theresa chose a seat on the loveseat across from him, her face white. Charles stood to the side, stoic as ever.

"You took her through the shadows?" Theresa questioned.

Gabriel pulled Parker's body closer to his, her head tucked under his chin. For the past two days, he'd waited for her to wake up again. Her slumber had been restless, her eyes constantly moving under her eyelids, breathless whispers keeping him awake. He'd listened as she'd cycled through each life, each name, each time they'd met. Each time they'd made love.

And each time she'd been killed by The Fold.

Those were the moments Gabriel needed to leave the room. He couldn't stand to hear her screams. Her pleading. Every time she'd called his name. The gurgling of her life being taken once again. His hands had clenched into fists at the sound. He promised her, during those times, he'd promised her that he would keep her safe, that he wouldn't let The Fold touch her again. "I will give my life to keep you safe," he'd whisper in her ear as he held her body. Held her as her mind replayed being murdered six times.

"Did you erase her memories again?" Mack asked the question softly.

Gabriel ran his fingers through her curls before raising his eyes to meet the older man's.

"Yes." What more could he say?

"How far back?"

"Before Boston."

"General…"

"It doesn't matter, Mack, it doesn't matter anymore because she remembers. It's all there, just below the surface of her mind." Gabriel sighed and looked around the room, his eyes landing on each immortal creature there. "She needs to know everything."

Mack nodded.

Theresa blanched.

Charles scoffed.

"To what end?" the fallen angel asked, crossing his arms over his chest. "What good does it do to tell her? And why did you never think it was a good idea to tell her during any other lifetime? The Fold will find her, and they will kill her…"

"Shut your *god*damned mouth," Theresa shouted as she jumped to her feet. "Christ, you original angels are all a bunch of hypocritical bastards." Theresa paced and muttered under her breath as she rubbed her temples. Gabriel and Mack both watched in amusement while Charles stared daggers at her. "Who is Maximus of Cordova?" she asked after returning to the couch, setting all her attention on Gabriel.

"Maximus of Cordova was another knight during the Crusades that rose through the ranks to lead his own army," Gabriel told her. "We crossed paths a few times, but I had no love for the man. His philosophy was to enjoy the spoils of war. He allowed his men the right to rape and pillage. Amongst his army were priests he'd pay for them to heap penance and forgiveness on his men, to absolve them of any guilt they may harbor for the crimes they committed." Parker stirred in his arms and Gabriel stopped speaking for a moment, looking down at her, hoping she'd open her eyes while simultaneously afraid she'd do so.

"I do not know what happened to him after the gates of Jerusalem fell," Gabriel continued. Absently, he ran his hand down through the curls of her hair again. "I came upon a group of Crusaders who had cornered a mother and her children." The rage built in him again, the black swirls of his anger swirling around his feet. Not once, in a thousand years, had Gabriel spoken about his own death. "I tried to stop them." Gabriel's voice broke. He looked up into Mack's eyes. "They killed the boy, and I attacked because I knew what was in store for those two women. Not even a woman yet, one of them. She couldn't have been more than ten if she was even that."

Theresa sucked in a shuddering breath and Gabriel watched her wipe a tear off her cheek and turn her head away.

"I tried, Mack."

"I know you did, General."

"Before the fighting started, when the priests came through and offered penance, I prayed to God to watch over my future bride. At that time, I had already decided I was done with war. I'd sent a messenger home to tell my father I would be returning and to start the search for my bride." Gabriel shook his head when Mack's mouth opened and closed but no sound came out. The other two angels remained silent.

"When I was on my knees, praying for forgiveness, God sent me a vision of the woman I was to marry. I didn't realize who until a few days ago. God sent me a vision of my future wife. I was shown a soft smile on a plump cheek, a curl of hair blowing in the breeze." While he said it, Gabriel ran his finger over Parker's soft cheek and through a curl of her hair. Mack's eyes followed the movement.

"Are you saying..." Mack started.

"Yes," Gabriel replied.

"A thousand years ago?"

"Time means nothing to God," Charles finally replied, something softening in his countenance. "The vision you had a thousand years ago could have been yesterday as far as time goes."

"What happened?" The softly whispered question came from the area of Gabriel's chest. When he looked down, it was into the gray depths of Parker's eyes. "What happened at the gates of Jerusalem?"

"Parker, I..."

"Tell us, *mon mari*." Shadows danced across her eyes. "Tell us what happened."

Gabriel swept the hair back off Parker's face, catching it in his other hand. She remained firmly in his arms, snuggled as close to his chest as he could get her. "I tried to stop them, *ma femme*. I attacked the one in front of me, not thinking, and was betrayed from behind. A Crusader's sword through my back. After that, I felt nothing. When the sword was pulled from my back, I staggered back with the motion until I hit the wall and fell to my knees. I watched the blood drain from my body and into the holy soil of Jerusalem."

"*Gabriel...*"

"I died right there, listening to the screams of that mother."

The entire room was silent. Gabriel felt a shudder run down Parker's back. Then, her eyes blinked quickly, and she sucked in a breath before sitting up suddenly and looking around the room. "How did I get here?" she asked, her eyes landing on everyone in the room. "Theresa," she said. "Charles." Her eyes stopped on Mack sitting on the coffee table. Parker's mouth opened and closed a few times. Her eyebrows drew together. "Mack," she whispered the name with an echo.

Parker pushed away from Gabriel, scooting on her butt until she'd put the entire length of the couch between them. She hyperventilated, and Gabriel turned toward her, concern on his face. Parker held a hand palm out, forcing him to stop. "You... You... I saw you. I saw a sword grow from your hand."

Gabriel sighed. "Yes, *mon ange*, that is true, you did."

"What... What..."

"My name is Gabriel de Priveaux. I was born in what was called Genova, in the Kingdom of Italy, in the year of our Lord ten-sixty-six. I was the second son born to my parents, so I did what was expected of me and became a knight of the Holy Roman Empire. I fought during the First Crusade, under the leadership of Tancred de Hauteville, who later became the Prince of Galilee."

Slowly, Gabriel moved closer to Parker. He saw the sheen of sweat on her skin. The throbbing of the pulse point of her neck. The way she barely dragged air into her lungs. The look in her eyes that said her flight response was kicking in.

"In July of the year ten ninety-nine, during my thirty-third year of life, we seized the holy city of Jerusalem, and the walls finally came down." He had to be ready if she tried to flee from the apartment. It wasn't safe for her out there, not with The Fold in the city. "I was ready to face God's judgment." An inch closer to her. "As you just heard, I was killed with a sword through the back."

Parker's brow furrowed again. She caught her bottom lip in her teeth. "Your blood draining into the holy soil of Jerusalem."

"*Oui, mon ange*, it is as you said. As you heard." Another inch closer. "I was awoken…"

"Awoken?" Parker scooted back until her butt was on the arm of the couch, half her mind telling her to flee and the other half telling her to throw herself into his arms and hold him tight.

"When I died, my soul was captured by an assassin's league. They've been holding my soul prisoner for almost a thousand years now, getting me to do their bidding with the promise that one day, I would be set free. That I could finally stand before God and be judged for my sins." He saw the war in her eyes, how her past lives wanted to reach for him, but the fear wouldn't allow it. "For four hundred years, I did their bidding, until I was sent to Paris, in the year sixteen twenty-three, with the instructions that if I killed this final soul, mine would be set free." An inch closer. Parker's eyes were wide open. He'd bet she didn't know that tears streamed down her face.

"And that was the first time I laid eyes on you."

It was night now. Parker knew it was night because Gabriel had opened the curtains and she saw the night sky. He'd followed her when she ran, but she hadn't gone far, just back to his room. When she'd tried to slam the door, his hand had been there. He'd barely gotten the door shut before Parker screamed. The last thing she remembered was Gabriel pulling her into his arms as a cloud of darkness rushed around her. At her heavy sigh, the bed creaked next to her, and Gabriel placed a hand on her shoulder. Maybe she'd finally gone crazy, but the longer she lay here in the quiet darkness, the more she remembered the dreams she'd been having the last week. Dreams that always included Gabriel.

"You were a widow of six months," Gabriel began, scooting closer to Parker's body, his hand trailing down her arm. "I was told that one last hit, and my soul would be set free. When I saw you, everything changed, *mon ange*." Gabriel twined their fingers together as he settled his body flush with hers. "Paris, sixteen twenty-three, I set my eyes on you for the first time." Parker drew their clasped hands up until they lay over her heart and Gabriel's head rested on the pillow with hers.

Over the next few hours, Gabriel told her everything. The story of their shared past, of the love they'd shared for hundreds of years. Of The Fold and every time they'd taken her life. How he'd hunted them while he waited for her. "I've never been able to find you, Parker. Outside of when you happen to enter the city close to me, I've never been able to find you. And I've looked, believe me I have. So, when you knew who Maximus was…"

"Max?" Parker finally said, looking at Gabriel over her shoulder.

"Yes, he is like me, except he enjoys this life."

Parker lay there for hours after Gabriel finished his story. Much as she tried, her heart and mind warred with each other. At this point, she was pretty sure she was crazy and sitting in a psych ward somewhere. Next to her, Gabriel's breathing was slow and steady, his arm secure around her. If only it were true, the idea that they'd been in love for hundreds of years, it would explain so much, but that was impossible.

Parker knew it was impossible. Well, her brain told her it was impossible while her heart insisted it was true. After slipping out from under Gabriel's arm, Parker dressed and quietly left Gabriel's apartment. She needed to walk, to move, to work this out in her mind. The sun would be up in a little over an hour, and Parker set off with no set destination in mind.

Before she knew it, Parker raised her head and found herself standing next to the Saint Louis Cathedral and Jackson Square. In her mind, she remembered the first day she'd been in New Orleans and how she'd felt stepping into this space. There, buried deep, was the memory of the last time she'd set foot here, when her name was Pippa and not Parker.

"How very fitting," came a voice from behind her. Parker swung around to the sound.

"Max," she said, taking a step back, further into the square, to move away from him. Max matched her step for step, following her into the secluded space.

"It's unfortunate that I wasn't here the last time your death took place in this square."

With those words, Parker turned and fled from him, wishing she'd never left the safety of Gabriel's home, no longer able to deny the story he'd told her. A scream escaped her lips when Max tackled her from behind, sending her stumbling to the ground. Max's body landed on hers, and Parker bucked her hips to get him off her. "I like it when they fight me," Max growled in her ear. Parker got to her feet and kicked back when Max grabbed her ankle.

A laugh sounded from behind when Parker was stopped at the entrance gates by two more men. They both grasped her by her upper arms and dragged her back into the square. Parker screamed and kicked, trying to break away. After a few more feet, one man swept her legs and then both men thumped her onto the ground. One of them straddled her chest, imprisoning her arms and upper body, but not her legs. Parker continued to kick and scream until she was given two swift kicks to each leg.

When a shadow fell across her face, Parker looked up into Max's sadistic face. "I'm assuming the Crusader doesn't know you've left the protection of his home." Max bent at the waist. "Otherwise, he would be here to protect you."

"So, I'm not crazy," Parker squeaked out.

"Oh, you're crazy all right, being out here by yourself." Max withdrew a large dagger and flipped the handle into his palm. "I'm going to enjoy this so much, I only wish the Crusader was here to witness me taking your last life, like I took your first one."

"How... How did you find me, in Chicago?"

Max bent down farther as Parker struggled with the man sitting on her chest. "Easy, I just followed your idiotic guardian angel around until she led me to you. She really is a dumb bitch, it's like God wanted you to fail at life so many times." Max laughed as he flipped the dagger in his palm again.

Parker watched, waiting for the moment. When he drove the dagger down, she brought her arms up beside the man sitting on her chest and pulled him forward. This slightly moved her, bringing his body forward as hers slid a few inches under his, but it wasn't enough to keep Max's blade out of her body. Instead of her heart, it stabbed into her shoulder. Parker let out the most bloodcurdling scream of her life.

"Hold her steady, you idiot!" Max screamed at the man as he pulled the knife out of her flesh.

Max raised the knife again. Before it could come down on her, a black sword stopped Max's dagger. Max was pushed back a few feet, and another dagger was forced into the neck of the man sitting on her. Parker watched in horror as Gabriel pulled the knife from the man's throat and used it to parry Max's attack. Blood splatter sprayed across her face, and Parker gagged while the man covered the wound with his hands. With one more bump with her hips, Parker finally dislodged the man from her when he slumped to the ground at her side, his life gurgling onto the ground.

Doing her best to crabwalk on only one arm, Parker tried to keep the black haze of pain away. When she felt a bench behind her, Parker wrapped her good arm around it, trying to haul herself up on her knees. The pain in her shoulder was so excruciating that it was almost numb. She felt the blood running down her chest and arm. A sound to her left had her looking up into the eyes of the second man. Before Parker could scream, Gabriel appeared out of thin air right behind him and drove a sword through his back and into the man's heart.

"Did you think I would let this go unpunished?" Gabriel whispered into the man's ear as he drove his sword into the body. "None of you will *ever* touch her again." Gabriel released his hand and the shadow sword disappeared. The Fold member crumbled to the ground; his eyes wide open in a death stare.

"Gabriel," Parker sobbed, tightening her arm around the arm of the bench.

"Parker." Gabriel kneeled beside her, pushing the hair off her face. "How badly are you injured?" His heart had plummeted to his knees when he'd woken up to find her gone. Unlike before, this time he'd followed his gut and shadow walked right into Jackson Square, not caring if she saw him or not. He'd already told her the truth about everything.

"Watch out!" she yelled, her eyes going wide at something behind him. Gabriel stood and parried Maximus's thrust as the man came at his back. Gabriel was able to push him away from where Parker had taken cover. He let the shadow sword grow to its full length as he and Maximus circled each other.

"I won't let you escape me this time, Maximus." Two steps to the right and Gabriel flicked his eyes to Parker, noting that she'd managed to get herself up onto the bench. Her one arm was tucked into her chest. Gabriel's anger grew at the amount of blood running down her body.

Gabriel allowed another dagger to grow in his empty hand.

"This is so unnecessary, Crusader. So much time wasted on this game." Maximus thrust forward, and Gabriel met his strike with one of his own. Both men reversed course and circled again. "I've no wish to kill you again."

That statement made Gabriel pause for a moment, but it was a moment long enough to allow Maximus to move in, slashing through the air with his sword. Even though Gabriel's sword was made of darkness, it clanged like metal. The square was filled with Parker's scream when Maximus beat through his defense and punctured Gabriel's shoulder.

Gabriel stumbled back, away from Maximus and toward the opposite side of the square, trying to keep the other man as far away from Parker as possible. Luckily, Maximus had stabbed him in his non-dominant shoulder, and he could continue to fight.

He'd fight until his very last breath to save Parker. "Explain yourself," Gabriel said, holding his sword out straight in front of him.

"When you tried to save that infidel whore and her children, Crusader. It's a pity you didn't check behind you. Well." Maximus chuckled. "It's a pity for you."

In his mind's eye, Gabriel could see that confrontation again, remembering the third crusader, whose face had been covered to protect it from the never-ending sand, being stabbed in the side by the boy. He twirled his sword, the black shadow metal making an ominous sound.

"How did that wound the boy gave you go?"

As he suspected, anger crossed Maximus's face at the mention of the stab wound he'd received. "Unlike you, it took three days to kill me."

Gabriel wanted to be angry, he wanted to rage, because standing in front of him was the man who'd killed him during his mortal life. The man who'd been hunting Parker for four hundred years. The man who... "How long have you been jealous of me, Maximus?"

Time slowed.

Maximus raised his sword, letting out a cry of anger and frustration. Gabriel braced for the attack, understanding that using Maximus's anger against him was the best chance to kill the man and protect Parker. He switched his stance at the same time a flash of blue invaded his peripheral vision. Parker's scream drew his attention. When Gabriel looked over, he saw another Fold member had started attacking her. Knowing he was leaving himself vulnerable to Maximus, Gabriel turned toward Parker, pulled back his hand, and whipped the dagger at the other man. The blade found its mark in the man's throat at the same time Maximus's blade entered Gabriel's side. The sword in Gabriel's hand disappeared.

"No!" Parker screamed, her eyes catching Gabriel's.

"Seems I've won again, Crusader."

Gabriel turned his head to look at Maximus, hating the smug expression on his face. The wound Gabriel had was fatal. There was no way he'd survive it. Blood already ran down his body. The sword eviscerated his vital organs. As soon as Maximus pulled his blade free, he'd fall to his knees and the man would go after Parker.

This had to end now. Gabriel heard Parker's tears.

He reached out and gripped Maximus's wrist, holding the man from being able to retreat. With what strength he had left, Gabriel pulled Maximus by the wrist, impaling himself further on the sword, not letting the man free. Quicker than he'd ever struck before, Gabriel swung his dagger and found its mark in Maximus's neck.

"You, and The Fold, will never touch her again. I've always been ready to sacrifice my life for her. I will burn this world down for her."

Maximus's eyes went wide with the knowledge that he was about to face the judgment he'd been running from for a thousand years. Gabriel let go of the dagger and the blade disappeared as he released Maximus's wrist. Maximus held his sword in a death grip, and it was torn from Gabriel's body when Gabriel kicked him away. His cry was agonized when he looked down at the wound pouring blood, and he brought his hand up to cover it.

"Gabriel." Parker was there, tucking her good shoulder

into his armpit, holding him up. Together, they staggered out of the park and onto the bricks outside the St. Louis Cathedral. Finally, at the steps, they both collapsed. "Gabriel," Parker sobbed again, placing her hand on his cheek and turning his face to hers. "I'm so sorry. I'm so sorry, Gabriel."

"Shhh, *mon ange*, do not worry." Gabriel drew one shaking finger across her cheek and through her hair, wiping her tears and hating the blood streak he left behind on her cheek. He leaned against her, his blood pooling at their feet, his vision blurring.

"Gabriel, I can't live without you." Parker pulled him closer, as close as they could get, and he wrapped his arms around her.

"I gave you my soul, *ma femme*. I will always be with you." Hopefully, now that Maximus was dead, they would no longer hunt Parker.

"You're the only person I've ever loved, Gabriel." Slowly, the only way he could move, Gabriel brought their lips together in the last kiss he'd share with her.

"My soul is yours and always has been, my only love." His vision went out before his hearing. Parker's wail of sorrow filled his ears at the same time the clock on the cathedral pealed. The last thing he saw was a soft smile on a plump cheek, a curl of hair blowing in the breeze.

CHAPTER SIXTEEN

Parker pulled her backpack closer to her, holding it tightly against her chest. She sighed when the bus made another stop. Maybe she should have rented a car, or taken an Uber, instead of being cheap and only spending two dollars on the bus fare. She pushed her glasses back up her nose, checking the map on her phone to make sure she got off at the right stop.

She was heading straight for Café Du Monde.

She wanted to eat a beignet and drink chicory coffee with steamed milk before the two blondes showed up and she had to pretend like she didn't eat food. Those two had intimidated her all through college and she was sure they still would. Parker didn't understand how Theresa and she were friends. They'd met in college and ended up roommates the first two years. The two of them couldn't be more opposite, the only similarity between them was the fact that they both had brown hair.

Parker's phone binged, and she pulled the cord to let the driver know she wanted to get off the bus. She planned on walking the last mile. It was how she justified eating beignets.

They were here in New Orleans for Theresa's bachelorette weekend. In four weeks, she was marrying the man she'd met in college. He'd just graduated medical school and was about to start his residency. It was almost every girl's fantasy relationship. Parker wished them the best. She hadn't been surprised when Theresa didn't ask her to be part of her wedding party, but she'd been caught off guard when she'd asked her to come for this weekend party. Aside from Theresa and the blondes, three more women Parker didn't know were coming. They were supposed to be sharing a condo somewhere in the Garden District and Parker was already extremely uncomfortable about sharing a place with these other women.

Parker stepped off the bus and traveled the last mile on foot, following the directions on her phone's GPS. When she stepped off the sidewalk and into the space between the St. Louis Cathedral and Jackson Square, she felt a strange squeeze on her heart.

Ignoring the sensation, Parker placed herself in front of the cathedral and took out her phone, snapping a few shots of the architecture. She was sure none of the women coming down for this weekend were interested in touring old churches and graveyards. Maybe she could suggest a moonlight jazz cruise, but she bet that wouldn't happen. Parker went over the pictures she'd taken as she turned and made her way into the square, rubbing at her scarred shoulder under the strap of the backpack. When she was younger, she'd fallen off her bike and impaled herself through her shoulder on a piece of metal. Luckily, she hadn't bled out on the street. It went along with all the other scars from injuries she'd gotten over the years. According to her mother, before her parents had adopted her at four years old, she'd been in a very abusive situation.

Parker didn't remember any of her life before being with her parents, and she was eternally grateful for that.

After making her way through Jackson Square and taking a few more pictures, Parker stopped before crossing Decatur Street and surveyed the line for Café du Monde. It was about forty people deep, and she didn't know how long it would take to get through, but this was literally the only reason she was here.

Parker joined the line, pulling her hair out of its bun, massaging her scalp, and putting her hair back up. It was way too hot and humid here to have it down. She'd never complain about the humidity back home again. It was only early June, and it was already ridiculously hot in Louisiana. Hours later, exhausted and sweaty, Parker arrived at the condo she was staying at for the weekend. She wasn't sure what she expected, but walking up to police cars surrounding the place and screaming women was not it.

"That's right, you bitch!" Theresa yelled at someone in the back of the police car. "Take your shit and get out!" The only thing keeping Theresa from hopping off the porch and heading toward the police car was the officer standing on the steps, his arms out to stop her. "Too much of a coward to face me. You had to call the cops!" Theresa continued to yell.

Parker glanced into the parked police car and saw her nemesis, Emily, in the back. The other woman also glanced her way and shot Parker her middle finger before the car pulled away.

Parker turned to look at the condo and noticed the other women surrounding a crying Theresa. The police officer, who must have decided the threat was over, nodded at her as he walked away.

"Theresa?" Parker questioned as she made her way up to the porch.

"Oh, God, Parker." Theresa flew down the steps and threw her arms around Parker, sobbing into her shoulder.

"What the hell happened?" Parker patted Theresa's back and looked up at the other women standing on the porch. Most of them shrugged and looked away.

"I just found out Emily and my fiancé have been sleeping together for years. Years!" Theresa shouted after she stepped out of Parker's arms. She wiped tears off her cheeks. "This just went from a bachelorette party weekend to a breakup party weekend." Theresa flung her hands in the air. "Let's get inside and decide what we're doing. I know you have some ideas, like you'd come here without researching first!"

Parker hated to admit it, but she ended up having way more fun that weekend than she thought she would. In the end, Theresa hadn't seemed that upset about the breakup and had agreed to everything Parker had suggested, including all the wine and beer they could handle. Now, she was sitting at her gate, waiting for her flight to start boarding. To her surprise, Theresa was on the same flight, and she was currently rummaging through her carry-on bag, looking for the small bottle of vodka she'd managed to get through security. "Hair of the dog?" Theresa asked, holding the bottle out to Parker.

"No, thanks," Parker declined. "I don't think I drank as much as you this weekend." Parker didn't drink much at all because she lost all inhibitions when she did and felt like shit the next morning. Theresa shrugged her shoulders before downing the entire small bottle of alcohol.

"Damn, girl, give your liver a chance to recuperate. You've only been single for two days."

"You know what we should do?" Theresa said after an unladylike burp. "We should go to Boston."

"I would love to go to Boston," Parker replied. "I've never been there."

"I know, neither have I." The two women sat in silence for a few minutes, and Parker couldn't keep from staring out the windows, back toward the city of New Orleans.

"Is everything okay?" Theresa asked her.

"I'm not sure," Parker answered. "It's like—" She gestured out the window. "It's like I forgot something, or someone, important. Which is weird because I don't know anyone in that city."

Theresa also looked out the airport windows, back toward the city, an indiscernible look on her face. "Did you remember your phone charger?" she asked, looking back at Parker.

"Yes, you jerk." Parker giggled at her, nudging Theresa's shoulder, before her eyes, once again, were drawn to the window. She really felt like she had lost someone, or something. Which didn't make sense because she didn't know anyone in this city. They'd done a sweep of the condo before they'd left this morning. Before she knew it, they were calling to start boarding. Parker stood and slung her backpack on when their zone was called.

"I was thinking," Theresa said to her as they walked down the jetway to board the plane. "Maybe what you were feeling has something to do with the guy you broke up with not that long ago."

"You mean Max, the guy who disappeared after I wouldn't let him go through my bank records?"

"Yeah, that guy was a douchebag, I'm glad you broke up with him."

"Yeah," Parker said softly, "me too." *But that's not it*, she thought as she slid into her seat. Feeling all kinds of emotions and not sure how to deal with them, Parker put her headphones on and pulled up her favorite old jazz playlist, a lot of the songs from the nineteen twenties. Theresa fell asleep for the entire two-and-a-half-hour flight, and Parker spent the time staring out the window, feeling like she was missing a part of herself and not understanding it at all.

After disembarking and while walking through O'Hare airport, Theresa pointed to a sign on one of the airport walls advertising a festival happening in Millennium Park in July. "Since I won't be on my honeymoon, we should totally go to that festival next month."

"I don't know," Parker said, squinting at the sign as they passed.

"Oh, come on, Parker, it's a wine and food festival. Look, there's some kind of French pastry food truck that's going to be there." Theresa pointed to the list of vendors. "Come on, it'll be fun. Maybe you'll meet some French-speaking, art-loving man and be swept off your feet."

"Right, Theresa," Parker said as she shook her head and hitched her backpack higher. "Your imagination is amazing."

Gabriel awoke with a start, fighting the blanket around him as he momentarily forgot where he was, the dream that woke him fading into his subconscious. He'd taken a red-eye flight to Chicago last night and hadn't lain down to sleep until almost two in the morning. The front desk agent had remarked on how lucky he was to have gotten a room considering the festival going on this weekend in Millennium Park. Gabriel had rubbed his eyes and remarked that he'd made this reservation a month ago, but that sometimes he just got lucky like that.

To be honest, he'd almost forgotten about making this appointment with the realtor. He also didn't remember *why* he'd decided to buy property up here. It had never crossed his mind before, even though Chicago had several very large museums and a world-class art presence. Gabriel drew back the curtain and surveyed the view from his room. He'd gotten a room at the Hilton on Michigan Avenue with a view out over Grant Park and, further away, Lake Michigan. He checked the time on his phone. It was already after nine in the morning and his appointment was at eleven.

A huge sigh left him as he turned back toward the bathroom. While he showered, Gabriel thought about how he'd almost canceled this appointment, but some feeling inside him had been so strong, like he had to be here. His assistant, Charles, had looked at him like he was crazy when he'd suggested canceling, but he'd changed his mind before Charles said anything, deciding he was still going to go.

"You have to go," Charles had said.

"I just told you I'm going," Gabriel remarked before heading to the back of the gallery, checking his inventory list for a shipment that had finally made it through customs. He'd flipped a few pages back and forth before returning to the desk where Charles had been. "I think we're missing a painting," Gabriel had told him.

"Which one?" Charles held out his hand for the clipboard, but Gabriel ignored him, his skin tightening as he looked over the manifest. "I believe it was called 'Wife of the Assassin' or something like that." Gabriel looked up at Charles when the man sucked in a breath.

"Right," Charles had said. "That one is currently unavailable again. Maybe soon."

Shaking out of the memory, Gabriel flipped on the hotel shower, ready to get this day started. After his shower and getting dressed, Gabriel decided he would walk since it was less than a mile and he wanted to see what the streets of Chicago were like. He didn't know why he'd never been here before, maybe because he spent too much time out of the country. Between that and Boston, most of his time had been accounted for. About a month ago, though, he'd started thinking about opening another gallery, letting Charles run the one in New Orleans, and opening one up here. O'Hare was a bigger airport than the one in New Orleans, so he could fly anywhere he needed to go. Gabriel was just crossing Balboa Drive with the crowd when his phone rang.

"Good morning, Charles."

"Did you make it to see the building yet?" Charles asked.

Gabriel had a tough time reconciling the two sides of the man who looked like a stuffy English butler but acted like a mother hen. He'd met Charles many years ago when he'd been in Marseille. After the death of his parents and older brother, he'd taken some time away from studying art history and hung out around the coast of France and Italy, discovering where his ancestors were from. It had been Charles who'd helped him pull his life together, and they'd been as inseparable as family ever since.

Gabriel continued down the street. "As it is the same time down there as here, you should know I have half an hour 'til it happens." He spoke in French, one of the many languages he knew, instead of English. This was a game

Charles and he would play, see how many languages they could stuff into a conversation.

"I know that you've been plagued by nightmares lately and haven't been sleeping well, so I didn't want you to miss it."

Gabriel frowned, stopping in front of the Congress Hotel, and stepping out of the foot traffic. "I didn't realize you knew about that." He realized that was what had woken him up earlier, the dream about being stabbed. Sometimes it was in the back and sometimes it was in the side. Always, in the dream, was the sound of a woman screaming and crying, and his frantic attempts to get to her and save her.

Always, he woke before that happened.

"It's been going on for a few months now. Of course, I knew about it. Mack called me after your last trip to Boston and told me he was worried about you."

Gabriel chuckled and resumed his walk, turning past the Congress to head toward where he would meet the realtor. "Who needs a mother when one can have two old men to watch out for them." He'd met Mack many years ago on his first trip to the museum in Boston to authenticate a painting, and they'd become fast friends. Since then, Mack and Charles had taken it upon themselves to become his surrogate parents.

Not that he minded.

"Listen," Charles continued. "I happened to be looking at events taking place in Chicago this weekend and I noticed a wine and food festival not too far from where you're staying."

"Yes, I did happen to see something going on a few blocks from here."

"I think you should stop by. I read about an award-winning French pastry chef having a food truck there."

"Really, Charles?" Gabriel stopped at the address he was to meet the realtor at. "Has it been that long since you've been to France? Like an award-winning French pastry chef would be in a food truck."

"Fine, maybe that was an exaggeration, but I think you should go. Maybe they'll have that bread you love so much."

An hour later, Gabriel stepped back onto the street, shook the realtor's hand, and marveled at the fact that he'd just spent way too much money buying the gallery space. But it was perfect for his needs, and he'd decided to trust his gut on this one. It hadn't steered him wrong yet. Gabriel made it back to the corner of Michigan Avenue and, instead of turning right and heading back to the hotel, he turned left and walked toward Millennium Park.

This was a fool's mission, but he hadn't had good bread since the last time he'd been in France, and that was nearly a year ago. He'd gone back every day to buy a loaf, it had been that good. That was when he'd started having the strange dreams about a woman to go with the dreams of blood and death. But, in the dreams with the woman, it was always poignant and erotic at the same time. Gabriel hated to admit how many times he'd woken hard as a rock after dreaming of her. And he never saw her entire face at one time. What he mostly got were flashes of a plump cheek and straight nose, or a soft smile and a curl of hair. So many times, he'd begged to see the whole package, like he knew that cheek and the roundness of her shoulder.

Sometimes, he'd glimpse the curve of a hip while her fingers danced over his skin. His fingers would clench because he wanted to touch her so badly. It was like he knew what her skin tasted like, and it vexed him more every time he dreamed of her. He'd never been the casual sex type, so he lived with the fantasies, taking care of his needs solo, and hoped one day he'd either meet the woman or the dreams would stop.

Finally, after wandering Millennium Park, Gabriel found the damned French food truck and got in line. Instantly, his eyes caught on a woman standing two people ahead of him, at the curl of hair trailing down her neck. She turned so he could see her profile, and his breath caught.

"How about you suck off?" she said into her phone.

"I'm in control of my life." The woman violently jabbed the off button on her phone and placed it back into her purse, muttering in French the whole time.

Gabriel couldn't help but chuckle.

Then his heart almost stopped when she took her hair out of the bun it was in and started massaging her scalp, every glorious curl of her hair begging for his touch. Gabriel fisted his hands at his sides and his skin got tight.

It was her.

The woman he'd been dreaming of.

She was real.

He'd bet all the money in his bank account.

"Excuse me," he said, taking control of his destiny and pushing through the people standing in front of him. There was no care in his soul for the shocked voices when he did so. Gabriel's heart hammered. He already saw her eyes in his mind. Had he ever seen her eyes? When she turned, he would know.

"Hello," he said to her in French. Gabriel stood so close, nearly touching, and he smelled the scent she was wearing, something deep and sensual. She turned, and her gray eyes widened when they landed on his. He held out his hand to shake, and she placed her hand in his.

"My name is Gabriel," he said as he took her hand, turned it, raised it, and hovered his lips above her ring finger. "May I ask what your name is?"

"Parker," she whispered, her eyes wide on his face. "My name is Parker." She swallowed hard. "Have we met before?"

EPILOGUE

Charles stood on the sidewalk along Lake Shore Drive, his hands behind his back, knowing the exact moment that Gabriel and Parker met once again. In it was a sense of satisfaction. Of knowing that he'd finally been able to break the curse and lead Gabriel to the fulfilling life he was always meant to have before it was stolen by The Fold.

A life filled with love.

"It's finally happened," Theresa said as she stopped next to him. Charles looked down at the other angel, whose face was pointed in the direction of where Parker and Gabriel were. He knew they'd already sat down together, drawn to each other, as they had been for hundreds of years, soulmates kept apart through no fault of theirs.

"Yes," Charles said, tears gathering in his eyes, one escaping down his cheek. Finally, after losing Gabriel's soul a thousand years ago, he was able to make right on the promise he'd made when he'd stood over Gabriel's mortal body and watched him die near the gates of Jerusalem.

Now that Gabriel was mortal again and the threat to Parker was gone.

Now that The Fold knew Gabriel had died soulless, that there had been nothing for them to take. And in that, his soul had finally been set free.

"I can't believe it," Theresa exclaimed, pointing at a man

walking toward them. He was about six feet tall, brown hair pulled back in a bun, white button-up shirt and red pants fitted to his strong body. On his feet, sandals. He had burnished brown skin, his eyes shaded by sunglasses, and looked around at everything with a smile on his face. He stopped in front of the two angels and tipped up his glasses, giving them both a wink.

"Je——" Charles started.

"I think I prefer the name Yeshu down here. What do you think, Charles?" Yeshu slid his hands into his pockets and continued to smile.

"If that is your preference, then of course, Yeshu."

"I just took a walk through the festival over there." Yeshu waved at Millennium Park. "I have to be honest; I wasn't sure your plan would work, Charles, but I'm happy to say that I was wrong." Yeshu looked around at the people on the street, smiling toward the festival. "Do you feel you've finally redeemed yourself as a guardian angel?" Yeshu's deep-blue eyes bored into Charles's and the angel nodded before casting his gaze back over the festival, over Gabriel and Parker.

For four hundred years, ever since The Fold's first attack on Parker's former incarnation, Charles had been trying to bring about this very ending. The more times her death happened, the longer it got between birth cycles, and the more Charles despaired that her soul would be allowed to be born again. He'd begged and pleaded for Parker to be born into her final life, laying the groundwork for this final meeting to happen. Even going so far as to grovel before Archangel Michael to get Theresa to play the role she also felt she needed to.

It had taken much longer than Charles had thought it would to get them to agree to allowing Parker her last incarnation. Her soul would have remained in limbo for as long as it was deemed necessary to protect her last life. Charles had bartered his own immortality to secure her release.

"And you, Theresa, does the outcome also soothe you?" Yeshu turned his gaze to the other guardian angel.

"All we've wanted was for them to have the life they deserve, Yeshu. To be together as they should have been for so very long."

"And they shall," Yeshu told them. "They most definitely shall."

AUTHOR'S NOTE

I hope you enjoyed coming on this journey with me as much as I enjoyed writing it. Sometimes, when I first start a story, even I don't know where it will lead. Or the twists and turns in the middle. And I'm very glad it led to Gabriel and Parker's happily ever after.

ABOUT THE AUTHOR

Jen has been a voracious reader from a very young age. Then, she discovered a love for writing and the stories in her head started pouring out. Who doesn't love a good romance? Page turning, hot and sweaty, makes you wonder, romance.

You know what else she loves? A happily ever after. And who doesn't?

Jen finds inspiration for her writing with her love of travel and each new adventure creates a new story.

Facebook.com/authorJenShaffer
Amazon.com/author/JenShaffer
Tiktok.com/@jenshaffer.author

Instagram.com/jenshaffer.author